For A

Happy reading,
Honeybee!

Come Undone

THE CITYSCAPE SERIES: BOOK ONE

JESSICA HAWKINS

Copyright © 2013 Jessica Hawkins
www.jessicahawkins.net

The Cityscape Series: Book One, Come Undone
Cover Photo © iStockphoto.com/VikaValter

All rights reserved. Except as permitted under the U.S.
Copyright Act of 1976, no part of this publication may be
reproduced, distributed, or transmitted in any form or by any
means, or stored in a database or retrieval system without the
prior written permission of the author.

This book is a work of fiction. Names, characters, places, and
incidents either are products of the author's imagination or are
used fictitiously. Any resemblance to actual persons, living or
dead, events, or locales is entirely coincidental.

ISBN: 061574642X
ISBN-13: 978-0615746425

PRAISE FOR
THE CITYSCAPE SERIES

"...a contender in the race for the most captivating and sexy contemporary romance series..."

—Autumn After Dark

"This series is incredible. It belongs on every best-seller list. Hell, it belongs on the big screen. FIVE STARS."

—Author Staci Bailey

"...the writing is fantastic, the emotional detail, involved, and the connections are so well explored, that we get to LIVE this story (the good, the bad and the ugly). Thoroughly. Intensely. Honestly."

—Maryse's Book Blog

"What is straight? A line can be straight, or a street,

but the human heart, oh, no, it's curved like a road through the mountains."

—Tennessee Williams, *A Streetcar Named Desire*

PROLOGUE

OLIVIA COULDN'T QUITE REMEMBER the first time she saw Bill, just that one day he was there. They worked in the same office building, thirty floors apart, and often met in the courtyard by the fountain— he for a cigarette break (a habit she would soon break him of) and she for a stolen moment of sunshine.

During their brief encounters, she'd test the waters with a glance here, a touch there, and find her herself both relieved and disappointed at the lack of art involved. Over time, her feelings for him grew fonder, and she came to look forward to their frequent meetings. She liked that he didn't ask too many questions, and he, well, he was smitten.

One day, about six months into a developing friendship, Bill asked her out. She peered at him from behind dark sunglasses and declined. He was undaunted by her refusal, which she admired, though it also made her uneasy.

That night she dreamed of him. He kissed her with gentle reverence and made love to her in the dark, where his touch was as real as if he'd been there in bed next to her.

When Olivia awoke the next morning, she started as the dream, which felt more like a memory, flooded over her. She thought of it all morning until, when they met the next day, she asked him to dinner.

CHAPTER 1

EVER SO SLOWLY, I touched the tube to my parted lips and glided on the Ruby Red. I'd always lacked the patience for lipstick and only used it for special occasions. Next came a translucent lip gloss that left threads of goop as I smoothed my lips together. I drew back slightly from the mirror to admire my work.

Perfectly coiffed hair, teased and styled into a long bob, floated just at my shoulders, every shiny brown lock suspiciously cooperating. In the trash laid the scattered teeth of yet another broken comb. I'd wrestled especially long with my tangles tonight, but looked particularly poised as a result; so much so, that if one thing were to tremble, everything else would come tumbling down. Or so it seemed. In that moment, I caught Bill's gaze in the reflection, his normally mild eyes watching me intently. I quickly forgot that feeling of unease.

"You look good," he said, admiring my emerald green dress.

"Your favorite color."

"Because it matches your eyes." I picked at a mascara smear on the mirror with my fingernail. "Do we have to go tonight?" he asked.

"What?" I'd successfully chipped off the mark, but now I was faced with the messy smudge of a fingerprint.

"Tonight. Let's stay in."

"Everyone's going to be there." I tossed makeup products back into the drawer and wiped the counter with my palm. "People pay good money for these tickets, babe."

"Whose idea was this again?"

"Andrew's firm got tickets for their clients. Not everyone could make it, so he invited us."

"But," he began. A quick glare in his direction silenced him. He held up his palms in defeat. I turned back to my reflection.

I checked my eyeliner one last time to make sure it was even. "I talked to my dad today. He'll be in Chicago for a night next month and wants to have dinner."

Bill groaned and slumped in the doorway.

"What? You don't want to go to the ballet, you don't want to have dinner with my father . . . . It's only one night."

"And you're so thrilled when my parents drive in."

"Touché." I flipped my hair over my shoulder and pushed a gold stud through my ear. "Well, you don't have to come, but I know he'd like to see you."

"Sure he would, where else does he get free legal advice?"

"Oh, please. He has plenty of corporate lawyer friends."

"Not for work, Olivia. For his divorce from Gina. Lawyer friends don't put up with that shit, they charge you for it."

"Well, get used to it, 'cause he's not going anywhere. I'm sure if you ever need advice on how to win over girls half your age, he'd be happy to help."

"Half my age?" he repeated as he came up behind me and encircled my waist. A piece of brown hair fell over his eye. He was overdue for a haircut. "Are you trying to get me locked up? I'd say I've got my hands full married to a twenty seven-year-old."

"Bill," I whined, swatting his hands away. "You'll wrinkle my dress, and I'm finally ready."

"Yes, darling," he said with a sly smile, backing away. "I'll pull the car around." I followed him out of the bathroom and then pivoted back quickly, grabbed a hand towel and wiped the smudge away.

~

We arrived at the performance minutes before curtain. Teetering in my heels, I clung to Bill's arm as we scoured the crowd for familiar faces. Sophistication perfumed the lobby, as if it had been bottled and sold to Chicago's elite. Smartly dressed women carefully stepped down scarlet-carpeted steps, passing beneath elaborate chandeliers that cast shadowy corners.

"There they are," Bill said. From behind, my two best friends, registering at just a few inches over 5 feet, could almost be sisters. Gretchen, in a revealing pink dress and boosted by spiky heels, gestured wildly to the group around her. Her long platinum hair bounced in signature curls with each exaggerated movement.

Next to her, Lucy dodged Gretchen's flailing limbs, anticipating her every movement. She wore a boat-neck black dress, and her short brown hair was fashioned into a perfect chignon.

Her boyfriend, Andrew, stood off to the side, wringing a program. Upon spotting us, he grinned toothily and beckoned us over. "Sorry, Gretch," he interrupted. "Everyone, this is Lucy's other best friend, Liv Germaine, and her husband Bill Wilson."

"What, now I'm the *other* best friend?" I joked, shaking hands with someone. "I only introduced them, you know."

Lucy looked up at me with big brown eyes before hugging me. "Look, we're the same height now," she said, showing off uncharacteristically high shoes.

"I don't know, shrimp," Bill said. "Liv's still got some inches on you."

"Anyway," Gretchen interjected impatiently. "The plane lands, and I rush to the station, just barely making the train. Since it's now one in the morning and I've been traveling for fourteen hours, I immediately pass out. When I wake up, the—what are they called—stewardess?—she says, 'Welcome to Chile!'"

"Chile!" one of the women cried.

"I'd gotten on the wrong train, slept through the entire ride, and ended up in Santiago."

Everyone laughed. I politely joined in, though I'd heard the story twice before.

"To make matters worse, it was fifty-something degrees outside, and I was wearing shorts and a tank top."

The man next to me guffawed loudly. He was the only one who'd been introduced without a partner; Gretchen's lure was cast.

"Oh, I think it's time," Lucy squeaked when the lights pulsed.

The single man sidled up to Gretchen as we made our way to our seats. "What do you do that you can take off to Chile whenever you like?"

"Entertainment PR," she said, batting her eyelashes at him.

"Hook, line, and sinker," Bill whispered, reading my mind. Gretchen turned and shot us a dirty look when I giggled. "Uh oh, Windex is mad," he said with a playful smile. Her face softened. She liked Bill's nickname for her. When I'd introduced them, he'd said hers were the bluest eyes he'd ever seen.

Once we were seated, he leaned over so only I could hear. "Are you familiar with the tale of Odette and Prince Siegfried?" I arched an eyebrow at him, and he passed me a program. "*Swan Lake.* Just another love story gone wrong."

I was unable to keep the surprise from my face. In the three years we'd been married, I'd never heard him mention going to the ballet.

"My parents took me as a teenager," he explained. "Culture, they said. Just another one of my mandated activities."

The lights dimmed, and Bill sat back, shifting to get comfortable. His long legs knocked against the seat in front of us multiple times before its occupant turned to raise her eyebrows. I suppressed a laugh just as the conductor lifted his arms.

Before long, the stage was awhirl with white tulle, hard muscles, prettily pink slippers. And those pink slippers, which curled and arched and lengthened unnaturally, seemed perfectly untouched. Everything about the ballet appeared smooth and blemish-free, from the dancers to the patrons. The graceful precision was one thing, but I was floored by the flawlessness of the performance. Everything in life should be so clean. When the curtain fell for intermission, I clapped gleefully with the crowd.

We spilled into the lobby, excitedly reviewing what we'd just seen as we maneuvered. Bill and Andrew left to get drinks as Gretchen, Lucy, and I broke away from the others, keeping close through the bustling crowd. The room was brimming with people, and I hoped that Bill wouldn't be in line the entire intermission.

"I can't believe my mother let me quit ballet when I was seven," Lucy said once we'd found a semi-open spot. "I could've been a star."

"I don't think it's as easy as that," I said.

. She shook her head. "I could have been a professional ballerina." Gretchen and I laughed at her sincere expression. "Fine, don't believe me," she said. "I'm going to the restroom."

"Oh, me too," Gretchen said. "Liv?"

"I'll wait here for the guys."

I craned my neck above the crowd to search for the bar, where I expected Bill would loom over everyone. My gaze lingered on different people, noting how their stiff, deliberate movements countered the elegance of the dancers on stage. To me, they not only seemed like strangers, but like aliens. Or maybe I was the one who didn't belong.

Since the abrupt divorce of my parents when I was a teenager, I'd never figured out exactly where I was supposed to be. Large crowds heightened that insecurity and left me feeling vulnerable. It was an unfortunate ability of mine, feeling spectacularly alone in a crowd, even when surrounded by friends and family.

I had the sensation of being watched seconds before I met a man's unfamiliar pair of eyes across the room. They were dark, narrowed intensely in my direction as if he were trying to place me. Everything slowed around me, but my heartbeat whipped into a rapid flutter.

Our gaze held a moment longer than it should have. My body buzzed. My pounding heart echoed in my ears. It wasn't his immense, tall frame or darkly handsome face that struck me, but a draw so strong that it didn't break, even when I blinked away.

I jumped at a hand on my arm. I'd been holding my breath for those stretched seconds, and it rushed out of me now, disjointed and erratic. I shifted for the passerby and spotted Bill winding toward me through the crowd. When I looked back, I gasped quietly.

9

The man loomed closer than necessary. Something about the lean in his posture was intimate and easy, yet the space between us was physically hot, igniting fire under my skin. I reminded myself to breathe. I bit my rouged bottom lip as I took him in—hair blackest black, short and unruly but long enough to run my hands through. His suntanned complexion appeared natural from time spent outdoors. Strong carved-from-marble facial features were softened by long, unblinking lashes. Involuntarily, I drew a sharp breath at the magnitude of his beauty.

A woman's voice cut into my consciousness and he turned, giving me the opportunity to regain control. In one swift movement I ducked away, exhaling audibly. Bill and Andrew were there then, shoving a wineglass at me as I shielded myself with their bodies.

"Where are the girls?"

"You like Pinot right?"

"What do you think of the show?"

I made a noise, an attempt to speak as the room spun with words and images.

"I'll take that," Gretchen's voice called suddenly.

"The line for the bathroom isn't bad if you have to go," Lucy said. I flinched when she touched my shoulder. "Liv, are you—"

"I think I will go to the restroom," I said, backing away. I only just saw her puzzled expression as I turned to struggle through a crowd dense enough to suffocate. Or so it felt in that moment.

~

I could not remember what he looked like. Our exchange was a mere moment, but I had felt the shift.

After, as I sat in the theater, the velvety red seats that I had not much noticed before pricked at my exposed skin, causing me to shift uncontrollably. Because each time I sat still, his heat enveloped me again. As hard as I tried, I could not remember what he looked like. I could only feel him.

I forced myself to focus on the second half. A bewitching Odette mournfully enthralled the crowd as her story unfolded. Why did it feel as though she watched me between sequences?

Back in the lobby, in the most unobvious way I knew how, I scanned the crowd for a clue or hint as to who the man might be. To both my relief and disappointment, I did not see him again, and tried to forget the feeling while we dined and drank into the night.

~

The heavy door of our Lincoln Park apartment threatened to slam behind me, but at the last second, I caught the knob and eased it shut. I yawned, hanging my coat and sliding out of my pumps. Bill flipped on the television set in the next room while I sorted through mail, tossing half of it into the trash. On the brown polyester couch his mother had given us some years ago,

I found him in his boxers, languidly watching replays of the basketball game he'd grudgingly missed.

Three glasses of red wine coursed through my veins. I stripped off my emerald dress in one sinuous motion and let it drop onto the floor. When he didn't look up, I shimmied over and settled myself onto his lap.

"Hi," I said in my sultriest voice. His hand righted a stray strand of hair as he glanced between the screen and me. I wet my lips and kissed him full on the mouth. I'd been humming with electricity since intermission and was impatient for human contact.

"Well, well," he said when we broke. "What's gotten into you?"

"It's late. Take me to bed."

His eyebrow rose, and his mouth popped open as if connected by an invisible string. He looked about to protest and then relaxed as he thought better of it.

In an uncharacteristically graceful motion he stood, with my body secured to his, and carried me to the mattress. Fingertips tenderly caressed the outsides of my thighs as he hovered over me.

"Shit," I said, just as his face dipped. I sat up in a panic. "I forgot to pick up condoms."

"It's fine."

My brows furrowed. "It is not fine. Not while I'm not on birth control."

He sighed, annoyed. "Come on, just this once."

"Nope. You know how I feel about no condom."

"There's one in the kitchen drawer," he said, rolling his eyes. I slid out from underneath him and shuffled to the kitchen. I rifled through the cluttered drawer until I found one in the back. "Liv," he called impatiently.

I grabbed it, checked the expiration date, and ran back, jumping onto the bed. "I'm sorry, babe, where were we?"

Frown lines faded as he propped himself up on long, wiry arms. I touched his pecs, trailing my fingers down to a soft midsection while goose bumps sprang to attention across his skin.

"My, my, Mrs. Wilson," he said. The designation always made me think of Bill's mom, but I'd managed to control my grimace over the years. It remained one of the reasons I hadn't officially changed my surname. "What big green eyes you have," he continued, touching his lips just above my cheekbone. "And such pretty blonde hair," he added, brushing a lock from my forehead. His hips ground against me in anticipation. I reached up and ran my hand through his floppy brown hair, cocking my head to the side.

"Not blonde, just plain brown," I said with a pout.

"What?" he asked with feigned surprise. "You must be colorblind. I see some blonde strands in there."

"You just want to tell people you married a blonde."

"Agree to disagree, then." He smiled. It creased his adorably crooked nose. He loved to say he'd broken it during one-on-one, but the truth was that it was just naturally that way.

He unhooked my bra swiftly, gently cupping my breasts in each of his hands. His fingers were long, and I didn't quite fill them up. From the living room, the unmistakable sounds of a heated basketball game blared from the television.

The motions were familiar. His touch had become defter, more confident, over time. And his usually awkward nature became more fluid. He groaned my name as he pushed himself into me, pulling my hips closer. I echoed his movements, my arousal growing with his satisfaction. I watched beads of sweat form on his brow, more apparent when his face screwed up with pleasure. He didn't kiss me again, but I'd become accustomed to that. Making out was for teenagers.

I inhaled his natural scent, enhanced by a salty concoction of unwashed hair and fresh perspiration; it was always sharper when we were making love. I felt a twinge inside and sighed softly, but then it was gone. It wasn't long before he came, squeezing his eyes shut as he called out and collapsed onto me.

"Sorry," he breathed into my ear after a moment. "Do you want—"

"It's fine," I reassured him, suddenly tired from the wine. "It was nice."

It took him less than two minutes to fall asleep; I knew because I often watched the clock as I waited. I untangled myself from his clutches and tiptoed out of the room.

Once the apartment was dark and still, and I'd washed my face of the day, I returned to cocoon myself in the soft sheets. He stirred and reached for me, but I expertly dodged his grasp. I'd had to learn to find the comfort in postcoital cuddling. I was always the one left with tingling limbs and uncomfortable sweating as I willed myself to sleep.

A twinge. Though the sex was comfortable and good, a twinge wasn't much of anything. I let my head roll to the side to look at my husband. At one point he'd wanted my orgasm as much as I did, but it was the one thing I couldn't give him. There were times when we'd been close, when the stars and the body parts had aligned, and I'd shuddered in response. But when it came time for the grand finale, I'd buckled under the pressure.

Bill had found comfort in the fact that it wasn't just him. I'd been with other men before him, mostly in college, but despite my efforts, had yet to find my slice of Nirvana. I couldn't find comfort in that, though. To me, it was my eternal flaw and as a wife, my greatest inadequacy. If things were the other way around, could I live with the fact that I couldn't pleasure Bill?

I was happy, though. I had other ways of getting myself off when necessary. I had my husband, who loved me in spite of everything. My life was pretty much as perfect as a night of good friends, wine, and sex. I lay in bed and watched the ceiling, waiting for sleep. Yes, I was happy.

CHAPTER 2

"DON'T FORGET, tonight is dinner with Mack and Davena." I rummaged in my purse for my building pass.

"Got it." Bill tapped his head and pulled the car up to the curb. "I'll meet you there. I can't get out of the office any sooner."

"I know, babe. That's why I scheduled it for eight o'clock. Luckily the Donovans aren't early birds."

"No shit. They're bigger partiers than us, which is depressing considering they're twice our age." He leaned down to peck me on the cheek. "I'll see you later."

"Thanks for taking me to work today," I said and winked. "I owe you."

"Love you," he called as I shut the door behind me.

"Oh, hello, fancy girl!" I heard from behind me. "Can't be bothered with public transportation like us common folk?"

"Hi, Jenny."

"I love Fridays," Jenny said as we walked to the front of the building. "They're so full of possibility. Know what I love more than Fridays though? Gossip."

"Where do you get all this?" I teased.

"Nothing gets by reception," she said, deadpan. "Beman's going to fire Diane."

"What?" I asked, stopping suddenly. "He wouldn't fire a senior editor with everything that's coming up. How do you know?"

"I just know. I also know that he's going to hire you in her place."

"You're joking," I said, trying to suppress a smile. "But isn't Lisa next in line? Are you sure?"

"Yep. Everyone knows you've been carrying Diane's load for years." I stiffened when she touched my arm. "Since we're early, want to grab a coffee with me?"

"No," I said with faux disappointment. "I want to get a head start on the day. I'll see you up there?"

"Sure thing."

I headed to the fourteenth floor and shook my head in disbelief. I'd been working hard under Diane for years but senior editor was a leap. Was I ready to step into her position? My dad's voice was clear in my ear: *Say yes to everything. Never pass up an opportunity.*

Coming off the elevator, I almost ran right into the editor-in-chief and balked as I was hit with the smell of his self-tanner. His face pinched, deepening the many wrinkles around his eyes.

"Good morning, Olivia," he said as we switched positions. "Nice to see you here early. Come by my office in an hour, I have something I'd like to discuss with you."

"Absolutely, Mr. Beman," I said as the elevator doors closed between us. I turned the corner to see Lisa through the glass doors, hovering over Jenny's desk.

Damn. I exhaled audibly and pushed through the doors to *Chicago Metropolitan Magazine,* giving her a quick wave. *What time does she get here anyway?*

I made sure to arrive at Beman's office exactly one hour after our conversation. It was all I needed to decide what my answer would be. I waited, seated before him, while he tediously tidied his desk. As always, his back was a little too straight, and the part in his white hair was a little too perfect.

"I fired Diane this morning," he said suddenly. I didn't have to fake my surprise because before I had a chance to respond, he continued. "I've been very pleased with your work as an editorial assistant. Not only do I think of you as an innovative editor, but your writing style fits the magazine very well."

"Thank you, Mr. Beman," I said, masking my shock at the compliment. "Your opinion means a great deal to me."

"It's not my opinion, it's just the truth," he said. "In any case, I'm moving Lisa into Diane's position and giving you her title of associate editor." My face heated with disappointment. I almost wished Jenny hadn't mentioned anything, and I definitely wished I wouldn't have to work as Lisa's inferior.

"Mr. Beman, if I may—I've been working closely with Diane for almost three years now. I'm ready to step into her position."

He eyed me carefully as I remained passive, watching him back. "As our associate editor, Lisa is technically next in line. You believe you're ready, though?"

"Yes."

"Let's try this then. We'll start with one of our most popular features: 'Chicago's Most Eligible Bachelors and Bachelorettes.' It's got potential to be our top-selling issue of the year. Let's entice advertisers with our best selection of people yet. Move into Diane's office for now and work with Lisa on the article, along with whatever other assignments Diane had coming up. I'll decide who I'd like to promote after the issue hits."

I nodded and stood to shake his hand. "I'm in. Thank you, sir." He sent me on my way with the news that Diane was already cleared out and then requested I send Lisa in to see him. She gave me a knowing, slightly triumphant smile as she glided past me to his office.

After moving what few items I had from my cubicle to Diane's office, I excitedly picked up planning where she'd left off. In my enthusiasm, I decided to enlist the help of an intern.

"Looks like we'll be working together on *Most Eligible*," I said, poking my head into Lisa's office on my way to the interns' station. She only grunted in response, never taking her eyes off her computer screen. Lisa was nothing if not passive aggressive, which would be fine if her bitterness didn't surface in other ways. "So I'll come by this afternoon, and we can get started. I can catch you up on where Diane left off."

She blinked up at me for a quick second. "Great, Liv. I'm crazy this afternoon, but I'll try to squeeze you in."

I gave her a tight smile, but she was already ignoring me again. Moments later I was staring at the back of a short blonde bob that ended in soft, pink tips. "Are you Serena?"

A young girl, who I guessed to be just out of college, turned suddenly. "Oh, yes. Mrs. Germaine? Or is it Ms. Germaine? Jenny wasn't sure." She glanced at my ring. "Or something else?"

"Whatever you like. Call me Liv if you want. About the article you e-mailed last night. You sent it awfully late."

"I know, I'm sorry," she said, her light eyes widening. "I was feeling so, like, inspired, and I didn't want to stop so I was up all night working on it. Next time I can wait to send it 'til the morning."

"No, don't worry about that," I said, waving my hand. "I'm just glad you got it in early. Makes everyone's job easier."

"Oh!" She covered her mouth with her fingertips. "I thought I was in trouble."

"Nope. Anyway, I liked the article, but there are some things I want fixed. I'll e-mail my notes. In the meantime, Lisa and I will be taking over the annual 'Most Eligible' issue. I'd like it to be the best selection of bachelors and bachelorettes that we can possibly find. Can you start narrowing?"

"Sounds good," Serena said as she made notes on a yellow pad. "How do I know what to look for? Like, looks-wise or . . . like . . . occupations?"

I gave her a tense smile, wondering if I'd given instructions to the right person. I made a mental note to follow up later. "Grab issues from the last few years to get an idea of what we're looking for. I know they've weeded out people already, but this year I want the absolute best options out there. No friends of friends or relatives. Set up interviews with the top picks so Lisa and I can decide from there."

"K," she said. Even though it was just a letter, her voice wavered, and her eyebrows met in the middle.

"I was an intern once too." I gave her my best attempt at a reassuring face. "You'll figure it out."

~

"Hello, dear," Mack said when I entered the restaurant that evening. I loved how his smiles deepened the wrinkles by his eyes because they were always genuine.

"Mack," I said with a kiss on his cheek. I leaned over to his wife Davena.

"How are you, honey?" she asked, her down-home drawl a stark contrast to Mack's clean British accent.

"Bill should be here any minute. He's been at work late every night the past two weeks, but he's on his way."

"No problem," Mack said. "Let's sit and get a drink." He indicated the hostess. I let them go ahead. Their hands never unlinked while they maneuvered through the restaurant.

"How's work?" Davena asked once we were seated.

"Wonderful," I said. "I just found out I'm up for a promotion. My colleague, Lisa, is more qualified on paper, but I know I can handle the position."

"I knew you'd work your way up quickly," Davena said. "I never put my stamp on anyone I don't believe in."

"Thanks," I said, grinning. It was Davena's recommendation that had secured me the internship years earlier.

"Don't waste your energy on the competition," she added, studying her menu. "If I know you, she's the one who should be worried."

"And your mother?" Mack asked. "How is she?"

"She's well."

"Anything in the works?"

"Sure," I said lightly. "Isn't there always?"

He grinned appreciatively. "I always tell everyone what an outstanding writer she is. Brilliant artist," he mused. "I look forward to her next novel."

"Well, she certainly has an artist's temperament," I muttered.

"You know that Max, from her first novel, was based on me? A sprightly British cad, come to university to terrorize the young ladies of the U.S. of A."

"Of course she knows that Mack, you remind her incessantly," Davena teased.

"Rubbish," he said, sneaking me a devious smile. "She was quite the girl, your mother. Walked right into the university's newspaper office and demanded they print her piece on corporate sexism. I knew then that we'd be great friends. No surprise she became editor of that paper soon after. A real go-getter, like our Liv here." I frowned, and he laughed.

I spotted Bill through the diners and cringed when his elbow accidentally struck a woman in the head. The restaurant's lighting turned his gold shirt mustard.

"I was here on time," Bill said, breathing hard, "but parking is impossible." He leaned over and gave me a lingering kiss on the cheek. "Congrats on the job opportunity." He turned to Mack and Davena, dragging his chair from the table. "What'd I miss?"

"We were just reminiscing about old times," Mack said. "Here, have some wine."

"What's new with you guys?" Bill asked. I looked at him gratefully. He knew how I hated to talk about 'old times.'

"Well, Mack and I are headed on a last-minute trip to the Amalfi Coast, so we've been shopping ourselves silly."

"Correction, *she* has been shopping herself silly," Mack interrupted. "I'm just the human credit card."

She waved him off. "I only needed a bathing suit that'd cover my new scar." She pointed to her side. "No more bikinis for me," she scowled, "just old lady one-pieces." I eyed her petite but athletic body—she was the picture of health with olive skin and cropped, wavy blonde hair. Her fiery eyes were surpassed only by her sassy attitude.

Even with the discovery of her breast cancer three years earlier, I'd never seen her without a twinkle in her eye. Pity was not a word in her vocabulary, and I'd learned long ago that normalcy was the best medicine.

"You really should go see my best friend Lucy," I said.

"Which one is Lucy?"

"Her college friend," Davena said. "Try and keep up."

"Liv and Lucy rushed the same sorority," Bill said. "When they were accepted, they decided they liked each other better than any of the other girls and dropped out together."

"Oh, isn't that sweet?" Mack smiled, ever the romantic.

"She's a stylist, right?" asked Davena.

"Yes, and she works just across the street from me. I'm sure she can help you find something that's cute and conservative."

Davena made a gagging noise. "I hate that word. Me, conservative? No, missy."

"Why do you think she made me move from Dallas?" Mack joked.

"So can you take Liv on this vacation?" Bill asked, nodding in my direction. "This girl needs some sun."

I pouted. "I'm not that bad," I said, pushing up my sleeve as the table laughed.

"You stay out of the sun, hon," Davena said. "Fair skin is in. Embrace it."

I laughed and nodded. "Sure it is. Pale is all the rage."

"Hey, Davena—get this. We just finished a case against a doctor who botched a mastectomy and nearly killed the woman."

"That's horrid, Bill. I don't want to hear that."

I almost rolled my eyes at Bill's inept social skills.

"Really, dear, how's mum?" Mack asked me with a lowered voice.

"I haven't spoken to her much lately," I confessed. "She says she's working on a new book but won't say what exactly. And since Dad no longer owes her alimony, she claims she's broke. But between a successful career and my father's support all those years, I just don't see how that can be." I found Mack's company comforting. Because of their history, he knew my mother in a way Bill and my friends couldn't. "Bill offered to lend her money, but I think it's bad idea. And we really don't have it to spare, since we're house hunting."

"Are you?" he asked, and clapped his hands once. "I'm so happy for you. You really are all grown up, little Liv. I still remember your first birthday—such a fabulous event your mother threw, and you, hardly able to enjoy it. She had that party for herself."

"What's so funny?" Davena asked when we both laughed.

"These two are house hunting."

"Oh, you know Mack and I own quite a bit of property, so we're nearly experts."

Bill smiled proudly and launched into a recount of our progress. It was his favorite topic as of late, so I let him talk and nodded at all the right times. Davena was sure to interject when she disagreed with Bill, and he made no attempt to hide his irritation. If there'd been an ounce of religion in my household growing up, Mack and Davena would've been my godparents. They'd always been protective, and Davena, being a natural know-it-all, didn't mind pointing out when Bill was wrong.

During dinner, I admired Mack and Davena's easy interaction. They touched often, as if Mack was reassuring her of his presence. Once, when he thought we weren't looking, Mack leaned in and kissed her between bites. She rolled her eyes playfully. I smiled at Bill, but he was looking at his phone.

When we'd settled the check, Mack said, "Don't worry too much about your mother. Leanore's always been able to take care of herself. Just remember that she may need emotional support more than she needs money." He patted me on the back. His words rang true, but unfortunately, emotional support had never been my strong suit. "And if we can be of any help with the house hunt, just call."

"Have a great trip," Bill said as we stepped out onto the sidewalk. He draped his arm over my shoulders and waved as they walked away. "Hey," he said, ruffling my hair. "Bad news. I have to go back to the office."

"What?" I looked up at him. "It's Friday night."

"I know, it's ridiculous. I'm so sorry. I'll make it up to you this weekend."

"It's all right," I said, running my hand down his long forearm. "I just don't want you to burn out."

"It'll all pay off when we buy our new home. Just think—you, me, peace and quiet . . . . It'll be so nice to finally get out of the city."

I opened my mouth to object and closed it again. Bill worked hard and deserved what he wanted, which was a spacious home in a calm neighborhood. It would be hard for me to adjust to that life after five years in Chicago, but I knew I would eventually get there. "You're right," I said. "It'll pay off then."

"So you're good to take the train?" he asked. "I might be late, so don't wait up."

~

I woke early but left Bill in bed to sleep. He hadn't come home until well past two in the morning, and I frowned to think of how hard he'd been working. I threw on my rattiest t-shirt and black spandex pants before raking my hair back into a ponytail. As I was grabbing my tennis shoes, Bill turned, muttered something, and hugged my pillow to him.

I started out the day with some Madonna and bounced down the street, taking a right, then a left, all the while humming along to "Papa Don't Preach." A few songs in, I yanked the headphones from my ears and pushed into the building. Telltale sounds of a bustling animal shelter pierced the air; high-pitched meows punctured low, deep barks. I'd been volunteering at the shelter twice a month since Bill and I had moved to the area, more if I could manage.

On my way to the back, I stopped at a floor cage to peer inside. "Well, you're new," I cooed to a miniature black-and-caramel mutt. His big eyes blinked up at me as he sat motionless. "Don't worry. You're in good hands." I righted myself and came face to face with George.

"Morning, Liv."

"Hi, George. How are things?"

His smiled waned. I knew the answer. Life at the animal shelter could be a lot of things: fun, rewarding, messy, sweet—and quite often, heartbreaking. Though there were no-kill shelters in the area, they got more volunteers than the ones that weren't. And that wasn't the fault of the animals. They needed exercise, food, and love too, even if they might not last until the end of the week.

"So put me to work then. What's top of the list today?"

"Eureka needs a walk," he said, making a face. "She's been bouncing off the walls all morning, and no one else wants to take her."

I laughed. "That's why I've got my tennies," I said, curling my leg up. "Bring it on."

Once I heard the emphatic clicking of four sets of toenails against the concrete, I braced myself. Eureka flew through the door and stopped short just as she got to me, straining against her leash.

"She's all yours," George called over her barking. As I took the leash, she jumped up to lick my face, and then sniffed my shoes, working her way up to my crotch.

"All right, girl, that's enough," I said, laughing as I pushed her snout away.

I mustered all the enthusiasm I had and ran her down to Lakefront Trail while fending off her overzealous attempts to french my face. Once we hit the path, we slowed to a walk, and I kept her close as we passed laughing children, zooming cyclists, and fellow dogs. When she'd calmed down a bit, we sat to people watch. She wagged her tail excitedly at everyone who looked our way.

"Hey. Olivia, right?"

I glanced up, trying to place the man standing over me.

"Rick," he said. "From the ballet."

"Oh, of course. Rick." I recognized him as Gretchen's would-be suitor. "What are you up to?"

"Just finishing up a run. Is this your dog?"

"No, no. She's from the shelter. We're just getting her some fresh air."

"Oh. A volunteer?"

"You got it."

"Well, she's a cutie."

"She is, but she has a lot of energy," I said, waving my hand for emphasis. Just then, Eureka stood up and sniffed Rick's leg. She sat back and watched him, panting and waiting patiently for him to pet her.

"You know, I had a Pit Bull growing up. I think she might be half." He examined her. "How old is she?"

"About a year. She should calm down soon, she just has that puppy energy right now." I watched him stroke her fur and murmur softly. "She also has all her shots," I added.

He looked up and smiled. "I know what you're getting at. To tell you the truth, getting a dog has crossed my mind. I just worry I don't have the time."

"I can put you in touch with dog walkers. A lot of city dwellers use them. And on the weekends you'd have a running partner."

He crouched down then and took her face in his hands, rubbing her head. "What's her name?"

"Eureka."

"Eureka. That's great," he said, laughing. "She is most definitely a Eureka. Well, Liv, I'll give it some thought."

"That would be great," I said.

"Where can I find her?"

"Here, give me your information," I said, handing him my cell phone. "I'll text you the info. One thing though . . . Eureka has been at the shelter for a few weeks now, and I don't know how much longer she'll be around."

"Isn't that a good thing?"

I shook my head slowly.

"Oh." He ran his hand over his chin. "Shit."

"I'm sorry. No pressure."

"Eureka, huh?"

"You could someone around, right? Single?"

He nodded. "Single. In fact, I took Gretchen out last week. She's great."

"But?"

"Very independent. So independent that I can't get her to return my calls."

I laughed. "I'm sorry. We grew up together, and I can promise you this: it's not you, it's her."

He waved me off. "Got it. Nice talking to you. Text me that info tonight if you can."

I stood and watched him run off, clasping my hands in hopes that he would come through. Sometimes things were just meant to be, and Rick hitting on Gretchen at the ballet seemed like one of those things. When I looked down, Eureka had wound herself between my legs, ensnaring me in a certified leash trap.

"What are you doing?" I sang, trying to detangle myself. Just then, a small dog across the way started barking, and Eureka bolted for her, knocking me on my back. "Eureka!" I screamed, restraining her with every ounce of muscle I had, which apparently, was just enough.

"Whoa, whoa, whoa!" I heard a man's voice call as he ran over and rounded her up. "Now there's an expression I haven't heard in quite some time," he said, bending over me. Bleached blond locks hung around his handsome, tanned face.

"I'm sorry?"

"Eureka."

"Oh." I grinned, taking his outstretched hands and noting how his toned arms flexed from his cut-off tank as he pulled me up. "No, that's her name."

"Ah, of course. That makes more sense." His smile was friendly. "Are you all right?"

"Just a little embarrassed, thanks."

"Don't be, it was a very graceful fall, all things considered." I blushed and shook my head, noticing his furtive glance at my left hand. "Well, I should take off before I lose my heart rate. Try to be more careful, Eureka," he called as he ran off.

"We'd better get you back before you kill me or someone else," I told the dog. We ran all the way back to the shelter, where I gathered her information to send to Rick.

CHAPTER 3

I WAVED TO GRETCHEN as I exited the building.

"Hello, spring!" she called.

"Not quite." I crossed my arms against the evening chill.

"Where's Lucy? Is she still coming?"

"Running an errand." I shrugged. "She'll meet us at the restaurant."

"Come on." She squeezed her hand through the crook of my arm. "It's Monday, and it's happy hour. Let's get toasty."

We made our way down the street, and it reminded me of my first year in Chicago. The three of us would meet at our apartment after work, change quickly, and end up staying out until the early morning hours without realizing it. It was a time when responsibility was just another word in the dictionary. Where had the time gone? Things were different now, there was no doubt. But something in particular felt amiss. With the onset of the new season, change seemed imminent, although I couldn't identify why that might be.

The man from the theater's presence was static cling on my skin. I still could not recall the exact details of his face, or even the way he was dressed. But those eyes, that warmth, that inexplicable feeling—they were the things I couldn't seem to shake. Had he felt it too? And what had he seen in my eyes?

"Dirty martini," Gretchen's voice cut into my thoughts.

"And for you?" the bartender asked. "Wait, let me guess . . . pomegranate margarita, on the rocks, no salt."

"What makes you say that?" I asked with a small smile.

"Pretty girls always want pomegranate."

Gretchen's huff did not go unnoticed by either of us. I leaned off the bar, suddenly embarrassed by his forwardness. "I'll have a Guinness."

He raised his eyebrows at me and nodded.

"And make mine extra dirty," Gretchen hissed. I stifled a laugh and went to find a table.

"John has a new girlfriend," Gretchen divulged once we had our drinks. I rolled my eyes and pressed her for more information. "Don't be jealous," she said, referring to the playful crush her brother had harbored for me since we were kids. "She's the new receptionist at his office so it's totally under-wraps. John's typical type: blonde, young, and one crayon short of a box."

I laughed loudly. "But John's a catch. How come he gets hung up on these bimbos?"

"I'm sure a short therapy session would reveal it's got a little something to do with the divorce. When my mom left, he never really forgave her for it. If your parents—"

"Cheers," I cut her off, raising my glass. "It's happy hour, Gretch, not depressed, wallowing hour."

"Oh." She grabbed her drink. "Cheers."

I welcomed the bitter alcohol as it slid down my throat.

"By the way . . . Guinness?" she asked. "Never once, since we started drinking in high school, have I seen you drink that."

I shrugged. "I panicked. I was going to order pomegranate."

She laughed and pointed at the table. "Your phone."

Apr 2, 2012 6:17 PM
Where are you?

The curtness of Bill's text message wasn't lost on me. I told him Lucy had called a last minute happy hour.

Apr 2, 2012 6:21 PM
Didn't we just see them?

Quickly, I tapped out a response.

Apr 2, 2012 6:22 PM
She said it's 911. Won't be long.

Gretchen also expertly navigated her iPhone.

"Where is that girl?" I asked. "She's usually the early one." As if on cue, Lucy appeared through the doorway. She spotted us right away and rushed over, almost breaking into a run. When she reached the high top, she took a deep breath, sat down calmly, and grabbed the plastic happy hour menu. Her face turned many shades of red as she sat unmoving, ignoring our gawking.

"What is it?" I pressed. Lucy held the menu up to her face, wiggled her left hand and then peered at us with smiling eyes. My mouth dropped. "Andrew proposed?" I asked, staring at the conspicuous ring.

"Yes," Lucy squealed. "Last night."

"What?" we exclaimed in unison.

"You've withheld this all day?" Gretchen was indignant.

"Well, I wasn't going to tell you over the phone."

"How did it happen?" Gretchen demanded.

"Sunday is *our* day, right? He was acting strange all afternoon, and then he asked if I wanted to go see a movie. Normally we stay in on Sundays, but he said he really wanted to see some action movie that everyone had been talking about at work. I said no, but he promised to take me for ice cream afterward, so I agreed.

"Well, we go out of the way to this small theater in Lincoln Square, that's totally not our regular place, and when we arrive, he waltzes right in without paying or anything. I'm like, 'Andrew, *what* is going on?' but he won't tell me. We enter an empty theater where there's an attendant holding a tray of two bubbling champagne flutes. Instantly, the screen lights up, and I recognize the first bars of "Moon River." *Breakfast at Tiffany's*, my favorite movie. We take the drinks and follow the man to the middle of the theater. There, resting on my seat, is that famous little blue bag. I begin to cry right away. Andrew pulls out the box, tells me how much he loves me, and asks me to marry him."

"Wow," Gretchen said, grinning.

I took Lucy's hand and admired the three oval cut diamonds, centered on a smooth platinum band. As she spoke, lost in some other world, I moved my left hand next to hers. My gold and diamond solitaire stone was an heirloom Bill had inherited from his grandmother. Lucy's ring, like the proposal, could've been designed by Lucy herself. I found comfort in the fact that Andrew knew her so well.

Bill had bent on one knee as our friends and family looked on. His pants had been short, riding up too high when he kneeled. Everyone looked, watching my every move, waiting for the magic word from me.

For the next hour, Lucy, Gretchen and I passed the news around like a hot potato, jumping from detail to detail. Lucy straightened her back as she envisioned aloud her dream wedding.

"And of course there's the matter of the bridal party," she said, pursing her lips. Gretchen and I broke into large smiles and nodded our heads in anticipation of the question.

"Gretchen Harper, Olivia Germaine," she started. "Please do me the honor of being the bridesmaids in my wedding! I've asked my sister to be the maid of honor, and that's it. My three girls."

We agreed immediately, having discussed this moment many times before.

"I can't *believe* you never took Bill's last name," Lucy said after I tilted my head back for the last sip of beer. "I can't wait. Lucille Marie Greene."

I twisted my mouth at her. "It's more hassle than you realize," I said. "Tons of paperwork." They raised their eyebrows at me. "What? It's not that I don't want to, I just never got around to it."

"Poor Bill," Gretchen said with a shake of her head.

I sighed. "Well, maybe that will be my project for the summer. I know it would make him happy. It's just that . . . Wilson? It's so . . ." I made a face. "I don't feel like a Wilson."

"Are you telling me this whole time you've been putting it off because you don't like it?"

They giggled. I shrugged.

"Maybe. Speaking of Mr. Wilson," I said, pulling out my phone to text him. "I wonder if I can get him to pick me up."

"I have to take off too," Lucy said. "My entire day is booked with appointments tomorrow."

"How is it you get to shop for a living?" asked Gretchen. "That makes me jealous."

"Don't be. You try reasoning with a sixty-year-old woman who only wants to wear ivory to her daughter's wedding. She insists it's not the same as wearing white."

"What's wrong with that?" I asked, then recoiled at Lucy's horrified look. "Joking. I promise—no white for your wedding. Or ivory."

"You'll be wearing whichever color I choose, bridesmaid, so tread carefully. Personally, I think you'd look lovely in lilac, Liv." I made a choking sound, and we dissolved into laughter.

"First order of business as a bridesmaid," I said as I pulled up the calendar on my phone, "don't plan anything for the Saturday two weeks away." I shot Gretchen a look when she opened her mouth to object. "Engagement party!"

Gretchen stopped short and nodded excitedly, wisely keeping whatever date or commitment she had planned to herself.

Lucy agreed readily. She'd been waiting for this moment her entire life. She listed off some ideas, all of which I'd heard before, but I listened anyway.

"Come over this weekend," I said to Gretchen. "We can work on invitations as we plan. *Gretchen and Olivia's Party Planning Service.*"

"I'll bring muffins," Gretchen said.

"And Luce, send over Andrew's contacts," I said and grinned. "That is, if he wants any of *his* friends to attend."

My phone pinged with Bill's response.

·

Apr 2, 2012 8:20 PM
Out front

"Ride's here," I said. "You guys need a lift?"
"I'm meeting up with people."
"K. Lucy?"
She shook her head.
I leaned over and kissed her on the cheek. "Congratulations," I said softly.

A cool blast hit me as I stepped outside. Bill's silhouette leaned over the seat to open my door, and I was greeted with Robert Smith's melancholy voice. Bill's mood could usually be determined by his choice of music; The Cure meant brooding in our house.

"Babe?" I asked.

"If you're going out, why can't you get the train home?"

"You could've said no." When I'd first been hired at the magazine, Bill would drop me off and pick me up whenever he could, because it meant a little extra time together. Now, it was rare with the schedule he kept. I glanced over in the darkness, wondering if he was remembering the same thing. "Next time I'll take the 'L'."

"These brakes are done," he muttered. "I have to take the car in again."

"We could get a new one," I suggested for the third time since January. "Maybe my dad's Shelby?"

"Why? This one runs fine."

"It's old, Bill. It's not like we can't afford a new one."

"We can't afford—"

"All right, maybe not the Shelby, but something else. Just because it works—like your mother's couch—doesn't mean it's the best option."

"We don't need the Shelby. It's not practical." He grunted and after a moment, slammed his palms against the steering wheel. "Come on. This isn't goddamn rush hour. What's the hold up?"

Ignoring his outburst, I excitedly told him about Lucy and Andrew's engagement. As I spoke, his shoulders relaxed. "That's great," he said. "Really great. They're a good couple."

"They really are," I said, looking out the window. Yellow street lamps and dark shadows blurred together as we picked up pace.

CHAPTER 4

GRETCHEN AND I SAT AT MY KITCHEN
TABLE, laptops open and address books splayed out.
We each sipped a cup of coffee on Saturday morning as
we prepared invitations to Lucy's engagement party.
Andrew had e-mailed me his contact list, agreeing to not
only host the event at their place, but foot the bill as well.
An expense I wouldn't have to justify to Bill.

Gretchen addressed envelopes as I leaned against
the counter, staring at the precise handwriting on my
stack of invitations.

"What is this, the break room?" Gretchen asked.

I blinked at her, absentmindedly blowing on my
drink.

"Back to work. Where's Bill anyway?" she asked
abruptly, as though she'd just noticed his absence.

"Basketball. Andrew's started playing with them. I
think they're getting pretty chummy."

"Oh." She coiled a roll of stamps around her finger.
"Do you guys do it on this table?"

I nearly spit out my coffee as I burst into laughter.
"No," I exclaimed with a reproachful look. "But I could

use some excitement in my life. I'm sure you have something juicy for me. Spill."

"I went out with that guy Rick from the ballet a few times, but that's about it right now."

"I forgot to tell you."

She cocked an eyebrow at me. "What?"

"I ran into him last weekend when I was walking one of the dogs from the shelter. For one, he told me you wouldn't call him back."

"Nah. He's sort of whack."

"He seems nice. Anyway, he was interested in the dog I was walking, Eureka, and I just found out that he adopted her."

"Well. That's sweet. Now I feel bad about not calling him back."

"Well you can't now, what if you end up together? I'd never be able to forget how you called him whack."

"All right, for your sake, I'll leave it be."

"Gee, thanks."

"There is something else, though," she said hesitantly.

"Spill," I demanded again, alarmed at the nervous look on her face.

"I got a message from Greg the other night."

"What?" I said, dropping my pen onto the table. "Why didn't you say anything?"

"I didn't know how to feel about it. I still don't."

"What did it say?"

"To call him."

I narrowed my eyes at her. "Did you?"

She shook her head vigorously, blonde wisps escaping from the bun on top of her head. I had flashbacks to the apartment Lucy and I had shared at Notre Dame, where the three of us would sit at *that* kitchen table talking about Greg.

During our first class of Introductory Biology, Greg and I were the only people who seemed to notice how crazy the professor was. We'd looked at each other across the room and made the same face. We became fast friends and turned out to be dorm neighbors too. He, Lucy and I would discuss lectures over cold pizza in the dining hall or stay up late drinking Kahlua hot chocolates under the fleece Fighting Irish blanket my dad had sent me. He was smart and charming, and I was proud to call him a friend.

He and Gretchen grew to know each other over the weekends that she would visit me from Chicago. They didn't make it official until junior year, but I had instantly seen how compatible they were.

When smart and charming Greg mercilessly broke up with Gretchen two days before graduation, he wounded all of us: me, Lucy, and the rest of our tight-knit college family. He'd told us that he'd accepted a job in Japan, an offer we'd heard nothing about, and that he was moving to start a new life. I knew he was afraid of how intense things had become with Gretchen, and I tried to get her to see that too. She spent the weeks following graduation wallowing at her parents' house, accepting little comfort. When she emerged, it was to sign the lease on our new apartment and she never mentioned his name again. Until now.

"Wow," I said softly. "Aren't you curious about what he has to say?"

She widened her eyes at me and shook her head again. "It's done," she said with finality.

We both jumped a second later when her phone vibrated against the wooden table. We exchanged a wary glance before she peeked at it without touching, as though it might bite. "It's just John," she said before answering on an exhale. "Hey. Yep that's fine, just send me—uh huh, okay—just send me the file, and I'll look it over." She put her hand over the mouthpiece and whispered, "Maybe he ought to hire a capable secretary instead of bugging me to edit his press releases. Nothing, just talking to Liv." She paused. "Sure, hang on." She held the phone out to me.

"Hi, John."

"Hi, beautiful. I miss you." I could hear the smile in his voice.

"I miss you too," I said. "How come you never visit your lovely sister and her awesome friends?"

"Just say the word, Germaine, and I'm there."

I laughed loudly and Gretchen, all too familiar with her brother's penchant for flirting, rolled her eyes.

"How are you?" he asked. "Really? No bullshit."

"Hanging in there," I said.

"Don't say that. You know I hate it."

"All right—I'm great. Better than ever."

"That's no good either. I want you to be happy, but not too happy. At least not 'til we get together."

I shook my head and reddened. "Will you ever give up?"

He chuckled. "Is Bill taking care of you?"

"Yes."

"And work?"

"Good. I'm up for a promotion, in fact. Speaking of work, I hear you have a new—" I stopped when Gretchen slapped my arm. "Er . . . a new stapler."

"Gretch told you. I do have a new girl. But quit trying to change the subject. Tell me something about your life that's not in the public domain."

"I don't really have much going on right now."

"Come on. You're holding out on me."

"Oh, I know. Bill and I—"

"Nope."

"I'm married, John. I hardly have a life of my own. How about this—I'm going to ask my dad for the Shelby. Bill doesn't know though," I added, looking at Gretchen.

"The '68? Livs, you spoiled brat. You always get what you want, ever since we were kids. That car is a trip. You'd look hot in it."

"Okay," I said. "I'm giving you back to your sister."

"Wait, Liv." He paused. "I'm glad you're doing well. Next time I want more though."

"Here's your sister."

"I didn't hear your side of the conversation," Gretchen said, "but Liv here is as red as that Shelby. You're lucky Bill's not around to see this."

I threw some muffin at her and immediately picked it up before turning my attention back to the invitations.

CHAPTER 5

TO MY SURPRISE, the engagement party was a success. It boasted a fine crowd that was neither too small nor too big. Guests brought tastefully-wrapped gifts, which slid off of manicured fingertips and onto a glass dining table. Lucy and Andrew's River North apartment was the perfect backdrop to the upscale crowd. Snow-white plush carpet spanned the living room where guests congregated. I idly wondered how Lucy kept it so pristine. Her spotless nature was enviable—she seemed to repel mess. Large windows framed Chicago's dotted skyline while dim lighting illuminated the overstuffed white leather couches, a sleeping fireplace, and a well-stocked bar.

I waved at Jack, a work acquaintance I'd hired as bartender for the night. He winked, expertly pouring a martini into the empty glass of Lucy's middle-aged colleague. She just watched, rapt.

In the nearest window, I caught the reflection of my very fitted white dress that dipped just off my shoulders. I'd be avoiding the dessert table for the night. Just beyond, the sky was starless.

It was easy to go unnoticed in this crowd. Despite Lucy and Andrew's high-society social circle, I was dissatisfied with the company. I overheard tidbits here and there of the same old fodder. A tap on my bare shoulder caused me to start.

"Just a little something for the party planner." Jack held out a glass of red wine, garnished with a dashing smile.

"Exactly what I need. How'd you know?"

"Bartender's sixth sense." He placed his cold hand on my shoulder, and my arm tensed. "Come find me later," he said.

Alone again, I took a sip of wine and promptly spilled on my dress. I cursed my clumsiness on the way to Lucy's kitchen.

With a damp hand towel pressed against the impurity on my breast, I turned from the sink. My gaze hit those hooded eyes from the theater. I froze. I was back there, as if no time had passed. I racked my brain. Had we invited him? I couldn't know. I had no idea who he was.

He flattened his hands on the surface of the island between us. "Tell me your name." His thick voice was my desire manifested. Words stuck in my mouth, choking me. It never occurred to me to question the intensity of his question, the urgency in his voice. "What's your fucking name?" It wasn't malicious, but pleading.

"Olivia," I replied levelly, not recognizing my own voice.

"Olivia," he repeated, momentarily satisfied. He reached a long arm over the island and placed his hand over my mine—the one that held, now clutched, the towel. Goose bumps lighted over my skin. He took the towel, and I dropped my hand as he rounded the island. His eyes never left mine. He pressed the cloth against my breast. "Olivia," he said softly. "I'm desperate to know you."

My lashes fluttered underneath him. I'd remembered his eyes as dark, but they were an indisputable light chestnut brown, intensified a thousand times by his jet-black, bushy eyebrows. His freshly shaven jawline was angular and ended with a cleft chin, the only soft curve among otherwise chiseled features.

I tore my eyes away and looked down, swallowing so I might say something. I didn't quite know if I should protest his brazen approach, or if I should listen to my body and move against him. Before I had a chance to respond, Bill's laugh floated in from the other room. I half-leaped back to the sink as he blew through the door with a leftover smile on his face. He came straight to me at the sink and linked his arm around my waist, leaning down to kiss my forehead.

His loud voice carried back into the party. "Livs, Hugh insists the Bulls are headed toward defeat so I had to set him straight."

"Your husband is this close to betting your down payment on the playoffs," Hugh called from the other room, "and I can't say I haven't warned him." I forced a small laugh for Bill, but my insides turned over, and my heart fluttered like a trapped butterfly.

"Anyway," he continued, "I just came for the sweets." He smiled, just for me, and placed an oversized cupcake into a red napkin. He walked away, and I glanced back at the man who'd never stopped watching me. His eyes slowly traveled the length of my left arm until they rested on my hand. I only had a moment to try and comprehend his fallen expression before I heard footsteps again. I moved around the island, distancing myself from his spell just as Andrew waltzed into the kitchen.

"Where've you been?" he asked, just as he noticed the mystery man whose face, I was sure, revealed too much. "Ah, David. Of course. Always one with the ladies." Andrew laughed casually, nodding toward the man.

David, I thought. A common name; nothing out of the ordinary. But now I repeated it to myself behind sealed lips, as though it were the first time.

"Actually, we haven't met yet," David said. I turned to glare at him. He was calm and unperturbed, as if everything were normal. Slowly, he scrunched up the sleeves of his black V-neck pullover and rolled up the cuffs of the white button down underneath.

I, on the other hand, had been startled into silence. I mimicked his relaxed stance, loosening my shoulders and releasing my death grip on the counter.

"I was just—getting her a towel," he said. "For the stain."

"Liv, meet David," Andrew said. "He's the lead architect on our new office building in the Loop. And I hope if I hang around him enough, some of his charm will rub off." He winked at me. "The ladies in my office can't get enough of the guy." He pulsed his eyebrows at David. "And you usually have your hands full. No date tonight?"

David let out a short laugh, shaking his head. He wiped his brow with the back of his hand.

Andrew shrugged the way Bill always did. Except when he was angry. I wondered, watching Andrew smile, if he switched as easily between temperaments as Bill.

My tongue shot into my cheek as I looked back at David. He must have women falling all over him. I cringed. Someone that confident—who could relax on command, and who was that smoldering—someone like that knew what he was doing. And was only interested in one thing.

"Well," I interjected, having returned to myself, who was a little indignant. "Looks like I'm all cleaned up. Andrew, where's Lucy? I've hardly seen her tonight." I stepped backwards, distancing myself. "David." I faltered so briefly, only someone watching closely would've noticed. "Nice to meet you."

I turned and strode away, finding Lucy within the next couple steps.

"Hey," she said, touching my arm. "Are you all right?"

"I'm fine." My voice was unnaturally high. "What a party. Professional planners?"

Gretchen, who'd apparently been keeping Jack company, waved and ran over.

"You guys are amazing," Lucy said, looking between us. "Thank you for doing this." An impeccably-timed server passed with a tray of bubbling champagne. Following Gretchen's lead, we held up our glasses to each other.

"To you, Lucy, and your *fiancé*,"—Lucy smiled at the word—"all the best!" We each took a giddy sip.

"*Who* is that?" Gretchen asked suddenly. I didn't need to turn to know. Lucy sought out Gretchen's mystery man and nodded knowingly when her eyes fixated behind me.

"That, my friend, is David. He's doing work for Andrew's firm. They've bonded over sailing." Noticing Gretchen's raised eyebrows she said, "I know."

"Sailing?" I asked.

"Oh, didn't I tell you? Andrew wants to get a *boat*."

"He is just . . ." Gretchen trailed off, and I could almost see the wheels turning in her head. A deceptively innocent smile touched her lips as she seemed to make eye contact with him.

He breezed by the three of us with Lucy and Gretchen's eyes conspicuously on him, and I was incensed that he might think we were talking about him.

"Look at that ass," Gretchen said, her mouth twisting into an appreciative smirk.

"Oh, Gretchen," Lucy said. "You're being vulgar."

"I'm just stating the obvious," she said. "Don't tell me you weren't thinking the exact same thing, Lucille Marie."

Lucy blushed crimson at the suggestion and looked away.

"That's what I thought," Gretchen said with a nod, and we laughed.

When I saw her sharp eyes still concentrated in David's direction, my laughter quickly faded. For the first time in a long time, I remembered the excitement that came from being unattached—excitement born of possibility and anticipation. "I'll have to introduce myself later," she said, more to herself than to us.

Panic descended. "I met him in the kitchen. He seems like a jerk. Andrew practically said he's a playboy, so I wouldn't bother." How many girls had he suckered in with those eyes?

Gretchen gave me a curious glance, but she shrugged. "Not looking to marry the guy."

Lucy waved down a passing tray and handed us each a mini tuna tartare. "It's true. Andrew says since he's met him, he's seen him with a few different women, and they were all striking. Andrew actually said *striking*."

Gretchen waved the appetizer away. "Are we still on for lunch this week?"

I pivoted to see David from the corner of my eye as he talked animatedly with someone. I strained to hear, but his endlessly deep voice just vibrated in my ears.

"Olivia," Lucy snapped. "What's with you? You're acting strange."

"What?" I asked. "What did I do?"

"We're talking about lunch on Monday. She asked if you're still coming?"

"Lunch?"

"Yes. Park Grill? Bridal magazine bonanza."

"Oh, lunch. I forgot." I tugged on my earlobe, still trying to hear while answering Lucy. "That should be fine, yes."

"Let's meet at your office at eleven thirty and walk together."

"Sure, of course," I replied. "Um, excuse me." I ducked across the living room, trying not to make eye contact with anyone. Was I crazy? Why was this stranger under my skin?

I needed to get out of the crowd, and I knew exactly where to do it. I pulled open the sliding glass door to the balcony, took a lungful of fresh air, and then coughed as smoke filled my throat. Two lit cigarettes floated in the corner. I recognized one smoker as Andrew's receptionist and nodded to her. She looked about to speak, but I left for the opposite end of the balcony before she could.

The iron railing was cool under my palms. I shivered and wrapped my arms around my bare skin.

Every time I looked out at the skyline, it was like the first time. Tiny blocks of light scattered randomly into the patterns of buildings, and I wondered about the inhabitants—what they were doing in that very moment. Leaning over the barrier, I examined the city below. It wasn't a long drop from the eighth floor, but it was enough to accelerate my heartbeat.

"Do you have any idea how that makes me feel?" my mother screamed. I hid behind the stucco wall and peered through the glass door as my father raised his hands in exasperation.

"Leanore, you're being ridiculous. Do you have any idea how that makes me feel? Like you don't trust me."

"How can I trust you when you're flirting with every woman in the hotel lobby. And in front of your daughter."

"Don't you bring Olivia into this," he said, sticking his finger in her face. "This is your problem, and you're ruining our vacation."

I turned away from the door and looked over the railing that hit right below my eyes. My fingers grasped the bars of the balcony, and I pulled on them as I lifted onto the balls of my feet. I wondered what it might be like to fly. Had anyone ever tried? Perhaps it was possible and nobody knew it. We'd learned about evolution in school. Maybe we had wings that would know the difference between flying and falling.

"Olivia." I jumped at the voice behind me. "Come inside, and fix your hair," my dad said. "I'll take you out for a milkshake, but not until you brush those tangles out."

For no reason at all, I turned and looked over my shoulder to find the man filling the doorway. His hands were fixed against the jamb, his head cocked as he watched me. He wore an open, black pea coat and dark jeans. *David.*

The smokers had stopped talking to gawk at him. He stepped out onto the concrete and stuck his hands in his pockets. As he walked toward me, I turned my attention back to the skyline. My mouth dried. My heart thumped. I couldn't let him know the effect he had on me. He came close, and I smelled his aftershave.

"You're married," he said to my back.

I drew a breath and nodded. "Happily." I glanced back again, and his face was solemn. Marveling at the believability of his act, I twisted to face him. Squaring my shoulders, I lifted my hands to the railing behind me in an attempt to appear casual. "And you're quite the Don Juan."

He seemed taken aback by my tone, but then a small smile touched his lips. "You look cold. Take my jacket."

"I'm fine." I shook my head as he moved to take it off. Never mind that I was wearing a coat of goose bumps.

He paused a moment, silent, before shrugging it back on. "Actually, I don't have much time for gallivanting," he said finally.

I shrugged with exaggerated indifference. "It's not really my business."

"I suppose it's not, but . . ."

From my gut, I urged him to finish his sentence.

He shook his head. "I have to get going."

My heart fell a millimeter before I stopped it. I glimpsed over his shoulder again at the women in the corner. They'd resumed their conversation, but Andrew's secretary glanced at us.

"I'd like to see you again."

My eyes whipped back to his. "What?" Lowering my voice to a whisper, I motioned at the others on the balcony. "There are plenty of women here—*single* women. If you're looking for company, I'm sure they'd be much obliged."

"I didn't mean anything romantic," he said smoothly. "You're clearly spoken for. But believe me when I say, if that weren't the case, we'd be having a different conversation."

His words burned into me. The intensity between us had never left, but it grew thicker in that moment. The truth was that I wanted to see him again. The thought of this being our last meeting sent a wave of dread through me. I gripped the railing.

"I should warn you, Olivia. I don't really take rejection well. I can be very persistent."

I looked him over, inhaling that intoxicating scent. I wasn't sure if he meant it as a threat, but his words thrilled me more than anything. "Nothing romantic?"

"No funny business. I promise." He held up his palms.

Without warning, emotions I'd been purposefully suppressing for years surfaced, threatening to fight back. Something was tugging at the locked door behind my ribcage.

If I could anticipate our meeting, at least I could manage it. Overcoming him would pose a challenge—a challenge that would earn me a gold medal in my Olympic games of self-domination. The image had me lift my chin in anticipated glory. I quickly swallowed the rising pang of guilt like a pesky pill.

"Tomorrow night," I relented. Bill would be leaving for New York in the morning to prepare for his latest round of depositions.

His shoulders squared as a smile slid slowly across his face. "Come to Jerome's on North Halsted at nine o'clock. I look forward to it, Olivia." The way he drew out my name felt like being touched. I exhaled the breath I'd been holding when he walked away.

"Having fun, David?" The secretary was loud, but I couldn't hear David's mumbled response. "Smoke?" She held out her pack. He responded, bowing his head. I was glad when he left and after a few moments, I followed, making a point not to look over at the smokers.

"Now, if you put the money in a Roth, it will grow tax free," Andrew was saying to Gretchen when I walked up.

"And that's better?"

"Well, yes, in your case—"

My heart jumbled with mixed emotions as David approached. He stopped, hanging behind Lucy. He rubbed his jaw and peered at me as her head moved back and forth between Andrew and Gretchen.

"There's the bride-to-be."

Lucy straightened immediately and turned to David. He dazzled her with a large smile, one that was almost too big for his face. One I hadn't yet seen.

"Congratulations again," he said. "And thank you both for having me."

"Anytime." Andrew settled his arm around Lucy. "We're glad you could make it. And I'll be taking you up on that offer."

"Oh, I don't know about that," Lucy said, suppressing a smile. "We're in trouble if he falls in love with your sailboat."

"Why don't you come too, Lucy? I'll take you both out."

"Oh," she said, covering Andrew's hand with hers. "I suppose I could be convinced."

"Sounds great. I'm off, then."

"Leaving already?" Gretchen asked. "It's not so late."

I looked away, focusing my eyes on anything but the impossible-to-ignore man in front of me.

"It isn't, but I have somewhere to be."

"Well, that's a shame," she cooed, holding out her hand. "I'm Gretchen, by the way."

"Nice to meet you," he said, but I knew his eyes were fixed on me.

CHAPTER 6

THE NEXT MORNING, I awoke to faint, early light coming through the windows. I closed my eyes and automatically slid from the edge to the middle of the bed. After a few moments, the clicking of metal forced its way into my sleep. I eased myself up. Once I'd wiped the sleep from my eyes, I focused on Bill's figure moving near the closet.

"Morning," he whispered, leaning over for a kiss.

"New York." I inhaled. "Right."

"Yeah. Sorry, babe. Stay in bed." He hoisted his brown leather bag over his shoulder.

I got up and followed him through the apartment.

"I'll be back late Thursday," he told me as we stood in the doorway. "But you knew that." With a quick kiss, he exited out to the hallway and then turned back to surprise me with a substantial kiss. "You look sexy right now," he said, slipping his hand into my silk robe.

"I doubt that."

"You do," he said, pinching my chin. "Bye."

A knot sat heavy in my stomach that day. In my unease, I couldn't bring myself to eat a thing. A sweet text from Bill at the airport had me feeling especially troubled. I reminded myself that my impending meeting was an end rather than a beginning. I would tell him what he wanted to know and then reiterate that I was married. I tried to find comfort in the thought but could not. It was the ending part that was bothering me.

In an effort to keep busy, I ran routine errands all afternoon. Even though I was alone for the next few days, and the thought of preparing meals wasn't exactly appealing, I picked up groceries. Dropped off Bill's dry cleaning. Took old linens to the animal shelter. Anything to keep me out of the apartment.

After what felt like a never-ending day, I surveyed the contents of my closet. What did one wear to such a thing as this? *To 'nothing romantic.'* I settled on a harmlessly beige silk blouse and tucked it into high-waisted black pants. My lipstick slid on darker than I expected, and I turned it over to check the name: *Vamp.* I yanked a tissue from the counter and held it to my lips but stopped short. The color was vivid against my pale skin. I let the tissue fall into the trashcan, deciding that maybe I'd be someone else tonight.

After clasping on a gold necklace and stepping into heels, I gave myself a once-over in the bathroom mirror. I drew my hair away from my face and instantly released it, feeling exposed. My wristwatch—a gift from Bill on our second anniversary—read eight o'clock. I bundled into my coat, hiked up the collar, and decided a walk would soothe my nerves.

On the way, my emotions ping-ponged between excitement and fear. I wondered if I could actually go through with it, if I'd actually go in and sit down and wait for him. I rarely backed down from a dare, but this was a different type of risk.

When I found the bar, I realized why he'd chosen it. Stone steps at the entrance led underground. At night, it was a place where people could spend the late hours as someone else—in the day, a place to hide from the sun. I looked down the stairwell that faded into black. The low swollen notes of a saxophone drifted up, beckoning me inside. Jazz looped through my ears and into my head, creeping into the dark corners of my mind. Like a devil on my shoulder, it willed me to take a step.

My eyes welled with tears. Whatever this was, I couldn't do it. I'd come too far in life to throw it down a stairwell. My watch read almost nine. I'd been standing for five minutes, entranced by the music. If I went back now, it'd be as though I'd never left. I turned to leave. And, as though he'd written it himself, he was there to catch me in his arms. His face came so close to mine that I could feel the heat from his mouth on my forehead.

"You're early," he said. The words rested against my skin. The skin near my face was dark with the shadow of fresh stubble and close enough to kiss . . . .

I jerked away, but like lightning, he caught my wrist. I went to pull back when I realized why; I was teetering at the edge of the stairs, the darkness ready to break my fall. When I caught my balance and he let go, we descended into the shadows together.

~

David signaled toward me from across the room, and the bartender nodded. He strolled back to where I was seated, as if he did this every night. He was at the table before my mind ran away with that thought.

We were an anonymous couple in the small crowd, cloaked in nothing but candlelight. I looked at my hands in my lap as I fingered my winking ring. "I don't know what I'm doing here," I said to the table.

"You look beautiful."

I didn't respond.

"From the bartender," he joked. "He wanted me to tell you."

I suppressed a smile. "Thank you. To the bartender."

I glanced at the waitress, who unhurriedly made her way toward us. She set down my wine, her eyes widening at David. She reached over his shoulder to place a tall, dark beer on the table. Something about the way her long hair grazed his shoulder made me squirm. He thanked her, and she idled a moment before leaving. I took a large sip of my wine.

"Shiraz?" I asked, inhaling.

He smiled as though he sensed my discomfort. "So, Olivia." There it was again, my name, but not like I'd ever heard it in my twenty-seven years. It sounded as though it were made for his mouth. "Do you work?"

"Yes," I said, dipping my head in an exaggerated nod. "At *Chicago M.*"

He leaned forward on his elbows. "Journalist?"

"Editorial assistant. Editor-in-training. I do contribute sometimes, but it's not ultimately what I want to do." It was hard to ignore the fact that he was staring at my mouth. "I don't really care for writing."

"But you like editing?"

"It's methodical. Like a puzzle. There are rules, and—do I have lipstick on my teeth?"

His eyes darted up. "No. Sorry. So, that's a no to writing."

"Basically."

"I've dealt with Diane at the magazine before. Do you work for her?"

I hesitated. "I did, actually. I was her assistant until recently. She was let go."

"I see. So you'll take her position?" The abrupt, intrusive question reminded me of my father.

"I'm in the running for it. I'm taking over some of her features, and if they go well, I may get promoted."

He sat back. I liked the way his molten brown eyes watched me, how they made me feel like the only person in the room. Jazz wooed us. Wine warmed my body. The private, dimly lit club was ideal for clandestine encounters. Why did he ask me here? And how many others had come before me?

"Another round," he said, jarring me from my thoughts.

The passing waitress nodded.

"How long have you been married?"

"Three years this summer."

"How did you meet your husband?"

"I used to work in his building."

"And he asked you out?"

"Not right away. We became friends over time." I fingered a button on my blouse, feeling suddenly too warm.

"How long?"

"How long what?"

"Before he asked you out." He'd leaned forward again, his focus growing more intense.

"Six months or so. Why?"

His eyes roamed my face. It felt like minutes before I spoke again. "What about you? Are you, you know, single?"

He raised an eyebrow.

"Don't read into that," I said. "I'm just making conversation."

The waitress was at the table with our drinks; how long she'd been there, I wasn't sure. She made a note on her pad, glancing up at David repeatedly.

"Am I single? I am available, yes."

Of course. He was a bachelor in the utmost sense. I knew the answer long before I'd asked the question.

"David."

"Yes, Olivia?"

"Why'd you want to see me tonight? What exactly can I do for you?" I sipped my drink and set it down, waiting. My fingers fidgeted with the stem as I looked at the couple at the next table, the floor, the liquor behind the bar. Anything but his unsettling gaze.

He reached over and steadied my hand with his. My nerves felt suddenly exposed, his touch rushing through me all at once.

"I think you know why I wanted to see you," he said, his eyes boring into mine. I licked wine from the inside of my lips. I had the sudden urge to see what he'd taste like, to put my mouth on his. My hand slid out from underneath his.

"Why do you do that?" he asked.

"Do what?"

He motioned toward my earlobe.

"Oh." I placed my hands back in my lap. "I don't know. Old habit." *Nervous* habit. But he didn't need to know that.

"Nervous habit?"

I straightened my shoulders. "A noble but unsuccessful attempt to change the subject."

He shifted forward in his chair and opened his mouth, then closed it. He pinched his bottom lip. "I can't seem to get you off my mind."

"David—"

"I'm very attracted to you." His words were directed right at my mouth.

I swallowed. "I'm married."

He looked up into my eyes. I was his with that look. The urge to taste him was suffocating.

"Yes," he said. "You are."

"And I love Bill."

He relaxed back into his chair. "Of course you do. You've never had an extramarital affair?"

My jaw dropped. "No," I said. "Not *extramarital* or otherwise."

"I'm relieved to hear that."

"I've never so much as fantasized about another man since I met Bill. Or even thought—I love my husband, and I wouldn't have come here if it weren't for—"

I couldn't grasp what I was reaching for. My fingers were curled into fists. My cheeks burned. He was so goddamn beautiful.

"For?"

"For nothing." I looked away. "I certainly wouldn't jeopardize everything for a roll in the hay at some bachelor pad."

"Where do you get that? Never in my life have I referred to my place as a 'bachelor pad.'" He shifted against the back of his chair. His brows were heavy as he crossed his arms, flashing a glint of his silver watch. From the look on his face, I wondered if anyone had ever turned him down at all.

"I feel this—something. Don't you? This is worth exploring." He shook his head. "No. That came out wrong."

"Exploring?" I asked. "And what exactly does 'exploring' entail? Don't answer that—I can only imagine. And after you've finished your 'exploration,' I'm supposed to go home to my husband and pretend nothing happened?"

"What I meant—"

"I'm not some notch in the bedpost. Marriage does not mean a challenge; it means I'm completely and totally unavailable." I waited, but he was statue still. "Sorry if that spoils your plans for the evening."

He glared at me from across the table, shook his head, and looked away. I followed his gaze after a moment. He watched our waitress across the room, fueling the ember of my anger.

"Also, I don't appreciate what you're suggesting. And if Bill knew, well . . . ." I snorted softly. *He'd do nothing.*

David's nostrils flared. His expression was not one of someone who was used to being rejected.

I waved my hand emphatically. "This city is littered with available women—single *and* married—who'd happily go home with you tonight. You shouldn't have any problem finding someone—"

He slammed is fist on the table. "I don't want *someone*." The bar chatter grew quiet. Lowering his voice, he said, "I'm not what you think."

My heart raced from his reaction. Confused and in shock, I fumbled for my purse, unlatching it with shaky hands.

"Olivia, wait." I threw down a bill and was on my feet in an instant. His chair screeched against the floor behind me. In my heels, I was no match for his long gait. He grasped my upper arm, whirling me backward. "Please," he said under his breath. "Don't go. Not yet."

I could've melted just from the intensity of his stare. I knew the emotions battling on his face: Anger, lust, fear, longing. I recognized them as my own. If I didn't escape now, I never would. With everything I had, I yanked my arm from his grasp and ran up the stairs, leaving him there to watch me flee.

CHAPTER 7

AS I EXITED THE STAIRWELL, it was everything I could do not to burst into tears. Over the years I'd studied composure as though I were being graded on it. Now I'd almost let a stranger undo me. I held my purse to my side and hurried down the street, desperate to climb into my bed. Thankful that it would be alone.

I walked as I halfheartedly tried to hail a cab. The night replayed in my mind. No detail was lost. I had questions; questions for David, questions for myself. Questions, I realized, that would never get answered.

Since our moment in the theater, whatever it was that drew me to him was already stronger. He was dangerous, but he compelled me. It was a broken explanation for why I'd agreed to meet him in the first place.

My apartment building loomed ahead. I'd walked all the way back without even realizing. Just then, the sound of glass shattering against the concrete made me jump. I kept my eyes forward. I'd enjoyed the dusky walk to the bar, but now it was dark and late. My ears pricked when I thought I heard footsteps behind me.

"Hey."

Bill had always told me, nonchalantly, not to pay the bums any mind, and they'd leave me alone. I'd never seen any on our block, but I was rarely out at this time alone. I hastened my pace.

"Hey!" It was a male's voice.

The phantom footsteps quickened behind me. Cursing my choice of footwear, I vowed to wear tennis shoes everywhere going forward. Fishy fingers grasped at my elbow—fleetingly at first and then, as he missed, more forcefully. He pulled me in the same spot David had, but I winced at his harsh grip. He jerked me back into a cloud of alcohol and stale cigarettes.

He wasn't a bum at all. His short build swam in an oversized hoodie, and his glossy hair reflected the one dim, yellow streetlamp.

"Does the name Lou Alvarez mean anything to you?" he slurred, tightening his grip over my twitching muscles.

"Let go."

He moaned against my neck. "You smell like flowers." Leaning in, his eyes closed with a deep whiff.

I lifted the purse I'd been clutching with my free hand and smacked him in the temple with all my strength.

He cursed, and I wrenched my arm away. I took a step before he caught me again and squeezed my arm so powerfully that my knees buckled.

"Olivia," he snarled. My breath caught in my throat hearing my name from his mouth. His misty eyes became clear as he bared his teeth at me. "It *is* Olivia, right?"

"Who are you?"

He got closer. "I'm here about my brother, Lou."

"What? Who?"

"Bill will know." He released me with an emphatic push.

I didn't take another moment. I ran to my complex without stopping. Once inside, I bolted the lock and leaned against the door, exhaling my relief.

Bill hadn't mentioned the name Lou Alvarez, or if he had, it wasn't enough that I remembered. I dug my cell phone out of my purse, located his name, and stared at the screen until it went black. How would I explain being out so late? Bill and I didn't lie to each other. There was never a reason. But the thought of telling him the truth made me put my phone away.

I headed straight for the bed, stopping only long enough to kick my shoes off. I lifted the comforter over myself and thought about what the man had said. What would he have done if he'd found Bill instead?

~

I reached across the bed for a body that wasn't there and woke with a start. I sighed remembering Bill was away and then again when the night's events flooded over me. The room was softly lit with the rising sun.

Scrambling out of bed, I went to the couch where I'd flung my stuff the night before. I prepared to call Bill, but my thumb just hovered over his name. Sleep had brought no answers. I was even more confused than before. I threw the phone back into my bag and decided it could wait until after a shower.

Hot water poured over my face and questions filtered in. Who was Lou Alvarez, and what was his connection to Bill? Did it involve one of his cases? I could say nothing to Bill, avoiding a lie about where I was. Or rather, whom I was with.

David. Would I ever see him again? Was he upset with me? My mind flashed to the eager waitress. How easy was it with him? Would she need to make the first move?

I shook my head. I had bigger problems than David, and thinking about him could only make things worse.

I wore a grey dress and black sweater to mirror my mood. Concealer covered dark circles from my halting sleep. I brushed on mascara in an attempt to open my sleepy eyes, but it didn't help much. I gave up, tossing the makeup back in a drawer.

~

Serena the Intern followed me to my new office with two cups of steaming coffee.

"Thank you," I said, accepting the drink and sitting across from her. "How was your weekend?"

"Awesome." Her eyes doubled in size. "Brock and I saw *Enter the Dragon.*"

"*Enter the Dragon?*" I wrinkled my nose. "What's that?"

"It's a martial arts classic," she enthused. "There was

a special showing downtown."

"Oh." I grinned. "Is martial arts an interest of yours?"

"Chinese cinema is, absolutely! Brock too."

"When did you get into that?"

"Hmm." She closed one eye as she counted silently. "Eight—no, seven—no, eight months ago."

"And you've been dating Brock for . . . ?"

"It'll be a year in a few months." She grinned, seeming proud.

I raised my mug. "Well, thanks for the coffee."

"Oh, a couple things. Mr. Beman wants you to refer to yourself as associate editor for now. He said nobody will take you seriously otherwise."

"Sounds like something he'd say," I mumbled.

"Also." She pulled a folder out from under her arm and handed it to me. "One of the guys for *Most Eligible* is available to meet today, but it's his only time. He sounds very busy."

"Busy is good," I said, opening the file. I scanned the profile sheet and nodded approvingly. "He sounds great. Can you get me a photo?"

"Oh, trust me," she said. "He fits the part. Lisa already approved him. I'll send one over but, like, can you do the interview? Or should I ask Lisa?"

I scowled. Lisa would just love to edge me out. "I'll do it. Just e-mail me the address, and I'll prep the rest." I straightened when I saw Beman's head bobbing through the office.

"Actually, he's coming here. He insisted."

"Oh. That's fine, I guess."

"Good morning, ladies," Beman said. Serena jumped. "I see you have Starbucks there. Anything for me?" He directed his glare at Serena.

She responded slowly. "I'm sorry. I can go back. What would you like?"

"Nothing," he snapped. "Please get to work. Olivia, a word?"

Despite his small frame, the office seemed smaller when he was in it. "How are you this morning, Mr. Beman?"

"I'd like an update on the *Most Eligible* article."

"It's coming along nicely. In fact, I have an interview today with a mister—" I opened the file and squinted, "a mister Lucas Dylan."

Beman raised his eyebrows. "The architect?"

I nodded, glancing down at the occupation field quickly.

"Excellent. But don't call him Lucas. He doesn't go by that." He waved a finger.

Luke it is.

"We've tried the past few years to get him involved, but he's very private, only does work-related interviews. Actually, *Architectural Digest* profiled him in last month's issue. Look it up."

I smiled on the inside, silently thanking Serena.

"This would be a huge coup, Liv," he continued. "If you manage to get him in the issue, well . . . " He paused. "It would be very *impressive.*" His lips thinned into a tight smile.

"Can I run an idea by you?" I asked.

He glanced at his watch and nodded curtly.

"In addition to the issue's launch party, I think it would benefit us to have an exclusive meet and greet for the top candidates. Since many of them are local celebrities, it would drum up some publicity."

"Publicity would be good. I'd like the issue to be a high point of the year." His jaw swung from side to side as he considered it. "Get me numbers by Wednesday. I'll see if there's a budget. We'll need sponsors to foot the majority of the bill."

"I can make that happen."

"Oh, and might I suggest a little lipstick before you meet with Mr. Dylan? No harm in trying to look nice for him."

He sashayed away, and I touched my fingers to my hair. What did it matter how I looked for him? I was interviewing him, not testing his make-out skills. The thought of Beman pimping me out to guarantee a bachelor made me laugh and cringe simultaneously. I wasn't sure he wouldn't do it.

The phone had become more conspicuous with every passing minute, and now it demanded my attention. I knew I had to call Bill and that it would be the first time I would really lie to him. But there was no way around it.

"Hi, babe," I said, when he picked up.

"Hey. Can I call you back? Just got out of a meeting and got another in ten minutes."

"Actually, this is important," I started.

~

The phone buzzed. I grabbed it automatically, my eyes fixed on the computer screen.

"Mr. Dylan's here." Jenny's voice was even more high-pitched than usual.

"Right. Can you have Serena bring him back?"

Serena hadn't sent the photo, but it was too late now. According to everyone else, he was a shoe-in. Quickly, I peeled my sweater off and grabbed my makeup bag, heading for the tiny mirror Diane had installed behind the door. My hair was actually behaving, and I patted it appreciatively. Balancing the bag on the couch, I smoothed on raspberry lip gloss, Beman's comment lingering in my head.

"Right back here," I heard. Just then the bag teetered over, spilling products all over the floor. *Shit.* I squatted and threw everything back in record time. A green Clinique lipstick tube caught my eye from behind the couch. *Leave it.* But I couldn't, so I steadied myself against the edge and reached an arm into the sliver of space.

"Hello, Olivia," I heard, just as I had grasped it.

Burnished, brandy-colored, leather brogues stared me in the face. My eyes drifted up a long body and landed on David's expressionless face. His hair was parted off to the side, gelled into one soft, cohesive wave. His sharp navy pinstripe suit looked as though it was made for him. It likely was. He wore his collar open with no tie so that I could glimpse the beginnings of his collarbone, and the sight of his exposed skin sent a thrill through me that ended in a tingling between my legs.

"D-David?" I said. If I thought the office seemed smaller before, it now felt tiny, especially from my current position. His presence could barely be contained. I rocked off my heels and stood, smoothing my hands over my dress.

"You're surprised. Were you expecting someone else?"

"Um, yes. Lucas Dylan?" I wiped excess lip gloss from the corner of my mouth.

"Do you always do this much research before an interview?" he teased. "I go by my middle name."

I eyed Serena, who stood in the doorway. This was her oversight.

"I'm sorry, you're right. Welcome." I stuck my hand out. Quickly, I attempted to sort through my thoughts, but all I could think was that I was glad I'd heeded Beman's advice about the lipstick. With a smirk, David took my warm hand in his icy one and squeezed it with a pump, sending a chill up my arm.

"Sorry for the cold hand. It's biting out there today."

"How about some coffee then?" Serena offered.

"Sure," I said, narrowing my eyes at David. Once we were alone, I gestured to a seat as I returned to my spot behind the desk.

"Mr. *Dylan*," I began, "I wasn't expecting to see you again."

His laugh was soft. "I should think not after the way you ran out on me last night."

"Anyone else might take a hint."

"I love what you've done with your office," he commented, gripping the arms of his chair and looking around. "Very colorful."

I hated its stark white walls and generic carpet. It was the matted and grimy type that you never wanted to touch with bare feet. The only personal thing I had was a photo of Lucy and me in college that Lucy had taken, printed, framed, and brought over my first week at the magazine. She even positioned it on my old desk herself.

"Well, I'm just borrowing it," I said.

He glanced around the room. In the daylight, he was no less mysterious. But in my office, with the desk between us, he somehow seemed less threatening. And if possible, more handsome.

"That's right. It must've been Diane's office." He looked back at me. "So, I want to apologize if I came on a little strong last night." Lowering his voice and leaning his elbows on his knees, he continued. "I don't know what came over me."

"You came here to tell me that?" I asked. "How did you know where to find me?"

"It wasn't hard." He winked.

My brows creased as Serena knocked and entered the room.

"Here you are, Mr. Dylan," she said, offering him a steaming mug. She set the tray on the coffee table and handed me mine as well.

"Thank you, Serena," I said.

David stared at me over the lip as he took a sip. I

shifted in my chair. He swallowed and cupped a hand around his drink, watching me like I was his next meal. In unison we glanced at Serena, who was lingering near the door.

"Thank you, Serena," I repeated.

She smiled at David, even though his back was to her, did some sort of curtsey and left the room. *Strange girl.*

"I'm not sure it's such a good idea, your being here." I straightened a pile of papers on the desk.

"Why not?" he asked. "Nothing's going on."

My face flushed. "So you went out of your way just to tell me that?"

"No," he said simply. "Diane had asked me to do the article this year, but I turned her down. I've changed my mind."

I set down the stack of papers. "Really?" I asked. "Why?"

"Don't make me answer that, or I might back out." His mouth kinked into a half-smile, but I chewed the inside of my lip. This would mean working with him until the issue went to press, since he was all but guaranteed a spot. Perhaps I was wrong about him, and his visit was purely platonic. As if reading my mind, he added, "I never mix business and pleasure. Ever. You have my word that I will be completely professional."

I narrowed my eyes at him without realizing it.

"You don't believe me," he said. His tone dropped. "Do though, as I don't like repeating myself."

"I don't really have a choice in the matter," I pointed

out, searching his face.

"Sure you do. It's your article. Don't worry about them." He waved his hand. "I'll say it's a conflict with my schedule if you aren't comfortable."

Part of me wanted to refuse, wanted to ask him to back out if it became too much. But I didn't know how to express that in so many words, and I didn't want to make something of nothing. Not only that, but it would put me some steps closer to the promotion.

"And I imagine you'll need a sponsor?" he added. "My firm would be happy to do it, providing I'm involved."

"All right," I decided, straightening my back. "Let's do it."

He answered with a large, boyish grin, pure and unassuming. I flexed my hands against my thighs. I'd never seen a smile like that before. It made me want to laugh and hug and kiss him all at once.

"Let's get started then," I said, blinking away the dreadful impulse.

I reached over the desk for his file, and he jumped out of his chair. My head snapped up. His jaw steeled, his gaze fixing on my arm.

"What the fuck?" he asked. I followed his eyes to find fresh, purple bruises forming along my bicep and elbow.

My eyes flitted between the marks and his face. I shook my head. "No, David—"

"Shit, Olivia. I am so sorry." He ran a hand through his hair and stared like he was physically unable to look away.

I shook my head harder. "No, no, no—you didn't do this. It wasn't you."

His eyes crept up to meet mine. I sat back in my chair, fumbling for my sweater. He rounded the desk and gently pulled my arm taut. His touch was careful when he encircled my wrist. His thick eyebrows met while he examined the bruises.

In a voice contrary to his touch, he said, "How did this happen?"

"It doesn't hurt." I doubted he'd believe me. It didn't hurt—I hadn't even noticed them earlier—but the marks were vivid.

"Olivia, tell me who did this." His voice wavered. "Was it me?"

I was reluctant to explain. I hadn't even had time to process it myself. He raised his eyebrows at me insistently.

I sighed and looked down. "Last night . . . after I left you, I was walking home—"

"What?" He dropped my wrist. "You *walked* home last night? Christ, I never would've let you walk. Do you have any idea how dangerous that is?"

I fluttered my eyelashes at him, and his expression softened a bit. I started to tell him that I'd done it several times but thought better of it. "Someone—a man, he . . . he was drunk. He tried to get my attention, but I ignored him. I guess he didn't like that. He grabbed me."

David's eyes widened.

"But," I said before he could speak, "I used my purse

to fight him off, and I'm fine. Here I am." I shrugged, tucking loose hair behind my ear.

"I shouldn't have let you go."

"You didn't *let* me do anything. I'm not your responsibility."

His lips drew into a straight line. "Right," he said. "You're not. What'd your husband say? The police?"

"He's out of town."

David closed his eyes and shook his head. "You slept alone last night?"

"Yes, of course."

He exhaled in a gust. "What if he'd followed you home?"

I looked at my lap.

"What aren't you telling me?" He waited a moment. "Olivia." It was a command, rumbling with warning, and it almost turned me to jelly. If I didn't respond, would he say it again?

"He was looking for Bill," I said.

"Your husband?"

"Yes. *Bill.* He's a lawyer, and it's related to one of his cases."

"Is that so." His jaw looked tense enough to snap. "So he was looking for him but found you instead. Do you know how?"

"It was in front of my apartment."

"He knows where you live? But you still slept there?" He rolled his head back and said something under his breath. He took his phone out of his jacket pocket, checked the screen, and cursed. "I have to get this."

"Of course. We can talk later."

He ignored me. "Dylan," he said into the phone. "Yes. No. No. How is that an emergency?" David looked at me as he listened. "I see. Fine." He hung up, never taking his eyes off me. "I have to go."

"Everything all right?"

"Just another fire to put out. Are you safe here?"

"Yes." I had no idea, but I wasn't about to admit that. "It's not as big of a deal as it seems. I'll be fine."

"It is a big deal. What about tonight? You can't stay alone."

"Bill wants me to stay with him in New York, but I haven't decided. I'll have to clear it with Beman."

David appeared to relax, but his guarded expression remained as we looked at each other. Knowing that I could sit and drink him in all day, I broke our stare and held out my card. "E-mail me. We'll do this another time."

CHAPTER 8

STATELY SILVER BUILDINGS, glowing in the last light of the setting sun, filled the tiny airplane window. Beman wasn't pleased about my personal emergency, but I'd assured him I could work remotely. His annoyance was tempered by the news that the elusive David Dylan had agreed to be in the issue.

A cab dropped me in front of Bill's New York hotel. At the front desk, I was given a note with a time and address for dinner.

"Is this far?" I asked the concierge, handing him the paper.

"Not at all," he said. I hadn't been to New York in years and was looking forward to wandering anonymously among the crowds until dinner. I thanked him, and after a quick refresh, left the hotel.

Boutiques had lowered their gates for the night, shielding exquisite works of art parading as clothing. Bass thumped from behind opaque glass. Two young women laughed casually, cigarette smoke wafting from between their fingers. Exposed belly buttons, long slinky hair, black studded booties—they seemed like nightlife regulars.

I huddled into my coat. They could've been models. I hadn't even brushed my hair before leaving the hotel. They were women that belonged to handsome, wealthy, charming men. *Men like David.*

I was hundreds of miles away, yet part of me was still back at the office, under his gaze. The rate at which my heart skipped had proliferated since we'd first made eye contact. I rewrapped my scarf around my neck as if to stem the direction of my thoughts.

Bill was early and waiting at the restaurant bar. His eyes were transfixed on a television above stacked bottles of liquor.

"Come here often?" I asked.

He jumped when I touched his shoulder. "Hey, babe. Didn't realize the time." He snaked an arm around my waist and planted a peck on my cheek. I nestled awkwardly against the barstool. "I missed you," he said, squeezing me to him. "I'm glad you're okay."

"Hungry?"

He grinned. "Always."

The hostess showed us to a cozy table in the corner and handed us our menus. After I'd decided, I looked up to find him watching me.

"I've been worried," he said.

"I know."

"I'm glad you're okay."

I smiled. "You said that already."

"Well, it's true."

"How serious do you think Mark's threat is?"

"He's a borderline junkie. Functional enough to deal, though. Could go either way."

"And he wants to get to you that bad?"

"He just got out of prison, but his brother'll be there another decade. Mark blames me for that."

"You said he and his brother were picked up for the same charge."

"They were, but Mark got two years and was released early for good behavior. His prosecutor couldn't link the bust back to the gang. When you can prove gang involvement, that's a big deal. I did. That's why his brother's right where he should be."

"How?"

He shrugged. "I'm better at my job. I think the real question is, what were you doing out that late by yourself? You were vague on the phone."

"Like I said, Gretch and I went out for a couple drinks. It was harmless." With my right hand, I spun my wedding ring around my finger under the table. "You and I walk around Lincoln Park at night all the time."

"Together, yes."

"I've done it alone."

"Whatever, Livs. You're safe. But Gretchen'll get an earful from me about this. She can do whatever she wants on her own, but I hate when she drags you out with her."

"She feels awful enough," I said. "She blames herself even though it's not her fault. Please don't bring it up with her."

He studied me a moment, and his expression relaxed. "Yeah, we'll see."

I smiled to myself, no doubt that I'd won.

"But I mean it." He set his elbows on the table. "You've been drinking with them a lot lately. There something going on?"

"No. Can we drop it?" I inched the chair out from the table. "Order for me. I'm going to the restroom."

~

The next morning, Bill left me barely after sunrise to work. For the first time since we'd been married, he suggested I 'hit the town, do some shopping.' When the door clicked shut, I exhaled against my pillow. We'd made love the night before, and he'd kissed the marks on my arm. I'd pulled my elbow away and told him to stop.

After twenty minutes of staring at the wall, I got out of bed.

Outlook popped up on my laptop, and the program pinged as e-mails filtered in. David's name flashed by. My heart threatened to leap, but I wouldn't let it. I started from the bottom, meticulously reading through each e-mail until I could no longer concentrate and skipped ahead.

From: David Dylan
Sent: Mon, April 23, 2012 04:26 PM CST
To: Olivia Germaine
Subject: Your safety

Olivia,

What did you decide about New York? Please let me know you're safe tonight.

How's Friday morning for our interview?

DAVID DYLAN
SENIOR ARCHITECT,
PIERSON/GREER

I smiled inwardly at his concern, resolving that he'd probably figured out I'd gone to New York. I proceeded to read through the remaining e-mails, but curiosity gnawed at me. I opened the search browser.

'D-a-v-i-d D-'

David Dylan. There he was. The first link was to the *Architectural Digest* magazine article. I opened it to see David's stern face staring back as he stood like a king in front of his latest masterpiece. I scanned the three-page article, noting that his firm, Pierson/Greer, was within walking distance from my office. Apparently he was one of the most in-demand architects in Chicago and a pioneer in modern design. I hit 'Back' and scrolled through more work-related links.

"GQS will acquire Multi-Parcel Express, CEO Gerard Dylan announces"

GQS? The *GQS?*

I read intently about Gerard, CEO of Global Quick & Speedy, the worldwide shipping company. I searched Gerard's name, which revealed endless articles, both business and personal. A profile of his home life presented four perfect smiles: Gerard, wife, Judy, daughter, Jessa, and son, David. There was no mistaking David's sister, who had the same obsidian hair that complemented clear brown eyes and long black lashes.

David was magnificently photogenic with a piercing gaze and sturdy features. I sifted through images of him, mostly working or at events. His tall frame and broad shoulders dwarfed anyone who posed with him. A profile shot with his sister, laughing and dressed in head-to-toe black, could've been from an advertisement.

A few rows down was an image of him on a red carpet, his arm placed behind a stunning, golden-skinned brunette with narrowed green eyes. Two more photos with her. And another with a leggy redhead. I clicked out of the browser. *So much for research. It's not news that he looks unjustly good in a hardhat.* I shut the laptop with a thud.

The late morning was balmy and warm. Shopping and people watching were two areas where New York was never lacking. Throngs of tourists filled the sidewalks, stopping abruptly to take pictures or admire the shops along 5th Avenue.

After hours of window shopping, I happened upon St. Patrick's Cathedral. Its dark beauty came through in hard, sharp edges of smooth, stone-colored marble. From base to sky-stabbing spire were breathtaking carvings. I climbed the steps and entered quietly behind a slew of other people. Observers wielded their cameras and phones, trying in vain to capture the power of the architecture. The candles flickered each time the cathedral door opened.

A ringing phone disrupted my trance. I was embarrassed to find it coming from my purse. I dug for my phone while bolting for the door. A hurried finger swiped across the screen silenced the ring. "Hello?" I asked breathlessly as I descended the steps.

"Olivia." That voice was no less powerful on the phone. "It's David Dylan. Serena said I could reach you here."

I rolled my eyes, imagining how he'd charmed my personal number out of her.

"Hello, Mr. Dylan," I said, trying to keep the butterflies in my stomach and out of my mouth. "What can I do for you?"

"I've been concerned."

"I'm *fine*," I exhaled. "Everyone is overreacting."

"How's your arm?"

"Healing beautifully. What can I do for you?" I repeated.

"Friday," he said, disregarding my clipped tone.

"If you don't mind a phone interview, Friday will be fine."

"I'd prefer to do it in person. I'll get in touch with a better date, then."

The phone pinged in my ear. I pulled it away to quickly read a text message from Bill.

Apr 24, 2012 4:17 PM
Headed back now.

"Is that it?" I asked David.

"Serena tells me you're in New York."

"You'd love it here," I said. "Some of the buildings are as jaw-dropping as the women."

"I've been to New York, Olivia. I travel there for business quite frequently."

I flushed. "Oh. Of course. Surely you must know intimately the type of women who live here."

He snorted, but his tone softened. "Where are you?"

I glanced around, squinting for a street sign. "I don't know, actually."

"What?"

"Well, I've just been wandering, and we were talking . . . I'm by St. Patrick's Cathedral. At least I was."

"Christ. Pay attention, would you? I'm about to hire you a bodyguard."

"A bodyguard?" I repeated. "Yet I've managed to make it this far without one."

"You're trouble." He said it so quietly that I almost missed it, but the words still stirred my insides. "You know," he said, "I waited a full twenty-four hours for your response to my e-mail. It was everything to restrain myself from calling."

"It hasn't been twenty-four hours," I pointed out.

"It's four-thirty," he stated simply.

I giggled. "Not in Chicago it isn't."

"You have a most enchanting laugh, Olivia Germaine."

I stopped, reddening. "David," I said, "don't call me here again. You can e-mail if it's important."

"Understood. Tell me where you are, though."

I read off the nearest street sign. "Madison Avenue."

"Not surprising," he said. "What, were you doing some shopping?"

"I tried, but I didn't find much."

"I think it might be fun to take you shopping." I could almost hear him smiling on the other end.

"Sounds good, Edward Lewis," I said, playing along.

"Edward Lewis?"

"Never mind. *Pretty Woman* reference."

"So that would make you Julia Roberts, then."

"No. That would make me Vivian."

"All right, well, *Vivian*—get a cab back, would you?"

"I'm going to walk. It's not often I get to see the city."

"Where are you staying? I'll tell you how to get to your hotel."

I toed the deformed sidewalk beneath me, thinking.

"Don't worry," he said. "I won't show up or anything."

I rolled my eyes but smiled. "Meatpacking District."

Twice he gave me directions on how to return to the hotel. The hotel where Bill would be waiting.

My plan to ignore David was not working, but I relaxed knowing I wouldn't be hearing from him for a while. My heart dropped a little, too.

That night, Bill surprised me with tickets to a show and a late-night meal at Sardi's. After making love, we agreed to extend our trip through the weekend.

I was content, as I'd always been, except that I couldn't shake the tiny knot at the pit of my stomach.

Something had been planted inside of me that I was finding hard to escape.

CHAPTER 9

GRETCHEN STOOD IN MY DOORWAY. She tossed her blonde curls over one shoulder. "Your new office is pretty fancy," she said. "How was the Big Apple?"

"No apples to be seen. Remember when you almost moved there?"

"For Ramon." She shook her head. "Asshole."

I laughed. "His cheating saved you, in my opinion. You could be a couple Puerto Rican babies deep by now."

"Would that really be so bad?" She smiled deviously. "It's just my own personal hell. Are you ready to go?"

"One minute to finish up this e-mail. Thanks for pushing this lunch back, by the way. Lucy's meeting us downstairs."

"What's new?" she asked, slumping her Louis Vuitton bag onto a chair.

"Nothing. You?"

"Worked like crazy. My boss had me there 'til eight o'clock three nights in a row, and Friday I went straight from work to an event. Then I went to a party with Ava and her friends—we drank way too much and I got into a

Twitter war with a fourteen-year-old. But before that, her hot co-worker was there, and—"

I shifted in my seat.

Her perfect eyebrow arched. "Why are you looking at me like that? What's up?"

I hit 'Send,' sat back in my chair, and then leaned forward again. "There's a reason I took off for New York last week. Sunday night, I was walking home from Halsted and was confronted by this guy."

"Confronted? What does that mean?"

"It means he grabbed my arm and threatened me. Bill was the prosecutor in a case against the guy's brother back when he worked as an ASA."

She rose from her seat, covered her mouth and sat back down. "Olivia," she squealed. "Where?"

I shushed her. "In front of my building. It's been over a week since it happened, and frankly, I'm sick of it. But I thought it would be a good opportunity to get out of town and spend some quality time with Bill."

"You know you could've stayed with me."

"Of course, sweetie, I know. But Bill suggested it and . . . anyway, it happened, and I'm going to be more careful in the future."

Gretchen leaned forward and put her hand on my arm. "I'm so sorry you had to go through that."

"I need a favor," I said, wiggling her off. She withdrew her hand. I could almost see the question forming in her mind. "If anyone asks—Bill, specifically— you and I were together having drinks that night."

"What's going on?" she asked, fidgeting with the clasp of the Vuitton.

"I can't really say."

Her head tilted to one side.

"It's nothing serious or bad," I said, "but I just don't want to talk about it. I need you to trust me. Please, just promise you'll lie if it comes up. Even to Lucy."

She didn't seem surprised but just nodded. "Of course. I'll cover for you. But if you need to talk about it, or if it gets serious or bad . . . come to me. I know you're not easily fazed, but I'm always here to listen." She paused. "I still haven't forgiven you for freshman year of high school. The way you clammed up after your parents' divorce wasn't fair. I wanted to be there for you."

"You're a good friend."

"I try, but sometimes you make it hard."

"Let's not get into that," I said. "And Lucy just texted. She's downstairs."

"You brought her earrings, right?"

"What earrings?"

"The chandelier ones. You were supposed to bring them today."

"I was?"

"She told you at her engagement party. We were talking about lunch, and you promised to bring them."

"I don't remember that."

She raised her eyebrows. "She'll be pissed. Apparently her outfit is unacceptable without them."

"I think she's already pissed," I said, holding up my phone to show her the text message.

"Hurry up," Gretchen read aloud. "All these bridal magazines are killing my back. Don't forget earrings."

She laughed. "You're fucked."

"We'd better go," I said, grabbing my purse. "And I want to hear more about Ava's hot co-worker on the way down."

~

Bill and I followed the maître d' through a crowded restaurant. I reached back to squeeze his hand when my father came into sight. Seated rigidly straight, his hair almost completely charcoal now, he sipped his signature whiskey on the rocks.

"Hi, Dad." I smiled, greeting him with a big hug as he stood.

"You look skinny," he said, holding me at arm's length. He stuck out his hand. "Bill."

"Mr. Germaine. Nice to see you."

"Is she eating enough?"

"Like a champ," Bill said, winking at me.

"I'm fine, Dad. What are you doing in town?"

He waved his hand. "Meeting with the VP at a local ad agency about doing some consulting there. Nothing exciting."

"How's business?" Bill asked, unfolding his napkin onto his lap.

"I just finished up a big project in Dallas that should get me some referrals. I'm considering trading in the BMW for a C7."

"Corvette, huh? Can't argue with that. Maybe we'll take that Shelby off your hands, then."

My eyes widened. "Really?"

"Don't make that face. You look like an owl."

"Who," I said, laughing.

"We'll be moving out of the city soon," Bill said. "You'll need your own car so I don't have to cart you around."

I smirked at him playfully.

"You still want the Shelby?"

I nodded at my dad.

"We'll see what happens with the C7," he said. "Any news at work?"

"Not since last month. Today I reworked one of Lisa's layouts, and my boss was very impressed."

"Does that mean you got the promotion?"

"I won't know that for a little while," I said. "I told you already."

"I know, kiddo. But maybe they'll give it to you early. Just keep thinking about the next step." He motioned across the room for the waiter. "Whatever'll get the boss's attention."

"It's only been a month since I heard."

"Doesn't matter. Keep your eye on the prize. Never turn down an opportunity, and make sure they see you working hard. Can we get some more water here?" he asked the waiter. He turned back to me. "Given any more thought to moving to New York? Isn't that where the top publications are?"

"Well—"

"We've discussed it," Bill interjected, glancing at me. "But it's just not the right move for us."

"That so? How come?"

"This position is still new for me. We love Chicago. Plus, my family is here."

My dad inhaled deeply. "I'm family, aren't I? How about coming to Dallas? I'd love to have her closer. Bill, I have plenty of friends in the area who own firms. Or maybe you want to think about starting your own. Dallas is a great place for that."

I resisted the urge to cover Bill's hand with mine while he played with his fork. "Thank you, sir. I'll keep that in mind."

"No, you won't," I said. "You know we're looking for a house, Dad. And I really want this promotion."

"I just want you to think big, baby."

"Did I tell you that Lucy's getting married?"

He grunted. "What about Gretchen? When's she going to settle down?"

"She's holding out for Kyle Korver," I said with a laugh.

"Who?"

Bill perked up. "Used to play for the Bulls. He's married though. Not sure that'd stop her."

I glanced at Bill.

"I'd like to see her meet someone nice," Dad said.

"It may be a while," Bill joked.

"Why's that? She's a great girl. Smart, too."

"Gretchen's doing fine," I said. "She's just having fun playing the field. She wanted to come tonight but couldn't get out of a work thing."

"So long as she doesn't turn into her mother. How about you, Bill? Things are good at Specter & Specter?"

"Absolutely. I'm on a few cases at the moment, one is pretty high profile. They're keeping me busy."

"Good to hear it." Dad looked around. "Jesus, do they not want us to order? Get whatever you want, honey. Dinner is on me. How's the market around here anyway, Bill? I don't want Olivia ending up with some bum property."

"We're being very thorough, sir."

Something flashed across my dad's face, but the approaching waiter caught his attention.

"What's new with the divorce?" I asked after we'd ordered.

"Finalized next week."

"That's good news," I said. "I don't imagine Gina is easy to divorce."

"Certainly not," he said, leaning back into his seat for the first time. "But nobody is, in my experience."

~

"That was exhausting," Bill said.

"It usually is."

"He spoils you." He raised an eyebrow. "I hope you don't expect that from me."

I laughed. "I'm his only child."

"Yeah, and you love it. He would give you that car if you asked."

"Maybe. But you saw how he nagged me about work."

"He thinks you can do better. In all aspects of your life."

"This again?" I shook my head at him. "He likes you, Bill."

"I'm so glad that, after almost five years together, your father *likes* me."

"He's your father too, so watch it," I said with a smile. "Let's go get ice cream. My treat."

"Ice cream?" He cringed, rubbing his stomach. "I'm stuffed. I just want to go home."

"I'll be quick."

"The car's right here. I have to get up early tomorrow, and your dad really wore me down tonight."

"Fine," I said. My tone was exasperated, but I took his hand. "Come on, old man."

CHAPTER 10

IT'D BEEN OVER A WEEK since my phone call with David. I stared longingly at my e-mail, wondering if he'd received my invitation to the magazine's Meet & Greet I was planning. Most others had responded to the message immediately.

I twisted the cap of my pen on and off. What would happen if he backed out of the feature? Would it cost me the promotion? Would I be able to move on and forget the things that were slowly awakening in me? A week was only a drop in the bucket, but it felt like ages. I wanted to hear that endlessly deep voice in my ear or see his eyebrows knit thoughtfully as he watched me talk.

A loud vibration against my desk jarred me from my thoughts.

"Hi, Davena," I said into my cell phone.

"Actually it's Mack. Sorry to bother you at work."

"No problem." I stood to close the door. "What's going on?"

"We aren't going to make it to dinner with your friends tomorrow night."

His tone had me steadying myself against my desk. "Is everything all right?"

"Things have been better. She's not well, dear." His voice broke, and he cleared his throat. "She insists she's fine to go, but I'd like to keep her home for now."

"What do the doctors say?"

"She contracted an infection a few weeks ago and has lost considerable weight. This happened once before, during her first round of chemo, and it took months to recover. After what she's been through, I'm not sure she has the strength to fight it off again."

"I'm so sorry, Mack. I've never heard you like this."

"I try to stay strong. For her."

"She's the toughest lady I know," I reassured him. "She'll be fine. Don't worry."

"She may not be, Liv. Just keep that in mind."

I couldn't picture it—not feisty, lively Davena.

"I should go," he said after a silence. "She'll be wanting some tomato soup just about now. I'm going to run to her favorite deli. Please give Lucy our regrets."

I hung up. As long as I'd known them, they'd fought hard and loved deep. In the end, Mack always stood by her, never letting anything touch her. The body that he'd loved so intensely was turning against him, and it was out of his control. I shuddered at the thought.

I wondered how my relationship compared to theirs. How would Bill deal if I were that sick? Would he know how to take care of me? Anticipate my cravings for tomato soup? Mack and Davena had been married over thirty years. Surely, in thirty years, Bill would know me that way.

~

"Catch that game the other night?" Bill called to Lucy's doorman as we passed through the lobby.

"Total destruction, man. On our way up."

"You know it."

"Did I mention you look handsome tonight?" I asked when we were alone in the elevator.

"Play your cards right, and you might get lucky."

"Is that so?" I teased. "Well I have a surprise for you if that's true."

"What is it?"

"I'll tell you later."

"What is it? I don't like surprises."

"Bill—"

"Seriously. What is it?"

"I started birth control," I said, grinning. "No more condoms. Actually, we can't start for a few more days, and I think I'd like to give it another week just to be safe—" I stopped when I noticed his expression. "What?"

He stepped off when the elevator pinged. "Unbelievable."

"What? I did a lot of research, asked the doctor all my questions. I've never been on birth control before. I thought you'd be excited."

"Bad timing, Liv."

"I thought I heard voices," Andrew said as he opened the door. "Come in."

Lucy was behind him, wiping her hands on a dishcloth.

"Something smells good." Bill handed Lucy a bottle of wine as Andrew squeezed me to him.

"Our brave girl," Andrew said. "Apparently you have quite the flair for self defense." He released me with an obnoxious pat on the head.

"You're just in time," Lucy said. "Have a seat, food will be out soon."

We found Gretchen and her date, an accountant she'd met in a coffee shop, snacking on bacon-wrapped apricots in the immaculate living room.

"How was New York?" Andrew asked, pouring wine.

"We found our way back, no thanks to Olivia."

"What's that supposed to mean?" I asked.

"Just that you couldn't find your way out of a shoebox." He looked at Andrew. "She said 'I've been here lots of times, Bill. Trust me.' I should've listened to my instincts and gone the opposite direction."

"Oh, please," I said with a playful shove. "You were even more lost."

He caught my wrist and kissed the back of my hand. "I'm happy to be your guide, babe." There was no trace in his eyes of whatever had happened in the hallway.

"Andrew, can you get everyone seated?" Lucy called from the kitchen.

We each took our place around the table as Lucy filled the table with delicious-smelling food.

"How are things at S&S?" Andrew asked Bill.

"Great. You? How's business?"

"All right," Andrew replied, cutting into his steak. Blood pooled on the plate. "I expected things to slow down more because of the economy, but we're doing fine. We've been lucky. Our New York firm was hit harder. I guess investment banking isn't so hot there right now."

"You should see their new building," Lucy said. "It's almost finished, and it's incredible. I'm excited for Andrew to be closer to home."

"Oh, yeah?" Bill asked.

Andrew nodded emphatically as he chewed. "The place is incredible, like Luce said. My boss owns the building, and I can't imagine the money he poured into it." He snorted. "And the architect is brilliant. He's from here but has studied in Europe and, I think, Asia. Really interesting guy. Plus, he owns a sailboat."

I stiffened. My mind flashed back to the night of the party, when Andrew had introduced me to David. I opened my mouth to change the subject.

"Interesting," Bill said before I could speak. "Maybe he does homes?" He raised his eyebrows at me.

"I'm sure he charges a fortune," I said.

"How's that going, by the way?" Lucy asked us.

Bill grunted. "We have an appointment with our realtor tomorrow afternoon. We picked the right time to start looking, but nothing has really felt right yet. At least not for this one." He jerked his elbow in my direction, and I nodded.

"You could always build from the ground up," Andrew said. "In fact, David—that's his name—he mentioned something about flipping houses as a hobby. I'll ask him about it."

Oh my God. Please don't do that.

"He was at our engagement party, Liv. David Dylan." Lucy cocked her head at me.

I shrugged, but Gretchen visibly perked up.

"Oh, come on," Lucy prodded. "Tall, gorgeous. He's unforgettable."

"You remember," Andrew said. I glared at him. "I introduced you guys in the kitchen. You spilled—"

"Yes," I said, seeing nowhere else to turn. "I remember now."

"Bill, this guy is something else. The women in the office go crazy whenever he stops by. I think they even have some sort of pool going to see who can score a date with him." He laughed heartily.

Bill just nodded and kept chewing. I pulled on my dress crossing and uncrossing my legs.

"If I were a jealous guy, I'd forbid Luce from working with him."

Gretchen and I dropped our forks at the same moment.

"What's that?" I asked.

"Oh." Lucy giggled. "He asked Andrew for my information because he could use a new personal stylist. I doubt anything will come of it, but I have to admit," she paused to look at Andrew, "he'd be a great client. I think he has money."

"Connections, too," Andrew added.

Gretchen noticeably gripped the table, while her date stared into his wine glass and sighed.

"Lucky guy," Bill said, forking a bite of steak. "Sounds like a catch."

"Lucy," I blurted, sending all eyes in my direction. I scrambled for a topic. "How's the planning coming?" I jabbed my fork at her ring, and her face lit up.

"We have news," she said, looking over at Andrew again. "We've set a date. First weekend of September."

"September?" I asked in shock. "Of this year? That's like four months away."

"I know." She hesitated. "It's not ideal. But Andrew's parents are leaving for their trip around the world in October, and it's really important to him—to *us*—that they be there."

"Why not wait 'til they get back?" Gretchen asked.

"They aren't sure when that will be. Andrew's mom has been planning this trip for a decade and they might not return for years. And there's my aunt, too."

"How is she?"

"She's stable," Andrew answered. "But that could change any day. We don't want to take the chance."

"Anyway," Lucy said. "That's the date, so clear your calendars."

She left into the kitchen and reappeared with a homemade cheesecake. We applauded. Her domestic skills never failed to impress me. She set a dish in front of everyone but Gretchen, who was 'stuffed.' Lucy continued with the details of the next four months—to Bill's chagrin, I sensed.

"Geez, Liv. I don't understand where you put all that," Andrew said, gesturing at me. Mine was the only empty plate. I turned red, and we all burst into laughter.

CHAPTER 11

JEANINE'S TURN SIGNAL CLICKED. Bill leaned forward from the passenger side, trying to get a glimpse of the house. The neighborhood's streets were quiet, save the almost imperceptible rustling of foliage. Old-fashioned, grand houses sat comfortably in their foundations, settled from decades of existence.

Bill turned to me in the back seat. "The commute wasn't so bad, was it?" He looked back out the windshield. "Oak Park is the perfect distance. You're still close to the city, and I can finally get a decent night's rest."

"It really is perfect," Jeanine said, glancing at him. "You also have the option of the 'L' train. It's maybe a thirty, forty minute ride."

She pulled up to the house, and to my surprise, it was magnificent. Its enormity lay in the imposing features rather than in square footage. The property was run-down and thick with overgrown brush, but somehow, it was alive with character. It was different from the houses around it with hard angles and jutting lines, but the neighborhood's atmosphere was still present.

I unbuckled my seatbelt and stepped out to get a better look. Dead grass crunched under my shoes as I used my hand to shield the lowering sun.

"Olivia?" Jeanine gestured to me as she and Bill crossed the street. "This one. Over here."

I looked behind her in confusion, noticing the 'For Sale' sign planted firmly in lush, green grass. I searched for the same sign on my lawn.

I crossed the pavement, looking once over my shoulder. In front of me stood another impressive house, yet it didn't inspire the same feeling in me as the one across the way.

Jeanine led us inside the creaky house and took us from room to room enthusiastically. We climbed the stairs to find a sprawling master bedroom. For Bill, that would be the exclamation point on this idea. While he and Jeanine lingered there to discuss amenities, I wandered down the hall into a smaller room that faced the street.

A cracked window allowed me to breathe in the fresh, spring breeze. The lawn below brilliantly green. Why had I been so afraid of the suburbs?

The house across the way seemed even more out of place on the street. From where I stood, it was an eyesore among champions. But with a trimmed hedge, a new stone walkway, a fresh coat of paint . . .

"What do you think?" Bill asked.

"I like the house across the street," I said with my back to him.

He was quiet for a moment. "And if you were on that side of the street, you'd like this one."

I turned to face him and his acerbic tone. "That's not fair."

"No? You haven't liked anything Jeanine has shown us. This is the best one yet. It's perfect. Good neighborhood, in our price range, and bigger than we'd hoped."

"It's an amazing place. I'm just not sure it's right. I can't see myself here."

"It's not just about you, though. I'm part of this too. And we have our *future* to think about."

"I understand that," I said, annoyed by the suggestion. "But buying a house is a huge decision, and I want it to be perfect."

He threw up his arms. "Perfect doesn't exist. There's always going to be something, Liv. It'll feel like home, you just have to give it time."

Jeanine appeared in the doorway. "I see you found the second room." She smiled dully. "Great for an office—or maybe a nursery?"

My eyes flicked between them. Bill laughed in a short gust. "We're not quite there yet," he told her.

"Forgive me," she said. "Most couples moving from the city are getting ready to start a family."

Bill's ears turned red as he looked at the ground.

"Of course," I said. "That makes sense. It's a beautiful home. What's the story with the house across the street?"

She strode over to the window. "I know. It's appalling. The owners live in California and stopped taking care of it a while back. I think a couple neighbors have tried to report housing code violations, so perhaps one day they'll sell or tear it down. I can find out for you."

I placed my hand on the glass. "It's rather charming."

"I suppose," she said. "But it's a mess. It needs a complete overhaul. This house, though . . . it won't be on the market long."

I turned back to Bill, whose lips were drawn across his face. "Let's get more information, then," I said. Without looking at either of them, I left the room.

~

Bill lingered in our kitchen while I prepared dinner. I had no desire to reopen the discussion, but I could see he wouldn't let me get away with that. I started in on washing lettuce, thankful for a task to distract me.

"About this afternoon," he said.

I grimaced with my back to him. "Here," I said, turning to hand him a knife and motioning to two red tomatoes on the cutting board. "Can you chop those?"

He began slicing. "What are you thinking?"

"About what?" I asked, back at the sink.

"Today."

"Can you be more specific?"

He was quiet. The knife hit the wood repeatedly. "That house is as close to perfect as it's going to get. We really can't hesitate."

"Yup, I got that. I said I'd think about it."

"And Jeanine's right. We're at the point where we should start thinking about a family."

I answered him with a heavy sigh. "I'm in the same place I was six months ago when we discussed this. And especially now, if I get this promotion—honey, I just don't feel ready."

"You might never *feel* ready. It's the same with the house. The timing will never be right. You just have to do it. The rest will come."

I stiffened. It wasn't that I just didn't feel ready. I didn't want it. And I worried that I never would. Before Bill proposed, when he and I would talk about our future, I'd assure him that one day I would get there. That there would be a right time for children. Did that mean I owed it to him?

"I need more time."

"I'm ready now."

I whirled from the sink to face him. "Now?"

He was quiet again, but this time he'd stopped chopping. His knuckles were white from gripping the knife.

"Bill, be reasonable. I'm not ready."

"I heard you the first time, but you are. We are. I don't want you to start birth control."

"Don't push me on this. It's too big of a decision."

"I'm ready, and so are you."

"Stop saying that," I cried. "You don't know what I am. What if you're wrong—what happens if we're not ready? I don't want to end up like—"

"Like what?" he asked, grimacing. "Like your parents?"

I turned so my back was to him again.

"That's completely different, babe. They didn't split up because of you. They changed. They fell out of love."

It was silent except for the running faucet. I knew I hadn't caused the divorce. But the year leading up to the split was the beginning of a painful downward spiral. Bill and I were happy now, but were we solid enough to bring a child into the world? And was that even what I wanted?

"Maybe you were right," he said after some time had passed. "Maybe you're not ready. We've been married for almost three years, and you still won't let me in. I don't know how else to get you to commit. I've been patient, but I want this, and that's not going to change. Promise me you'll give this some serious thought."

I heard the knife clatter on the table before he left the kitchen.

~

"It's Gretchen."

I took the phone from Bill's outstretched hand so he could return to sulking in silence. They were the first words he'd spoken to me since the night before. Fortunately, the latest James Patterson novel had kept him occupied for most of the morning.

"I think I told you about the chef I've been dating?" Gretchen said. "His restaurant's soft opening is tonight, and he wants me to invite people. You guys up for it?"

"You couldn't have picked a better day to ask," I said so Bill wouldn't hear. "Let me call you back."

I hung up the phone and Bill looked over.

"We're invited to a new restaurant tonight."

"With?"

"Gretchen and friends." I shrugged. "She's seeing a chef."

He stuck his finger in his book and closed it. "I thought you wanted a quiet weekend."

"I do," I said. "I did. But I think we could use the distraction."

"Babe, no. I'm not in the mood."

I dialed Lucy as Bill reopened his book. "Are you guys going tonight?" I asked when she picked up.

"Not sure yet. Andrew is throwing a tantrum about it. I guess there's a game on."

"Oh, is there?" I raised my eyebrows at Bill, who ignored me. With my finger over the mouthpiece, I said, "A game? Really, Bill?"

He barely looked up, and I rolled my eyes.

"Perhaps we should make it a girls' night then," I suggested.

"I was thinking the same thing. We can dress up too. I'll just check with Andrew."

"Come on," Bill started as I hit 'End.'

"Off the hook," I said on my way out of the room. "You're welcome."

I disrobed and waited for the shower to heat, watching steam curl over the door. I looked at my slim figure in the mirror. My hands ran over my breasts and down my stomach, stopping at the small, raised scar on my side.

I'd gotten what I'd wanted: distance from David Dylan. I still hadn't heard from him. But that distance hadn't helped. If anything, I thought of him more often. I wondered what he was doing, why he hadn't called the office. I thought of him now, as I stood naked in my bathroom. In *Bill's* bathroom.

I'd told him not to phone, and it was for the best. After the argument with Bill, it was important that I focus on the life we were building—imperative, in fact. I blinked from the thought, finding my image distorted in the foggy mirror.

~

I surveyed my closet, deciding on a gold, one-shoulder, sequined dress.

Bill shouted for me from the other room.

I grabbed my black platforms and went to meet Lucy at the door. "Don't you clean up nice," I said when I saw her.

"Not so bad yourself, Germaine."

"Is it too much?" I asked.

Bill looked over then. "Won't you be cold?"

"I'm taking a coat."

He shifted as he looked me up and down. "Is this restaurant thing a big deal?"

Lucy shrugged. "We just felt like getting fancy."

"You both look gorgeous." He unmuted the TV. "Just don't leave me for the head chef, honey."

I never knew which way his mood would swing, so I took advantage. I leaned over the couch, letting my hair fall over his shoulder. "Don't wait up," I said, planting a wet kiss on his cheek.

~

We found Gretchen at the bar with her roommates, Ava and Bethany. The three of them talked vivaciously, as though they didn't see each other every day. Lucy and I tried our best to sew ourselves into conversations about love, sex, and dating.

I could appreciate tales from the other side, but my stories had run out. At least, any stories these girls would be interested in hearing. Ava, who was husband hunting, would surely be disappointed with Bill's and my no-frills lovemaking. And Bethany, who was proudly unattached, would be bored by it. It didn't upset me; I'd happily left singledom behind.

One drink in, the hostess approached and interrupted us mid-laugh. "Harper?"

"That's me," said Gretchen, sliding off her stool.

"I apologize for the wait, Ms. Harper." She stepped back, allowing us to gather our things. "Jeff wanted us to prepare a special table for you as his guest."

She walked us to a round table in the restaurant's center.

I turned back to Gretchen on the way and asked under my breath, "Jeff the chef?" Lucy and I burst into a fit of giggles.

She rolled her eyes. "Grow up."

Gretchen insisted on facing the door to keep tabs on the crowd, and we molded ourselves around her. Almost immediately, the waiter arrived with what I recognized as an expensive Bordeaux and poured us each a glass. Another appeared with a plate of appetizers, and our girl talk took up warp speed as we indulged. Gretchen dished on Jeff, telling us he'd been wooing her for weeks but she'd only just agreed to a first date.

"I could get used to this," Bethany said. "I can't wait to see what happens when you actually sleep with him."

"Seriously," Ava said as she finished off another glass.

My ears tuned to a bass in the hum of the crowd. I tensed and hunched down in my chair, feeling instantly exposed. Gretchen had stopped talking and was staring over my sequined shoulder. Lucy, who was thoroughly tipsy, broke into a smile and waved.

"Well, if it isn't my lucky day."

The hairs on the back of my neck rose. I lifted my head and reeled at the sight of David. He was devilishly handsome in a pea coat that hung open to reveal a V-neck sweater and exposed checked collar. His eyes caught mine and that familiar electric current passed between us.

Then I saw her, the girl from the Internet. She was almost as tall as him in sky-high heels that lengthened already long, dark legs. Caramel-colored hair fell in waves over her shoulders, and her skin-tight, red dress showed off an athletic figure.

Envy flooded so quickly that I dug my nails into the seat cushion. She was the epitome of Latin beauty, and her dark complexion melded flawlessly with his bronzed skin.

I looked David straight in the eyes. He swallowed, glancing at her and then back at me. They were joined by a man just shorter than the woman, whose beady eyes lingered a little too long.

"Lucky day, indeed," he said in a distinct French accent, leering over each one of us. My skin tingled when he reached me. I touched my earlobe.

David cocked his head, and I pulled my hand away, embarrassed. No, mortified—mortified that he was here with his stunning girlfriend. I chided myself for even thinking I could hold his interest.

"I didn't realize you'd be here, David." Lucy's voice pitched into my thoughts.

"Arnaud, my associate, graciously invited me and Maria for the opening." He indicated the slight man next to him. "This was his project."

"It's wonderful," Lucy chirped. "Congratulations."

Gretchen nodded emphatically, her eyes darting between Arnaud and David.

"Thank you," Arnaud said.

I focused ahead and clasped my hands in my lap. I knew my back was unnaturally straight.

"Gretchen knows the head chef," Lucy said as an explanation for our attendance.

"A friend of mine," Gretchen interjected quickly with a laugh. "Just a friend."

"David?" the woman whispered silkily. I couldn't help sneaking a peek. She seemed disenchanted, staring straight ahead and ignoring our table.

"Hmm?" he asked without looking at her.

She motioned toward the waitress who was standing at their table patiently.

"We'd better sit down," David said. "Nice to see you again, Lucy. Gretchen, Olivia, ladies." The way my name rolled off his tongue—it was as if he was saying it for the first time in the kitchen. I evaded his eyes but felt him hesitate. Nobody noticed my unusually rude behavior because they were all staring after him as the three of them moved on.

"He remembered my name," Gretchen whisper-squealed.

"I just said it," Lucy pointed out.

Ava and Bethany leaned over the table. "Spill," one of them demanded.

"He's a friend of Andrew's." They turned their attention to Lucy. "And get this—he made an appointment for a consultation with me next week."

Gretchen gaped. "You lucky bitch. You'll get to see him naked."

Lucy turned a color I'd never seen on a person and shook her head. "My job isn't like that, Gretchen!"

"Was that his girlfriend?"

"Not sure," Lucy said. "I think he has lots of them . . ."

Everyone giggled.

"Hook a girl up," Gretchen said.

"Yeah, this girl," Ava said. More giggling.

"I don't know," Lucy said. "He's Andrew's friend. He seems really nice, though."

"Liv, are you all right?" Bethany asked, glancing over at me.

"You're going to be working with him?" I asked Lucy.

She nodded. "Why?"

"I think I might've had too much wine," I said.

The table fell into an unwarranted fit of laughter, and this time I joined them. We'd all had too much, I figured, and we were all feeling good.

I rose from my seat. "I'm going to use the restroom."

Those eyes were on me in a heartbeat. I knew, even though I wasn't looking at David. "Anyone else need to go?" I asked.

"I could go," Lucy said.

Gretchen stood. "Me too." She flicked her long, blonde ringlets over her shoulder as she shimmied out of her seat; a shimmy that was surely for David's benefit. He had a perfect view of her rear, which is exactly what he'd be seeing if he was still looking in our direction. I moved quickly through the tables to the bathroom as Gretchen and Lucy followed.

Gretchen was first to the mirror, fixing her lipstick and touching her hair. I admired her pointed nose and aqua eyes. She really was beautiful. If someone could capture David's attention, it would be her. I frowned.

Lucy joined us to check, fix, and reapply. "I think I found bridesmaid dresses," she said. "Can you guys make it one day next week for a lunchtime fitting?"

"Duh," Gretchen said. "I'll move some things around."

Lucy looked at me, and I shrugged my shoulders helplessly. "Duh," I mimicked. She clapped her hands with delight.

"What do they look like?"

"Very simple. Since we're doing navy and ivory, I thought a wine red would be a really nice accent. You'll both like the style, don't worry."

"Sounds beautiful," Gretchen said.

Back at the table, there was a new sampling of dishes, and I forced myself to partake to mitigate my drinking. Just as I had bitten into a duck spring roll, my clutch vibrated on my lap. Everyone was engulfed in conversation, so I checked the screen. It was a text from an unknown number. Quickly, I scrolled through my call history to confirm my suspicion: it was from David.

CHAPTER 12

May 5, 2012 8:43 PM
Why the cold shoulder?

May 5, 2012 8:45 PM
I'm not sure what you mean.

"More wine, Liv?" Bethany asked, filling my glass.
"Thanks," I muttered. I reread David's text again.
Cold shoulder? My phone vibrated.

May 5, 2012 8:46 PM
You do, don't be coy.
How are you getting home?

May 5, 2012 8:46 PM
Why?

I heard Gretchen's words, but I wasn't listening to
her story. My fingers clutched the phone as I tried to pay
attention.

May 5, 2012 8:48 PM
You're drunk.

> *May 5, 2012 8:48 PM*
> *So?*

May 5, 2012 8:50 PM
I'll come over there & ask in front of everyone. How're you getting home?

> *May 5, 2012 8:52 PM*
> *Thought I'd hitch a ride with legs over there.*

May 5, 2012 8:53 PM
Very cute. I'm coming over.

> *May 5, 2012 8:53 PM*
> *No!*

I scurried to type a response, taking only a second to shoot a harried glance in his direction.

> *May 5, 2012 8:54 PM*
> *I walked w Lucy. Why's it matter?*

May 5, 2012 8:55 PM
You know it does.

I took a larger sip and inhaled.

> *May 5, 2012 8:57 PM*
> *I haven't heard from you.*

May 5, 2012 8:59 PM
I've been out of town.

I didn't see how that mattered. I unfastened my purse to put the phone away, but it pinged before I could.

May 5, 2012 9:00 PM
& you told me not to call.

> *May 5, 2012 9:01 PM*
> *I meant my cell.*

May 5, 2012 9:01 PM
Same for texting? ;)

I typed a brusque *yes* and decided the conversation was over just as Jeff the chef approached.

"Thank you," he said when we applauded. "How is everything, Gretchen?"

She tossed her hair. "Delicious, Jeff."

"Great," he said, visibly reddening. "I'm sending over a special dessert just for my table." He eyed Gretchen as he spoke. "I have to get back, though. Good evening, ladies."

As I watched him walk away, my eyes fell on David. Maria gestured as she spoke to him, but he didn't appear to be listening. He was looking at me. Arnaud was enthralled, even though she was clearly ignoring him. I turned back to the conversation at my table. When I looked over again, his seat was empty.

~

I stood too fast, swaying with a red-wine head rush. David had returned to his table and was talking heatedly with Arnaud. Lucy and I said our good-byes as the group went to the bar to wait for Jeff.

The restaurant had cleared out considerably, but we'd barely noticed. When Lucy and I stepped out into the fresh air, a cab driver leaning against his car signaled to us.

"We probably should," I said.

"Hell yeah," Lucy said. "My feet are killing me."

"Where to?" he asked.

"Two stops. River North and Lincoln Park."

"Yep." He nodded, nearly pushing us through the door. I rolled down my window as soon as I was inside.

"I think I could've stayed for another drink, but I couldn't handle Bethany's voice another minute," Lucy said.

It was unlike her to say anything unkind, so I poked her in the ribs.

"What?" She giggled. "It's so shrill."

"It is a little, yeah," I said, sticking my hand out the window. "Tonight was fun."

"Hey. Everything all right with Bill?"

I snapped to attention. "Yes. Why?"

"I don't know." She hesitated. "It seemed a little tense when I was over earlier."

"Oh. No. Everything is fine. We had an argument yesterday. Sorry if it was uncomfortable."

"It wasn't, something just felt off. What was it about?"

"Hmm?"

"The argument."

"Nothing really. Just the house hunting stuff. It's stressful." I poked her again. "You'll know soon enough."

"I'm not so sure. We love our apartment."

"If you ever want to have kids though . . ."

Her eyes widened. "Are you guys—"

"No," I said, looking back out the window. "Bill just wants the space and, well, you never know I guess."

"That would be so exciting." She sounded miles away from me.

"Please," I said quietly, "I don't want to talk about that."

"Gretchen says tomorrow is your mother's birthday," she said.

I rolled my head to face her and sighed. "So?"

"Are you going to call her?"

I pursed my lips. "I hadn't thought about it."

"You should. I'm sure she'd like that."

When I didn't respond, she scooted over, wrapped her arms around me, and planted a kiss on my cheek. "I'll see you next week, okay?"

I looked out the window at her apartment building. "Sure." I smiled. "I can't wait to see my bridesmaid dress."

I refused her money and waited until she disappeared into the building. When we pulled away, I took out my phone and read a text from earlier.

> *May 5, 2012 9:09 PM*
> *Btw... killin me in that gold*
> *dress, honeybee.*

My insides tightened. I should've been indignant at the brazen comment, but the thought of his eyes on me, watching me move, sent my mind spinning. I stared at the text almost the whole way home until, with the swipe of a fingertip, I deleted the entire conversation.

The cabby pulled up to the curb. "No charge this evening."

"I'm sorry?"

"No charge." He smiled into the rearview mirror.

I narrowed my eyes at him. "Why not?"

He looked away. "There's no charge, lady. Get out before I change my mind."

I scoffed. "Thanks?"

As he drove away, I replayed the exchange with David in my head. He'd orchestrated this; I was sure of it. The question was why. And how he knew I'd accept. His ability to read me—women in general—was well honed. I wasn't sure how long I stood there before finally heading up to my apartment.

~

I sighed, stretching out my legs. The wine had put me into a mini coma, and I woke groggily. Bill reached and pulled me closer. His hand slid over my front, and he was hard against my backside. He nuzzled my neck and kissed my jaw.

"I can't," I said softly. "I'm hungover."

Bill flopped over and sighed. "How was last night?"

"Nice," I said. "Spirits were high, and the food was good."

"And the head chef?"

"Seems really sweet. Poor guy doesn't stand a chance against Gretchen, though."

He laughed. "How does she do it? She's hot and all, but damn. I wouldn't touch her."

I sat forward and looked down at him. "Why not?"

"Who knows how many guys she's slept with? She's always seeing someone new. Gives me the creeps just thinking about it."

"Babe, she doesn't sleep with all the guys she goes out with." I got out of the bed and pulled on a t-shirt. "Even if she did, who cares?"

"I'm just saying, it'd be a deal breaker for me."

"So if you'd found out I had a reputation, you never would have gone out with me?"

He was quiet. I went to the kitchen to make coffee.

"I couldn't deal with knowing half of Chicago had seen my wife naked," Bill said behind me. He kissed the back of my head. "I'm not going to find that out, am I?"

"Bill."

"I'm teasing. You're nothing like Gretchen."

I turned to face him. "What do you mean by that?"

"Babe. Seriously? Sometimes she's dating more than one guy at a time. That's disgusting."

"She's your friend. Don't call her disgusting."

"Let's be honest, she's a little slutty. One day it'll catch up with her. And she's *your* friend."

I set my jaw and let his comments slide.

"Who knows?" he said. "Maybe I'm wrong. The chef could be the one. Look at me—I never thought I stood a chance with you, yet here I am." He sipped his coffee.

I smiled in spite of myself. "Oh, please."

"It's true. I thought you were way out of my league." He winked. "Guess I got lucky."

"You're making me blush."

"All right." He squatted down and pulled out a pan. "How's an omelet sound for my hungover girl?"

I grinned. "Just what the doctor ordered."

~

My cell phone knocked against my leg, and I looked up.

"Where'd you get this?" I asked, retrieving it from the end of the couch.

"Your purse in the kitchen." My confusion morphed into panic when I remembered last night's texts.

Suddenly I couldn't remember if I'd deleted them or even exactly what I'd said. I opened my mouth.

"You should call Leanore," he said.

I blinked and deflated back against the couch. I pulled a pillow over my face, hiding. "Why does everyone keep saying that?"

"You can't ignore your own mother on her birthday."

"I'm not ignoring her," I said. "Why don't you call her if it's so important? Get Lucy on the line too, make it a conference call."

"Liv," he said. "Come on. Call her."

I pulled the pillow away and looked at my phone again. "I don't know what to say."

"Just wish her a happy birthday. Tell her you love her. Tell her you miss her."

I made a face as I dialed.

"Hello?" she said into the phone.

"Hi, Mom." There was a pause on the line. "Mom?"

"Olivia?"

"Yes. Unless you have some secret daughter I don't know about. Are you there?"

"Yes, yes. How are you?"

"I'm fine, Mom. Just called to wish you a happy birthday."

"I didn't think I'd hear from you. It's been months."

"I know. Things have been crazy here. How are you?"

Bill cleared his throat, and I picked at something on the couch.

"I'm well," she said. "I keep trying to get in touch with your father. Money is tight. I don't know what I'll do in a couple months. He won't take my calls."

"He doesn't owe you alimony anymore," I said. "As if I need to tell you."

"I don't understand why he can't just help me out. He has the money."

"You know why, mom. Don't play the victim. Anyway, he has just finalized his divorce with Gina, so he has his hands full."

"That's what she gets for breaking up a marriage," she muttered, her usual response. *She didn't break up a marriage. You did.*

"How's the book coming?" I asked, hoping to change the subject.

"All right."

"Care to tell me about it?"

"It's not there yet."

"I see. You're keeping busy though?"

"What do you mean by that?"

"Nothing. Just making sure you aren't . . . bored."

"Stop insinuating."

I sighed. "I'm not, Mom. You sound well."

"How's Bill?" she asked with a lightened tone.

"He's working a lot, but he's good." I looked over at him. He was engrossed with something on his phone. "He says 'hello.'"

"Good boy. He works hard so he can take care of you. You got lucky with that one."

I pursed my lips at the backhanded compliment. "I suppose I did."

"I should get going. I've had a long weekend. Thank you for calling, and give Bill my love."

"Happy birthday." I hit 'End' and sighed. When I looked up, Bill was watching me.

"That was pitiful," he said.

"You know how she can be."

"I know how you both can be."

"What's that supposed to mean?"

"It means that this way that you are, you learned it from her. When it comes to you and your dad, she's cold, even if she doesn't mean it."

"I am not like her. She's never been good at expressing herself. It's always been one extreme or the other: great indifference or irrational madness. I don't know how to make her happy."

"It sounds like she hasn't been happy since you guys left. Maybe she wants you to come back."

I shook my head. "When my dad and I left, it just gave her an excuse to be unhappy. And something to crucify us for."

"That's understandable, don't you think?"

I was silent. Was it? She'd left us no choice, but Bill couldn't understand that. "Does that mean you think I'm cold?"

"Sometimes, yeah," he said, touching his chin.

"Oh." It wasn't an entirely unfair assessment, but it was nonetheless painful to hear out loud. I never meant to be cold.

"She thinks you blame her for the divorce. Because you do."

"You're being a little harsh."

"Sorry, babe. I just hate that you guys fight. I want you to be happy."

"I am. And we don't fight. But maybe that's the problem."

He didn't speak for a beat. "Could you tell if she was drinking? On the phone?"

"I don't think she was."

"We can send her some money."

"Dad doesn't think we should. I believe the word he used was 'enabling.'"

"She's fifty-something. She's not going to change."

"She could change, but not until she admits there's a problem."

"Maybe there isn't. As far as we know she only overdrinks once in a while. I don't think that makes her an alcoholic."

"I don't know. Maybe—"

"You're too hard on her. So she's not a perfect mother. Who is? Don't make something out of nothing."

I nodded and shut my mouth. He always took her side anyway. It wasn't worth fighting over.

He didn't understand my relationship with my mom. Nobody could, except maybe Gretchen and her brother, who'd been there for the divorce and everything that came after.

I looked over at him as he flipped through his book, trying to find where he'd left off. How could I make him see that I wasn't always the bad guy? If I tried to get him to understand, and he didn't . . . would that mean he was right? That I was to blame?

I'd lost count of how many times I'd opened my mouth to explain what it was like. How it had felt to live through the divorce knowing that she cared more about losing my dad than me.

"Don't make something out of nothing."

Maybe he was right. "I'm going to take a nap," I said, sitting up. "Whoa." I steadied myself on the armrest and groaned.

Bill laughed. "All right. Go sleep it off, champ."

~

I woke up later in a daze, confused by the setting sun and the warmth of a heavy blanket draped over me. "Bill," I called from the bed.

I closed my eyes again, ready to give in to a second round, when he responded from the doorway. I opened my eyes and reached out. He climbed in next to me, tented the blanket, and kissed my naked shoulder.

"Do you still think I'm cold?" I whispered, looking up at him.

"No." He rubbed a smooth cheek against me. I lazily pulled him on top of me and ran the soles of my feet over his long calves. The inside of his mouth was hot and soft, and when he pulled away, I almost pulled him back. Instead, I told him to get a condom.

We made love under that too-hot blanket, sweating and groaning into each other. After a second time, we lay panting on the bed until I heard my phone faintly singing from the couch.

"Birth control alarm." I swung my feet over the side of the bed and went to leave when Bill caught my forearm. I turned to meet eyes that were asking me to stay. The moment stretched as we stared at each other in the almost-dark that was punctuated by chiming from the living room. I bit my lip in consideration. Slowly, I slid my arm through his hand and left to take the pill.

CHAPTER 13

From: David Dylan
Sent: Mon, May 7, 2012 08:23 AM CST
To: Olivia Germaine
Subject: RE: Chicago M – Meet & Greet Invitation

Olivia,

Thanks for the Meet & Greet invitation. I'll be there. I'm headed over to my latest project in a few hours. Come along & we can discuss my bachelor status.

DAVID DYLAN
SENIOR ARCHITECT,
PIERSON/GREER

This was the interview I needed. Needed, yes. But also wanted. Curiosity about David was living and breathing in me despite any attempts to smother it.

From: Olivia Germaine
Sent: Mon, May 7, 2012 08:31 AM CST
To: David Dylan
Subject: RE: Chicago M – Meet & Greet Invitation

I'm all yours. When & where?

Olivia Germaine
Associate Editor,
Chicago Metropolitan Magazine
ChicagoMMag.com

From: David Dylan
Sent: Mon, May 7, 2012 08:33 AM CST
To: Olivia Germaine
Subject: RE: Chicago M – Meet & Greet Invitation

Music to my ears. 11:30. Lunch is on me.

DAVID DYLAN
SENIOR ARCHITECT,
PIERSON/GREER

~

At eleven thirty on the dot, Jenny buzzed me from the front desk. I smoothed a hand over my hair and swiped on pink lip gloss before heading to the lobby. I was thankful for my conservative outfit—a short-sleeved, white button down and navy, high-waisted pencil skirt. Clutching my briefcase to my chest, I found Serena and Beman talked giddily with David.

"You didn't mention an appointment with Mr. Dylan today," Beman said. He nodded approvingly when David turned to me. "We're so thrilled you've agreed to be part of the piece this year, David."

David rubbed the back of his neck. "This isn't the type of publicity I usually engage in. Hope it doesn't turn out too bad."

"It will be quite the opposite. I expect you'll receive an emphatic response." Beman batted his eyelashes. "I've followed your work since that piece in the *Tribune* years ago. I'd love to come along and see the space?"

"Mrs. Germaine and I have set aside this time for our interview. With my hectic schedule, it's the only time I could spare."

I smiled at Beman.

"I completely understand," he said. "Please consider Liv at your disposal."

David turned to me and set his hands on his hips. "You ready?"

I indicated the door. "After you, Mr. Dylan."

"No." He shook his head and chuckled, swinging the door open with ease. "After you."

In the hallway, once alone, my shoulders depressed. David seemed to both wrack and calm my nerves.

"That guy tells anyone you're at their disposal again, and I'll throw him through the wall."

I tilted my head up at him, searching his face for teasing but there was none. After a deep breath, he smiled. "How are you?"

I arched an eyebrow, confused by the shift in mood. "Fine," I replied. I crossed my arms when he glanced at my elbow.

He tapped his foot and peered down at me while we waited for the elevator.

"And how are you?"

"Better," he said with a beatific smile, taking a hammer to my resolve.

~

David led me to a classic, black Porsche 911 so shiny and spotless, it must've taken a deal with the devil to keep it that way. Especially in this city.

"This is your car?" I asked when he opened the passenger door.

"Get in." I crouched down to slide onto the leather seat.

"This car," I said once he was behind the wheel. I examined the interior. "*And* it's a Turbo."

"You a car girl?"

"Not really. My dad always had a different sports car when I was growing up. I don't really care, but the faster the better."

"That doesn't surprise me. Hungry?"

"Starved," I said.

He looked over. "Really?"

"I eat a lot," I muttered. "Guess you aren't used to that."

He laughed and pulled into midday traffic. "You must work hard to keep such a great figure."

I blushed. "Did you have a nice time Saturday night?"

"Moderate," he said. "I went to support Arnaud, but you were quite the distraction. I'd have rather been at your table."

"No doubt, considering it was a table of five women."

"I meant that I'd have preferred your company."

I scoffed. "*My* company? I'd say you had your hands full with—what was it? Mar-*eee*-ah? She was the most beautiful woman in the room."

He raised an eyebrow. I feigned interest in something outside.

"Do I sense a hint of jealousy?"

I looked harder out the window.

"I do go on dates, Olivia."

I turned back to him. "You can call me Liv, you know. Everyone else does."

"Don't change the subject."

The hairs on the back of my neck prickled. That always worked on Bill. "All right," I said. "Okay. So you're dating."

"Is it something you wish to discuss?" he asked.

My chest tightened. I let myself appreciate his profile while he drove. His nose was strong—there was no better word for it—and it ended in an acute tip. Though smoothly shaven, I could see a shadow forming. His long lashes blinked and bushy eyebrows furrowed as he focused on the road, deepening the crow's feet around his eyes. Defined muscles strained against a crisp shirt when he shifted gears; my hand twitched, desiring to reach over and feel them.

It was something I desperately wished to discuss. How could I tell him the things that had crossed my mind lately, the things that tore at my insides? I couldn't. Not how the closer he drew me in, the further I stood from Bill. Not how I'd begun to question my marriage or if it would be enough.

He looked over at me, waiting.

"No," I said quietly.

We rode in silence the rest of the way.

~

"Good afternoon, Mr. Dylan." The hostess's sleek ponytail, low-cut top, and smiling red lips didn't seem to catch his attention, but I had to admire her effort.

"This place is close to the site," he explained. "We're here a lot."

"What exactly is the project?"

"A resort hotel on the river."

Just as we sat, I recognized an approaching man as Arnaud, the man David had introduced to the table Saturday night.

"Dylan," he said in his strong, French accent.

"Arnaud, you remember Olivia Germaine. She writes for *Chicago M*."

"Of course." He stared at me the way he had in the restaurant. "Hello again, *mademoiselle*." He held out his hand and bowed his head.

"*Madame*, actually," I corrected, reluctantly allowing him to kiss the back of my hand.

He lifted his bent head and raised his eyebrows, looking between the two of us. "I'm sorry. Madame."

"Are you going back to the office?" David asked.

"Yes."

"I need you to go and look at those light fixtures we discussed. Today. We can make a final decision when I get back later." He returned his attention to me, effectively dismissing Arnaud.

"Germaine," David mused once we were alone. "That's not your husband's name, is it?"

"How'd you know?"

"I did my homework," he said, a gleam in his eye.

"It's not. And before you ask, I haven't gotten around to it, and you can address me however you prefer." I smoothed a hand over my hair. "Makes no difference to me; I'm changing it soon."

"I see." He smiled into his menu.

"Since you're a regular and all—what's good here?" I asked.

"Do you eat meat?"

"Definitely."

"I know just the thing." He took my menu and set it on the edge of the table. I was about to object, but the excitement in his eyes stopped me.

While he ordered for us, I took a large gulp of cold water. It coated my insides, extinguishing the heat his nearness inspired. Only it didn't. Not even close.

I swallowed. "So, David. Tell me about yourself. What do you do in your spare time?"

"I try to keep busy with work."

"But you must blow off steam somehow?" I blushed at the accidental insinuation.

"I sail," he said, letting me off the hook. "And swim whenever I get the chance."

Wet. Shirtless. I shook my head. Was there a swimmer's body under that perfect suit?

He leaned in on his elbows. "How about you," he paused, his eyes concentrated on me, "*Liv?*"

His hand bolted out to catch my wrist before I could touch my earlobe. We sat that way, frozen for a moment. He released it slowly and eased back into his chair.

"Work," I said, but it came out squeaky. "I work a lot and spend my free time with—well, Bill, obviously—and also Gretchen and Lucy. Normal girl stuff." I shrugged. "I also volunteer at the local shelter. You know, when I need a dose of reality."

He looked down into his water glass.

My brows knit. "Do you like dogs?"

"Yep." He nodded. "Our family dog is sick. It's tough on everyone."

I reached to console him but thought better of it. "I'm sorry about . . ."

"Canyon." He smiled. "His name's Canyon."

I raised my water glass. "To Canyon's speedy recovery," I said and was rewarded with a bigger smile.

The waiter set down two juicy, stacked burgers with leafy side salads. I'd almost finished my salad when I noticed him grinning at me.

"I take it you like the salad."

"Actually, I don't really like salad."

"You're eating it like it's your last meal."

"My dad always made me eat my salad before I touched anything else."

"You know your dad isn't here, right?"

"It sounds stupid when I say it out loud. A habit I don't see the point in breaking, I guess."

"Interesting."

"Hmm?" I asked, chewing.

"Just soaking up everything I can about the elusive Olivia Germaine."

I casually stabbed lettuce with my fork, now conscious of my eating habits. "Well, don't. We're here to discuss you, not me. How long have you known Arnaud?"

"Since I started with Pierson/Greer. Eight years or so."

I went to grab my briefcase, but he touched my wrist. I drew back, startled by the unexpected contact.

"Let's just talk," he said. "We can do that later."

"All right." I sat up again. "So, Arnaud—he's also an architect?"

"He's the other senior architect. A brilliant one, actually."

"Is he married? Single?"

David's face fell. "Why? Are you considering him for the article also?"

I almost choked. "God, no. Just getting to know the elusive David Dylan."

He laughed. "Arnaud's single. Eternally."

"Must be a hazard of the job," I said with an amused smile.

"It is," he said. "We work constantly. Developing a relationship takes time we don't have."

"I get that," I said. "The firm's always sending Bill— he's a lawyer—out of town. Since he's in the no-kids club."

"I love what I do, though. I choose to do it. Women say they can handle my schedule, but they always want more."

"That might not be great for the article."

"Don't get me wrong," he said. "I want to give more. To the right person."

"Is that why you agreed to do the issue? To find that someone?"

He examined his plate and looked up. "No. That's not really why I decided to play along."

I took a bite of hamburger and chewed slowly. He watched me back, daring me to ask.

I swallowed my food. "So, if this were a formal interview, the next thing I might ask is where you went to college."

"Yale for undergrad, and then Architectural Association in London. You?"

"This isn't about me, David."

"Indulge me."

"Notre Dame."

"My father went there."

"Mine too."

"What are the chances?" His dimples deepened with a large grin. "Wonder if they know each other."

"What does he do, your father?" I asked.

"He was the CEO of GQS."

"That's . . . a good job."

We both laughed.

"He's retired now. They're back in Illinois. What—"

"How'd you like London?" I asked.

"Beautiful. One hell of a place to study architecture. Have you been?"

"With my parents as a child."

"What do your parents do?"

"My dad's a consultant in Dallas. My mother writes. Books. She's a novelist."

"A novelist in Dallas?"

I shook my head and looked at the table.

"Divorced?" he asked, tilting his head to catch my eye.

I nodded.

"When?"

"Right before high school."

"That must have been hard."

I just shrugged and wiped my mouth with my napkin.

"How'd you end up here?" he asked.

"Lucy and I met at Notre Dame, and we moved here after graduation. Gretchen went to University of Chicago."

"Did you always want to live here?"

"I thought I might end up in New York City."

"Really?"

I tapped the table. "Back to you. We're getting off track."

"If you could go anywhere in the world, where would you choose?"

I sighed. "I don't know. You?"

"You do know," he said with a half-smile.

"I don't have time to think about that." I sat back in my chair. "And Bill doesn't like taking vacations."

"That's a shame. Surfing perfect breaks, gorging on oysters . . . nothing to dislike about my vacations."

Wet. Shirtless. Surfboard. Oysters. My face warmed.

"Wherever it is you have hiding in your head, you'll get there. You seem like a girl who knows what she wants."

"I'm hardly a girl," I bristled.

"How old are you, anyway?"

"Well, Mr. Dylan. I reckon that's not a very polite question."

"I see. Is politeness something you look for in a gentleman?"

"Is that not a defining characteristic of the gentleman?"

"Touché. Is politeness something you look for in a *man*?"

My smile wavered. "Let's leave the personal questions to me," I said, folding my hands. "And I'm twenty-seven, anyway."

"Just a baby."

"Why? How old are you?"

"Thirty-four." He winked. "Practically ancient."

My heart thumped once. "Good choice," I said, nodding at my plate. "Very tasty. Now I'm full."

"Really? I could eat another one."

I laughed, and he pulled out his wallet.

"I should be able to expense this," I said, reaching for my purse. "Beman would be thrilled to—"

"I've got it." His tone was stern.

"But—"

"Olivia," he said with the same authority that had caught my attention before.

"I'll allow it this once." I smirked. "Since I paid for our drinks at Jerome's."

"You didn't. Sherry didn't charge us. Something about me looking upset. Said I could use a break."

I gaped at him. "Did you . . . ?"

"What?" he asked.

I blinked furiously, trying to decide if I should laugh or scream.

"You think I went home with her because she comped my bill?" His laugh filled the restaurant. "Relax. I'm not as bad as you think. She got a decent tip though, thanks to you. Don't pull that again."

I nodded mindlessly. I watched him settle the bill, surprised at how natural his company had been. Like we'd been longtime friends. It was just one more thing to feel confused about.

CHAPTER 14

THERE WAS SO MUCH MORE I yearned to ask David. The hotel was on the river, so we walked from the restaurant, winding our way along the water.

The sun was high. Fluffy, dense clouds spotted the sky. The Chicago River gleamed with the reflection of light, as if covered in gold sequins. We walked most of the way in silence. It was easy. Like everything was just as it should be.

"That's it," he said eventually. I tilted my head back and took in the imposing building. I'd seen it before because it was impossible not to notice. The lobby's outside was slate grey base, and everything above it mirrored silver glass. The building defied logic by curving outward along one side, dipping in and then bowing out again slightly, almost like the letter "B".

"What do you think?" he asked.

"It's something else."

"Is that good?"

I turned to face him. There was no humor in his expression. "Do you really need me to tell you?" I asked.

"Yes."

I looked back, squinting against the sun. "It's unexpected. I love how the glass reflects the blue of the sky and the water, but also the sun. Against the stone slabs—which are somehow both smooth and sharp, it's almost . . . fluid?" I rolled my eyes. "But you're the architect. I have no clue. You should be the one telling me."

He shook his head quickly. "You're right though. And I love watching you talk." He stuck his hands in his pockets and started toward the entrance while I stared after him. "Coming?"

I had to take long strides to catch up.

Large palm trees sprung from the ground, greeting us as they lined the walkway. "Palm trees?" I said.

"This will all be grass." He motioned toward the empty lots by the entrance. His face lit up. "And the lobby opens up. These glass doors slide open during the warmer months."

I walked over and touched the stone at one corner. It looked smooth but felt rough. Clean grey edges and long rectangular windows structured the front of the hotel. It made me think of waves crashing and foaming on black sand beaches.

He slid one door and motioned me through. "Welcome to Revelin Resort."

"Dave," someone called from across the hollowed out room. A sturdy man approached, engaging David in conversation about an issue that seemed urgent.

I wandered the room, envisioning what it would become. It wasn't much to see because of the construction, but windows filled the room with sunlight.

I looked back at David. Three people surrounded him now, each one looking to him for something. His presence at my office was strong, but it was just as much so here, even in all the empty space.

He stopped talking suddenly and searched the room until he spotted me watching him. That familiar current lasered between us. There was much unspoken, but we seemed bound to each other in an inexplicable, supernatural way. He came directly to me, leaving behind questioning faces. I crossed my arms to keep from reaching out to him.

"Are you okay?" he asked as he approached.

I didn't trust myself to speak, so I just nodded, trying to convey what I felt with my eyes. He placed a hesitant hand on my shoulder. Heat seared through my blouse, stinging the flesh directly beneath it. His broad shoulders shielded anyone who might be watching our restrained contact. Realization hit as a pain in my gut: Even this was too close to be to him. Any nearer could mean consequences.

The creases in his face deepened. "I don't want to push you," he said, dropping his arm. "You need to make your own decisions."

"Decisions?" I repeated with knit eyebrows. "My decisions were made years ago." My chest constricted with a deep breath. "I need you to be strong for me, David. If we want to have any type of friendship I need to know that—"

"I know," he said, shoving his hands back in his pockets.

"That text the other night—what if Bill had seen it? And now you're working with Lucy?"

"Is that a problem?"

"I haven't told her about the article yet."

"Why not?"

"I don't know." I hesitated. "I guess it feels wrong."

"Why? It's work."

"Please. I'd really like us to be friends."

He grimaced.

"Just—be careful. Don't mention anything to Lucy yet."

"I'll back off." He folded his arms across his chest and focused on the wall behind me.

"Thank you," I said to deaf ears. Inside I was like the building: hollowed out, gutted. I attempted a smile.

"Wait here," he said. "There's something else I want you to see."

He returned with a conspicuously red helmet on his head and another in his hand. He held it out. "Put this on."

I wrinkled my nose at it and then looked up at him in full pout mode. My hair didn't need another reason to act out. His face was stern, so I took it reluctantly, placing it atop my head.

I followed him through the scaffolding and over to the hoist. I stepped in the cage, testing the sturdiness of it. He followed a second later, and it jolted to life, carrying us up. When we approached the roof, I stood on the tips of my toes.

"This will be accessible to the guests in the penthouse suite," he said as we stepped into breeze and sunshine. "This gutted area, next to the deck, will be a private infinity pool. It has a glass bottom so you can see into it from the suite."

"How voyeuristic." I followed the line to the edge. "It hangs over the side?"

He led me to the edge. "It's cantilevered so you can swim out of the building and over the city. Listen," he warned, "as you can see, there's no barrier, so keep back. I just wanted you to see the view."

I rotated to take in the full view since the hotel appeared to be one of the tallest buildings in the city. The sun shone brilliantly, just warm enough when I stood directly in it.

I edged closer, exhilarated to be high above everything and completely alone with David. His handprint remained on my shoulder from earlier, still buzzing with the feeling of him. I craned my neck and took another step. And then another. What would it take to feel him again, to get that rush of electricity? I rolled on the balls of my feet. *A little more lean . . . .*

He gently gripped my arm and pulled me back. His touch was no less stimulating, despite my plea to behave. It needed a knob. I *needed* to turn it down.

"It's. . ." I looked out at the water, trying to find the words.

"Humbling," he finished.

There wasn't anyone else in our world, not one person who could see us on that glass mountain. The breeze kicked, blowing my hair in my face. I removed the hardhat to smooth it away, tucking it under my arm. I couldn't not look up at him. Another whip of wind blew strands into my lip gloss. The air crackled with a charge that quickened my breath.

Finally, he turned his head to return my stare. He wet his lips so quickly I almost missed it. I yearned to know how his mouth would feel on my skin; it had to be written on my face. Any woman who looked as I must have right then knew exactly what she was doing.

David's face was unreadable, but my breath shallowed in anticipation. I leaned closer still, readying myself for what was coming. The wind lashed violently. He turned his head, squinting into the skyline.

The helmet slipped from my grip and bounced on the ground. He swooped and grasped it effortlessly, handing it to me.

"Don't take that off again," he said, avoiding my eyes. "Let's go."

~

The fourteenth floor was quiet when I returned. I sneaked to my office to avoid Beman's third degree.

In the car, the mood had changed already. David seemed distant and although it bothered me, it was for the best. It was what I'd asked him for.

After working steadily for an hour, I needed a break. Serena and Lisa were giggling over yogurts in the break room.

"Where've you been?" Lisa asked.

"She had an appointment with David Dylan," Serena said.

Lisa looked away.

"Have you seen this?" Serena asked, picking up a magazine. "Beman brought it." She flipped through and held it open for me. I stared at the *Architectural Digest* article, and then glanced at Serena. Despite my messy afternoon with David, controlling my reaction in front of most people was second nature.

"He's so hot," she said. "And, like, even better in person."

I shrugged. "Sure."

"Too bad you're married, Liv," Lisa said. She looked me up and down. "How'd you land him?"

"He's a friend of a friend," I said. It was the only answer I had. I'd been wondering the same thing myself.

"Well, aren't you lucky. Lucky Liv," she said with a face that looked as though she'd just bit into a lemon.

"Seriously. If it weren't for Brock . . ."

"Yeah right, Serena." Lisa scoffed. "If David Dylan even looked your way, you'd be on your back in a second."

"I would not. Brock and I are, like, soul mates, I guess, and . . . ."

We waited for her to finish her thought, but nothing came.

I rolled my eyes. "Can I keep this? It'll be good for his file."

"You'll have to take that up with Beman," Serena said. "He might want it for his own private file."

We laughed, stopping abruptly when he waltzed into the kitchen.

"Olivia," he said. "There you are."

"Here I am." I grinned at Serena and tucked the magazine under my arm before following him to his office.

~

Davena flipped over the *Just Listed* postcard for the house in Oak Park. "Lovely place," she said. "I agree with your realtor. I think the neighborhood is great for a young couple."

"You think?" I asked. "Bill really likes it. I'm on the fence."

"Why's that?"

"I guess it just doesn't feel like the right place. Across the street, there's this eyesore of a home. I shouldn't like it, but I do. It has character." I indicated the postcard. "That one didn't inspire anything for me. But Bill—it's in his sights."

She sighed loudly. "Well, sometimes you have to compromise a bit."

"I'm already compromising," I said, relaxing against the sofa.

"How?"

I pursed my lips. "I'm happy in the city. I'm not ready to leave."

"Why are you then?"

"Bill's the opposite. He wants something quieter. And he's preparing for children."

"And you don't?" she asked. "Want children, I mean."

"Maybe. Maybe not. I'm just not able to give him the answer he wants. Why didn't you and Mack have kids?"

"We did," she said. "I had a child many years ago, but he didn't make it a day."

I gasped. "I had no idea."

"You were a baby," she said, waving her hand. "God's plan. I just didn't have the heart to try again, and Mack was supportive. Next thing I knew, I was just too old. I don't regret it though—kids aren't for everyone." She smiled to herself. "Mack would've made quite a father, though."

She left the room but returned a minute later in her bra with a brush. She teased her short hair in jerky, upward motions. "You know, not everywhere is going to feel like home right away. It takes time. It's about whom you're making a home with. If you love Bill, which you do, it doesn't matter where you live."

As she spoke, I couldn't peel my eyes from the large bandage on her ribcage and the purple bruise spreading from both ends of it.

She stopped brushing and dropped her hand to her side to catch her breath. After a moment, she sat down next to me. "The doctor says it's not looking good." Her sunken eyes twinkled anyway. "I'm not in pain though, okay?"

I nodded.

"How's everything else? Bill doing well?"

"Davena—"

"Please. I want to talk about you. I want to know about your life."

I swallowed down the lump in my throat. "He's busy, but he's all right. I think we're going to go to Waukegan this weekend. He's been working late this whole week, so it'll be nice to get away."

"Wonderful idea. Show that Bill of yours how much you appreciate his hard work." She lowered her voice. "Get yourself over to La Perla before you go. Look for Alejandro. He's gorgeous, but he knows shit about lingerie." She winked. "So when you're done looking at him, ask for Joanne. Tell her to put it on my account."

I laughed loudly. "You are something else. Do you ever stop?"

"Never. It drives Mack crazy. But you only have one shot at life, Olivia, and take it from me, you don't want to miss anything. If you want something, say it out loud. If you love him, tell him so. Seriously."

Even when she'd revealed her diagnosis to me, her expression wasn't so grave. Her eyes lingered on mine a moment while her words hung in the air, and then she looked away. "Listen, sweetie. Can I keep this postcard for the house? I know Mack would love to put in his two cents."

"Keep it. Have Mack call us when he gets a chance. I'd better get home."

She walked me to the door and kissed me on the cheek. "Ta-ta, dear."

On the way to the train, Bill called from his office, triumph in his voice. "Cabin is booked. I can't wait for a weekend away. I might even get to relax."

"Have you called Andrew? He's been looking forward to getting away too."

"You just want Lucy there."

"That's not true," I said. "It's so you have someone else to go fishing with."

He laughed. "I'll give him a call. See you at home, babe."

CHAPTER 15

BRIAN AYERS SWUNG THE DOOR OPEN. "What is that perfume?" he exclaimed. "It reminds me of Paris!"

I giggled. "I'm not wearing anything." I held out my hand. "Olivia Germaine, *Chicago Metropolitan Magazine*."

"Pleasure to meet you, Miss Germaine."

"Thank you for agreeing to be a part of the "Most Eligible" feature. You're just the type we're looking for."

"If that type is no type at all," he said, smiling. "Hang on a moment. You look familiar. Have we met before?"

"I don't believe—"

"Eureka," he said, clasping his hands.

"Eureka?" I repeated.

He broke into a sudden, boisterous laugh. "I was just picturing the way that dog took you down."

I nodded as I grimaced. "That's right. At the park. So much for a first impression."

"Darling, that was the most endearing first impression anyone's ever made in the history of first impressions." He grabbed my hand before I had a chance to pull away. "If you weren't wearing this lovely ring, it'd be a damn fine beginning to our own romantic comedy."

"*Leashed by Love*," I said. "Starring Paul Walker. In a suit."

"Paul Walker?" His eyes crinkled with a smile. "It's the blue eyes, isn't it? Have a seat. I'll get us a drink."

"That's not necessary, Mr. Ayers."

"Please, call me Brian."

His studio apartment felt bigger than it was because of its large windows, but almost every surface was covered with papers, negatives, paintbrushes and more. He seemed inclined to use coffee cups as paperweights. Gritty, intrusive portraits, backdropped by Chicago's streets, lined the walls. "You have a lovely collection here, Brian."

"Why, thanks. That means a lot."

He handed me a glass of white wine and set a platter of cheese and olives on the coffee table.

"I really shouldn't," I said.

"It'll be our secret." With a wink, he brushed his hands over his trim blazer and straightened his striped, knit, skinny tie. He motioned for me to sit across from him.

"I can see why everyone says you're so charming," I said, following his lead and sitting across from him. "You're serving them wine right off the bat."

He ran a hand through his bleached, shoulder-length hair. "You guessed my secret. But keep it off the record. I wouldn't want anyone else catching on."

"Got it," I said, pulling out my notepad. "Have you lived in Chicago long?"

"Lauren Bacall."

"I'm sorry?"

"You have her voice and, I think, her attitude. That's who I'm casting you as in our romantic comedy: a young Lauren Bacall."

"I haven't heard that before, but I'll take it as a high compliment."

He crossed his ankle over his knee, exposing grey socks with white polka dots. "You have wonderful bone structure. Such cheekbones. And your eyes. So sentient! Perhaps I can photograph you sometime."

"Perhaps," I said. "But first things first. Tell me a little about yourself, Brian."

~

I knocked at Lucy's door and poked my head into her office.

"Come in," she said. She was on her knees in front of David Dylan, tugging the hem of his pants.

"Oh, I . . . I'm sorry," I said. "Your receptionist said to just go in—"

"It's fine," she said with a pin between her teeth. "Come in, Liv."

David's head snapped up and caught my eyes in the mirror's reflection.

"You remember David Dylan," she said, removing the pin to stick in the pant leg.

"I do." I shut the door behind me and entered the office. "Actually, David here is a bachelor in our 'Most Eligible' issue next month."

Lucy beamed. "Really? Did you know, David? How wonderful."

"Yes," he said slowly. "I met with Olivia about it earlier this week."

"You're going to be great. And you'll be best dressed without a doubt. Liv, we're running a little behind. Do you mind?" She glanced up at David. "We're going to a bridesmaid dress fitting after we get something to eat. You should come. To lunch—not to the fitting." She giggled. "I'll be right back. I need more pins."

She rushed from the room, leaving us in complete silence.

"I'm surprised to see you," he said finally.

I shrugged. "I didn't know you'd be here."

"That's too bad." His eyes scanned over me. "I'd kind of hoped you'd worn that outfit for me."

I made a startled noise and looked down at my fitted black dress. "What's wrong with my outfit?" A snakeskin belt cinched my waist, accentuating my slight curves. The neckline scooped, revealing a small glimpse of cleavage. I was wearing higher-than-usual pumps, but they matched the belt—unavoidable. With the four inch boost, I figured my lips would come right up to his neck, or maybe just past, to his chin . . . .

"If you expect me to behave, don't wear things like that," he said.

"Noted. Beman says I'm to adhere to your every request."

His eyebrow shot up. "Every request?"

I glanced at my feet and blushed.

"Well, what do you think?" he asked. His arms were open, displaying the tailored, slate-colored suit. "Is it me?"

Within seconds I'd leapt into his arms, covering his face with kisses. I lingered on the soft spots and relished the coarse ones. I pressed my willing self against his hard body, locking those snakeskins around his lower back so we were perfectly aligned . . .

I blinked, forcing myself from the fantasy.

"It's nice," I said, bridling the heat rising in me. My eyes darted to a rolling rack with four crisp suits. "Are these all yours?"

"Seems that way. Lucy thinks outside the box. She's not afraid to take a risk. I like that."

"A three-piece suit?" I asked, tugging at a jacket's lapel. "Outside the box, indeed. I'm not sure I could picture Bill in one of these."

"She said women find it sexy."

I suppressed my smile. "Did she now?"

Lucy returned and practically pushed David into the fitting room with the next suit. I perched at the edge of her desk, fingering my earlobe as she bustled around me. Behind the door just feet away, David was shedding one suit for the next. Those long limbs and hard muscles. I closed my eyes and heaved a deep sigh. *Get it under control.*

"What do you feel like?" Lucy asked.

"What?"

"For lunch? Where should we eat?" She lowered her voice. "Do you mind that I invited him?"

171

I opened my mouth to answer.

"I was not wrong about you, Lucy," David said as he reentered the room. "I never would've chosen a three-piece suit for myself. It's something new."

"You look positively dashing," Lucy said in a mock British accent, flattening the tie into the vest. David straightened his shoulders in the mirror and tugged on the sleeves.

My mouth went dry. I swallowed. Our back-and-forth from lunch filtered through my head. Standing tall in the urbane suit, he looked every bit the refined gentleman. *And gentleman becomes him.*

When Lucy was occupied pinning again, I noticed David's black American Express on the desk beside me. I blinked to the price tag of one of the suits and almost fell over. $2,985. *Exactly how much do architects make?*

The desk vibrated under my thighs. David's phone lit up, and the name *Brittany* bannered across the screen. He didn't make any effort to move or see who was calling, so I didn't mention it. *Brittany? Doesn't exactly sound like work.*

"I brought snacks." I heard the cheery voice of Lucy's receptionist before I saw her. She entered the room back first and turned around. "Goldfish, apples, croissants . . ." She nodded as she named each thing on the tray. With a goofy smile plastered on her face, she set it on the coffee table and turned to David. She cleared her throat, trying to catch his eye in the reflection. "Um, is this all right, Mr. Dylan? Would you prefer something else?"

"I can't move," he said, nodding his head toward Lucy.

"Oh, of course." She nodded enthusiastically, picking up the tray.

"No, that's all right," he said when she started toward him. "I'll grab something later."

I stifled a giggle, wondering if women were always this uneasy around him.

"Of course." She set it down again. "Well, if you need anything—"

"I'll take an apple," I said.

"You're welcome to it." She motioned toward the tray as she left.

David grinned, but silence fell over the room in her wake.

"Liv's up for a promotion if the article goes well," Lucy said to David. She looked up at me and back to the pant leg. "Do you think you'll get it? Are you nervous?"

"I'm optimistic," I said.

"It's my favorite time of year," Lucy said. "Liv gets to work with all these hot guys while I live vicariously through her. Don't tell Andrew." She blushed as she smiled.

"Women too," I said.

David just stared at his reflection.

"I don't care about the women," she said. "Who else are you interviewing?"

"Actually, I just got back from meeting with a freelance photographer at his apartment."

"Hold still, David," Lucy said. "I might accidentally stab you!"

"His name is Brian Ayers," I continued. "Really interesting guy—beguiling, actually. Don't tell, but he fed me wine and cheese."

"While you're working?" Lucy asked.

I widened my eyes at her and nodded.

David looked at me finally. "Brian Ayers?"

"Do you know him?"

"For a long time. We run in the same circle." I thought I detected a hint of a growl, but I couldn't be sure.

"What do you think?" Lucy asked. "Would he make a good Bachelor?"

David's nostrils flared, but Lucy worked intently on the hem of his blazer. "He's a good guy," he said, rolling his eyes. "I suppose some women might find him attractive."

"Liv?"

I thought about meeting him on the Trail and how different he'd looked earlier. "He looks like a distinguished beach bum if that makes sense. Like, I could see him hitting the waves before a board meeting. But he doesn't have board meetings, because he's a photographer. I don't really know how to pin him down, which is why he'll be great for the article. He'll appeal to different demographics."

"Distinguished beach bum." David snorted. "Maybe that should be his headline."

"David, would you mind answering some questions for me so I can determine your wardrobe needs?" Lucy looked at me. "Grab the clipboard from my desk and take notes?"

"You're putting me to work?" I asked, reaching for the clipboard.

"We're almost done, promise." Her eyes pleaded with me. *If she only knew. I could sit and watch this all day.*

"Aside from work and the occasional event—"

"Frequent. I have events weekly."

"Right." Lucy nodded. "Frequent events. Side from that, what else are you shopping for?"

"How do you mean?"

"You mentioned you're a swimmer," she said. "What're your other hobbies?"

"I don't have much free time. Right now, Arnaud and I are flipping a house in Evanston, but for that I just wear a t-shirt and jeans."

My mouth twitched. He was trying to break me. Between gentleman, swimmer, and construction worker, he was hitting all the right triggers.

"Do you need trunks?" I asked, trying to be helpful. "For swimming?"

He glanced at me in the reflection and a smirk twisted his mouth. "I'm all set."

I smirked right back. *Two can play at that game.* "How about undergarments? Boxers? Briefs?"

He shook his head. "That won't be necessary. How about you? Anything you need?"

"I'm good," I said, fighting the blush that was creeping upward. "Bill has great taste in that department."

Lucy raised her eyebrows at me, but I pretended to make notes on the clipboard.

"Glad to hear it," David said. "You know what I could use though? Shoes. Size fourteen. And a half." He winked. "They're hard to find, so don't forget to write that down."

It took me a second to realize I'd dropped my pen. Lucy froze, and I was sure I saw her sneak a peek up from where she was crouched. David watched me in the reflection again.

"Shoot," Lucy said, causing me to break the stare. "I pricked myself. I need a Band-Aid. I'm done if you want to get dressed, David."

She left the room, and David walked toward me from the mirror. "Brian Ayers? Do you really think it's wise to go drinking wine in strangers' apartments?"

"I thought you knew him."

"He's a stranger to you."

"Is he a bad guy?"

"No, but that's not the point," he said, running his hand over his face. He exhaled loudly. "And in that dress?"

"It's just business."

He inclined forward, and I stiffened instinctively. "Do you really find him attractive?" he asked near my ear while he picked up his phone from the desk. His hair was styled into that lustrous wave again. When he stood back, there was a hint of men's hair product in the air.

I shook my head slowly without breaking eye contact. "I suppose some women might think so," I echoed his words. "But, no. He isn't my type."

David only raised his eyebrows and nodded.

I grabbed my apple from the desk. "Speaking of which, how's Maria?"

"We can call and ask if you'd like." He waved his phone at me, and I scowled. "Listen, I'll tell you anything you want to know. You just have to ask."

I looked into my apple, searching for an answer it couldn't give me. I even shook it slightly, hoping for a Magic-Eight-Ball miracle.

David disappeared into the other room, this time leaving the door ajar. The image of Maria's perfectly browned skin and slitted green eyes had haunted me since the night I'd seen her at the restaurant. But did I really need more details to torture myself with?

"So?" he called from the other side of the door.

"Okay." I took a bite of the apple and chewed slowly. "Is she your girlfriend?"

"No."

"Do you have sex?"

He chuckled a moment and fell silent. "Yes."

My heart dropped, and my insides tightened simultaneously. Although I tried to look away, I couldn't help noticing flashes of his tanned skin through the sliver of doorway.

"We have an unspoken arrangement. She usually accompanies me to events." He paused. "We sleep together sometimes. But we're not exclusive."

"Not exclusive?" I asked.

He reentered the room, crossing his arms and positioning himself in front of me.

"No." He looked me in the eye. "We're allowed to see other people."

"I thought you didn't gallivant."

"It's hardly gallivanting," he said, lifting his chin fractionally. "It's cut-and-dry. I don't have much time to seek women out, but sometimes things develop."

"Are you seeing other women?"

"Not technically at the moment," he said. "But I can, and I do."

I didn't know why his honesty startled me. I'd known all along that he was a player—casual encounters and all. I'd been right about one thing though: I wasn't the only person to experience such a connection with him.

I suddenly felt out of my league, which was becoming an all too familiar feeling around him. My indignation from our first introduction resurfaced. He couldn't notch me on his figurative post like the others, and I was grateful for that.

"Well," I said, at a loss for words.

"Anything else?" he asked.

His words were measured. He'd heard my request for restraint earlier in the week. I got the feeling there was something he wanted me to ask, but he was playing indifferent. I decided I'd heard enough, though.

"No." I forced a smile, a front for my confusion. "What is it?"

"Nothing." I shrugged. "I should check on Lucy."

"Olivia." He paused. His shoulders loosened. "I've been reading your articles online. You write very well."

My heart somersaulted, but I shook my head. "You have it wrong. My mother is a writer. I'm an editor. I only contribute once in a while."

"Don't sell yourself short. You're talented."

"Thanks," I said, embarrassed that it came out sounding like a question. We sat in silence for a moment. Before he could say anything else, I tossed the apple rind I'd been holding into the trash across the room, sinking a perfect shot. My fists shot in the air. "Three-pointer."

He grinned. "Basketball fan, huh?"

"Bill is. You?"

"I'm a Bears fan myself."

"Football? I could see that."

"Oh?"

"Sure. I can picture you as a quarterback, working the field. Leaving a trail of cheerleaders in your wake." I bit my lip as I smiled. "Did you play in high school?"

"Yes, though I would've preferred to focus on the swim team."

"Quarterback? Linebacker?" I paused, running my hand along the edge of Lucy's desk. "Tight end?"

"QB."

I nodded. "Thought so. I had a crush on our high school quarterback." I cocked my head. My eyes wandered down. "He looked a little like you, but not as tall."

His hand twitched, and he quickly crossed his arms tighter. "What are you doing?"

I shrugged one shoulder, staring him down. "What?"

"You're flirting with me, even though you asked me to back off. Just like on the roof the other day."

I blinked at him, unsure of what he'd say next.

"Olivia, I'll put on a show in front of your friends, at your work, whenever we're in public. But I'm growing tired of pretending when we're alone. Don't tempt me," he warned.

His tone meant to scold me, but my body thrilled with his words. *Pretending. What is he pretending?* For a quick second, I wished I were single so I could find out what he didn't want to pretend anymore.

Lucy burst through the door and showed us the bright pink Band-Aid around her finger. "Sorry. I had to go all over, but I finally found a mom with one in her purse. I doubt it's even bleeding anymore."

Despite the carnal reaction my body was experiencing, I couldn't help but smile at her; she could be so clueless at times.

"So, David, I think we're all set. You can take your card back. Did you want to join us for lunch?"

He hesitated for maybe the second time since I'd met him. "I would love to," he said and then looked directly at me. "But I really shouldn't. Thanks for your help today. Good luck with the, uh, dresses." He picked up the rest of his things from the desk and backed away.

"I'll have your items delivered as soon as they're altered." Lucy turned back around, but I stared at the door even after he was gone.

~

"Thanks for being flexible," Lucy said. "I don't think we have time for anything other than fast food."

"No problem." I slid into the booth across from her. "I supersized the fries."

"Rebel."

"We're indulging. Before a dress fitting." I unwrapped my burger. "Gretchen would not approve."

"I'll have an apple for dessert so I don't feel guilty."

"I'm having a milkshake."

"Olivia," she scolded. "Should I have asked for a size four instead of a two?"

I laughed. "Shut up. I haven't even seen Gretchen since the restaurant opening."

"I was a little wasted," she said.

"I think we all were." I dipped a fry in ketchup. "What's the latest on the chef?"

"She's still stringing him along, in true Gretch fashion. Sometimes it really bugs me, the way she treats those guys."

"I know what you mean. I think she likes making them squirm."

"Exactly. That's what bothers me about it."

"It takes two," I pointed out. "Sometimes I think they like it."

"I don't see why. Was she always this way?"

"No," I said, swallowing food. "Growing up she was kind of shy and always hid behind these big glasses. A little pudgy too, but don't tell her I said that. She's so smart though, you know. When she met Greg, her appearance changed—she started doing her hair and lost some weight. That started a few weeks before you guys met. And when he left, well, you sort of know since you were there. That's when something inside changed."

"Greg was great," Lucy said. "But I hate him."

"Me too." I laughed before pausing to think. "He was one of the closest friends I've ever had. After five years, I still consider him a close friend. I didn't really get to grieve his abrupt departure since I had to be strong for Gretchen."

"There was always something about him though," Lucy said as if she hadn't heard me. "Sometimes I felt like he was living behind a glass wall. Like I could see him, and he could see me, but I couldn't quite touch him. Sometimes I wonder how I ever fit in with you two."

I laughed, wiping my hands on a napkin. "What do you mean? I never heard you say that about him."

"We weren't really supposed to talk about him after he left. I just think you guys were similar, which is why you got along so well. And Gretchen and I aren't necessarily alike, but I'm surprised by how close we've become."

I nodded in agreement. Even though I'd introduced them, I sometimes envied their relationship. Their connection had developed quickly, and I'd often thought that they'd have found each other regardless.

"And Andrew, well . . ." She smiled. "He'd get along with just about anyone, so I'm not surprised that he fits so well into the group. I'm just thankful I snagged him before anyone else did."

"He's a good one. But you guys were meant for each other."

"Do you really think so?"

"Without a doubt."

"Do you feel that way about Bill?"

I stopped chewing before swallowing with a gulp. "Of course I do, Luce. But, you tell me: where does poor Bill fit into all this?"

"Bill? Well, he's . . ." Her face became still as she thought. "He and Andrew are becoming close, which I'm so happy about. It's a dream come true that we found guys who get along so well. And he loves you so much."

"He loves me so much? That's a cop out compared to what you said about everyone else."

She touched my wrist. "I'm sorry. I didn't mean it like that."

I waved my hand. "It's fine. Are you ready for our fishing expedition?"

"Andrew's over the moon." She pulled out her phone. "His text from earlier: 'Gonna catch you a big one tomorrow.'" We both burst into laughter. "Did I mention he's excited?"

"Bill too."

"We make a good team, the four of us." Her head inclined toward one shoulder. "I mean that."

I smiled. "We should get going."

CHAPTER 16

I STOOD WITH MY ARMS PLANED and my lips pinched, holding in a laugh. The seamstress pulled at the armhole of my bridesmaid dress. "It tickles," I said to Gretchen.

"Told you."

I looked over my shoulder at the plunging line of the dress. "Backless dresses. Bold move."

"Stay still," the seamstress said.

"You'll both look fantastic," Lucy said. "I promise. Red is really your color, Liv."

The wine-colored dress richly contrasted my fair skin. It grazed the floor, and the neckline, suspended by razor-thin straps, dipped into a "V" between my breasts.

I grimaced. "That feels a little snug."

The woman blinked up at me briefly and continued working.

"I'm on a strict diet until the wedding," Gretchen said. "I do not want to look like a porker in the photos."

"Don't you trust me?" Lucy asked. "I'd never send you out there looking like a porker. I have a flair for this, you know."

"I should hope so since you do it for a living," I said. "What about your dress?"

"No luck yet. I'm still searching."

"Bring magazines this weekend."

"What's this weekend?" Gretchen asked.

"Fishing," Lucy said.

"Do you want to come?" I asked. "We're going to stock up on Pinot Grigio and tear apart bridal magazines by the fire while our men forage."

"I'm sure I have plans," she said. "Have a blast, though."

"Don't be jealous that we'll be in flannel pajamas while you're running around in four-inch heels." I paused. "Never mind. You win."

"Finished," the seamstress said. "Go change."

In the fitting room, I slipped out of the dress and checked the price tag before handing it back to her.

Lucy and I said good-bye to Gretchen and walked the quarter mile back to work.

"I have the car today," I told Lucy before she turned for her office. "Bill carpooled with a colleague. Want a ride home?"

"That'd be awesome. My last appointment should be done by five."

I squeezed her arm. "See you at five, then."

~

I flipped through *Vogue* in the waiting room of Lucy's office. The receptionist stood, so I looked up.

"I'm off," she said, checking her watch, "but they should be done any minute."

Moments after she'd left, Lucy appeared from the hallway. She nodded at me and walked her client to the elevator. They shook hands when the doors opened.

She turned to me. "My crown came out while I was eating my stupid dessert apple. That was the most uncomfortable appointment I've ever had."

I scrunched up my nose and looked away when she tried to show me.

"Sorry. I forgot you hate that stuff."

"You would too if you were brainwashed into daily brushing and flossing as a child. My dad made the dentist show me detailed, gruesome photos of dental procedures while I was stuck in the chair."

"Gross. I spoke to my dentist earlier, and he's staying at the office late for me. It shouldn't take more than an hour to fix, but I have to go now."

The desk phone rang.

"I'll give you a ride," I said.

"Did my receptionist leave?"

"Just now."

"God forbid she stays a minute after five."

"I'll be your receptionist," I said with a wink. I grabbed the receiver. "Lucy Forester's office."

"Olivia?"

I froze. "Yes?"

"It's David. David Dylan."

I lowered myself onto the edge of the desk. "Oh. David? How'd you know it was me?"

"With that voice?"

I cleared my throat. "What can I do for you?"

"Actually, I was looking for Lucy."

"Right," I said. "Of course."

Before I could pass the phone, he continued. "I have a bit of a situation."

I shrugged at Lucy while she packed up her purse. "Go on."

"I've been invited last minute to a black-tie gala at the Museum of Contemporary Art tonight. My only tuxedo is in my New York apartment. If Lucy can find me one fast, I'll pick it up on my way."

"Hang on." I hit the hold button. "It's David Dylan. He needs a tuxedo for a black-tie event tonight."

She groaned. "My boss would kill me."

"What do you mean?"

"Just that David's turning out to be one of our best clients. I can't say no. I'll just have to go the weekend without seeing a dentist."

"Where would you even get a tuxedo right now?"

"We have some rented tuxedos here from an event the Chicago Bears attended recently. David's got a similar build to a couple of the players. Not a perfect solution, but it could work in a pinch."

"That's lucky."

"For him," she muttered. "Not so much for me."

"Let me help," I said. "What can I do?"

"Unless we can swap mouths for a few hours, not much."

"I meant here. Maybe I could get David the tux."

"Oh." Her eyes lit up. "He just needs to pick it up, right? You could wait for him here and lock up afterward."

"We won't leave for the cabin for a few hours anyway."

She took the phone from my hands. "David? It's Lucy. I have an emergency dental appointment—no, I'm fine—but I have something here that should work for your event. Liv will wait for you at the office. Come by on your way. You can change here." She paused, and I released the breath I'd been holding. Her eyes jumped to mine. "Sounds great. She'll see you in half an hour."

"You'd better get going," I said when she hung up.

She handed me a set of keys. "The tuxedos are in the walk-in closet down the hall. Bring the rolling rack; most of them should fit. There are shoes and dress shirts in there too. He's a huge client—"

"I've got this," I said. "Go."

She hugged me quickly. "Thank you. You're a lifesaver."

The moment she disappeared into the elevator, my stomach knotted. I went to the closet and looked at myself in the floor-length mirror. What had I agreed to? I turned away before I could answer myself.

I'd just set a pair of dress shoes in Lucy's office when my phone rang.

"Jack?" I said.

"Hey, Liv."

I sat at Lucy's desk and swiveled her chair to look out at the cityscape. "I haven't talk to you since Lucy's engagement party."

"I went to our hotdog stand today. It made me think of you."

I laughed. "I remember that day we bumped into each other and had lunch. One of the best dates I've had in a while."

"You wish that was a date."

I scoffed. "You mean *you* wish."

"Yeah." I could tell he was smiling. "Something like that."

"How are you?"

"Some of us are headed to Navy Pier later for a drink. There'll be people from your office there. You should come."

"Wish I could," I said. "Bill and I are going north for the weekend."

"Still with that guy?"

"He's my husband," I said, unable to hold my laugh in.

He sighed. "Yeah, okay. Maybe next time? You know where to reach me."

"Have fun tonight, Jack."

I hung up the phone and shook my head, smiling. When I turned around, David was leaning in the doorway.

"I didn't hear you come in," I said. "I hope you weren't waiting long."

"Jack?"

"An old work friend. He was the bartender at Lucy's engagement party, actually."

He raised his eyebrows. "That guy? He likes you."

I waved my hand dismissively. "He doesn't. I'm not even sure he's straight."

"He is straight, and he's into you."

"And you can tell that from a one-sided phone conversation?"

"He was flirting with you at Lucy's party."

My smile faltered. My only interaction with Jack at the party had been right before I'd spilled my drink. Those chestnut browns were on me before I'd known David was there. Watching. Observing.

"Yes, I saw you," he said, reading my expression. "I followed you into the kitchen to find out your name, which I did, and to ask you out. Which I did not."

I automatically touched my heart when it fluttered.

"In any case, he likes you."

"He's headed for disappointment then." I wiggled the fingers on my left hand. He looked at my ring and back at me. "So here we are again," I said before he could respond. "Lucy should really start paying me for my services."

"Lord knows I pay her enough to share the wealth." He grinned.

I nodded at the changing room. "The tuxes are in there. You have a few options. We do not take sartorial emergencies lightly."

He disappeared into the room, and I exhaled loudly. Being near him was proving harder and harder each time. I brushed hair from my face and took another deep breath.

David reentered the room soon after, closing up his dress shirt. Each button swallowed up a little bit of his tanned chest. His hair was black marble, styled in its sophisticated, slight ripple.

"How this one?" he asked, walking over to the mirror.

My breath caught as I watched his reflection.

"Olivia?"

"It has my vote."

He looked down, slipping into the shoes I'd set on the floor.

"Why is it every man looks even more handsome in a tuxedo?"

His eyes caught mine in the reflection. "Sold. I'll take it."

I laughed. "It actually fits surprisingly well."

"First time's a charm."

I walked over and took his wrist to help him with the cufflinks. "But it's only on loan for the night."

"Can't I just buy it?

"It belongs to someone else."

"I doubt he'd miss it." His dimples deepened with a smile.

"I'm sure he would," I said, scrunching my nose at him. "A lot."

It was becoming hard to ignore the palpable heat that was building between us. His stare followed me when I moved to the left cuff. A deep breath filled my nostrils with his spicy aftershave. I kept my eyes on his shoes.

"They're too small," he said softly.

"They only had size fourteen. No half. You'll have to make it work."

I took a step back and admired him. The bowtie hung loose around his neck, the final piece of the puzzle. He took both ends of it, furrowing his brows.

"Let me." I slipped between the mirror and him. The spicy scent, now mixed with something fresh— something from a recent shower—intensified as I leaned in. Reaching up, I deftly molded the fabric into a neat bow. I'd fixed my dad's bowties when I was younger, and the motions were automatic.

As I pulled the bow taut, my fingers stilled and lingered. I could no longer avoid his penetrating gaze. I watched the rise and fall of his chest until my eyes traveled up his exposed neck. His Adam's apple jumped as he swallowed. The ends of his hair looked damp. Creases around his lax mouth remained, though his smile did not. Finally, our eyes locked.

In one slow, measured movement, he wrapped an arm around my waist and pulled me to him. His other hand rose and raked through my hair, tilting my mouth upward. I pulled away as he closed the space between us, but his hold was firm. My eyes fluttered shut. His lips touched mine, testing the new territory. Warmth pulsed through me with his purposeful but tender touch. My mouth parted, and he answered with a harder kiss, opening me with his lips. An ache blossomed between my legs. My head swam with the hot breath and heady taste of another man.

He cupped my face and backed me against the mirror as the kiss became needier. His hands moved down my neck and over my collarbone. They covered my shoulders, pressing me into the glass. That ache grew painful, eager for relief. I yearned to reach up and touch him, but I was immobilized by his grasp.

I moaned without realizing it, and he tore away. We gasped for air, staring at each other.

He released my shoulders and stepped back. "Fuck." Suddenly his back was to me, his hands running through his hair. "*Fuck*," he yelled and pounded his fist against the wall. He whipped the door open and stalked out.

I just looked at the empty space, covering my tingling mouth. I picked up the office with jerky movements. My hands trembled as I folded the clothes he'd left behind and told myself over and over: *This can't happen. This has to stop.*

~

Physically and emotionally, I was drained when I returned home. The idea of a weekend sojourn, beginning with an hour car drive, seemed impossible. When I entered the apartment, I heard noises coming from the bedroom.

"Livs?" Bill called.

"Yep."

"We should probably eat before we pick them up."

I walked by the pile of fishing equipment at the door and into the bedroom, where Bill was folding clothes into an open suitcase. "You should start packing too."

I had the urge to turn and run. I looked away and pointed to my suitcase in the corner. "I already did. I'll make something to eat."

"Okay. Hey. Wait." He reached out and pulled me over. My every muscle tensed, but he didn't seem to notice. He kissed the top of my head and tucked some hair behind my ear. "How was your day? Work late?"

"It was good," I said, curling my lips into what I hoped was a smile. I wiped my mouth with my hand quickly, trying to erase traces of David. "I'm not feeling well though. Would you mind soup for dinner?"

He crinkled his nose. "I hate soup."

"Please," I said. "I'm not up for making anything."

"I'll get something on the way." He pressed the back of his hand to my forehead. "What's wrong?"

"I'm sure it's nothing. I just need a good night's sleep."

"And you're going to get one," he said. "Soon we'll be under the stars, away from all the noise. Doesn't get much more peaceful than a cabin in the woods."

For me, the best lullaby was the telltale sounds of a city not quite asleep. But Bill saw things differently. He longed for the sort of tranquility that only nature could provide.

"Can't wait," I said. "I could use some fresh air."

After a can of chicken soup, I didn't feel any better. I needed to cleanse, not consume. Despite Bill's protests, I flipped the shower on, promising him it would be quick.

"Quick?" he called through the door. "Then you have to do your hair and makeup. I'm almost ready to go— can't it wait 'til tomorrow?"

"No," I snapped. "The steam will help my head." I peeled my dress off, letting it fall on the floor. Bill opened the door and stuck his head in.

"Babe, I'm not going to do my hair or makeup," I said, exasperated.

"Damn right," he said. "We don't have time for that."

"I get it. I'll be fast. There's a twenty in my purse— take the bags downstairs, and get yourself food from the corner. I'll meet you in fifteen minutes."

He grunted and turned away.

"Honey, the door. You're letting all the steam out."

He pulled it shut as I stepped under the showerhead. I dumped too much body wash in my hand and smoothed it over my skin where the water burned. *God. Oh, God. What have I done? And what do I do now?*

I forced David's face from my mind. His lusty eyes had tormented me, reeling me in before his body cast me aside. I imagined my hands were his and squeezed my shoulders as he had, but my grip was pitiful in comparison. I ran his hands over my breasts, caressing taut nipples.

I opened my eyes and shook my head, begging myself to stop. I twisted the dial closer to red and forced myself in the water's punishing path. The ache from earlier gnawed at me, dragging my hands downward. My chest heaved as I gave in to the memory, gave in to the feel of David's lips against mine.

My palm pushed against the mound between my legs, slippery from the soap. I circled my opening, massaging the skin as my arousal mounted. *David.* Two fingers slipped inside. *Firm, strong hands. Holding me still, on my skin . . .*

I shot my other fist against the wall across from me, pressing into it as I lost myself in thoughts of him. With my back flush against the slick tile, I lifted one leg onto the opposite wall, continuing to pump and rub with my other hand. I gasped for air as my imagination took over, as David pulled open my blouse, hiked up my skirt, and rubbed against me. He threw me on the desk, opened me with his fingers, and shoved inside me.

I pushed my foot into the tile as the waves crested, throwing me into a fierce, blinding orgasm that seemed to continue for minutes.

I waited until my heartbeat slowed before removing my foot. My skin was red and raw everywhere. I continued to wash myself. I wanted to cleanse myself of him, of his presence, of the ache he had inspired. Instead I felt filthier than ever.

CHAPTER 17

THE DRIVE TURNED OUT TO BE a welcome distraction from my thoughts. Only once, while Bill and Andrew excitedly planned their morning on the lake, did I look out the window into the darkness and feel David's unrelenting clasp on my shoulders. And then his surprisingly tender lips claiming mine. The memory was made of details, unlike my furious fantasy in the shower.

"Enough," Lucy said in exasperation, tearing me from my reverie. I imagined her rolling her eyes in the backseat as she scolded Bill and Andrew. "No more fishing talk until I'm out of earshot or extremely drunk."

"Then the same goes for wedding talk," Bill said.

"Bill."

He glanced over at me. "No way. You girls can talk cake and centerpieces 'til you're blue in the face once Andrew and I have left in the morning."

Lucy made a noise. "I don't talk about the wedding that much."

"You don't," I agreed. "He's just being mean." I swallowed, wincing at the early sting of a sore throat. "How many bridal mags did you bring? Be honest."

"Well, nine. But it's because I'm so behind, and I need your help. For one, I can't stand white shoes. I need an alternative."

"Tsk, tsk," Bill said, shaking his head. "Tomorrow."

"One more thing," she said. "The tailor called. Your bridesmaid dress will be ready a week from Monday."

Bill's eyebrows shot up. "Bridesmaid dress? How much is that going to be?"

"Not now," I said.

"I'll have to budget it in for the month. You didn't mention it."

"We just had the fitting today. What do you want me to do, not be in the wedding?"

"I didn't say that. I just asked how much it was." He glanced in the rearview mirror. "Let's not get into it now."

I sighed. "What would you like to talk about? Sweetie?" I added as an afterthought.

"Andrew, what's the score now?"

Lucy and I groaned.

"Actually, man, there's something I want to ask you."

"Maybe now's not the best time," Lucy whispered.

"What is it, Andrew?" I asked.

Andrew cleared his throat. "Since Liv's going to be in the bridal party, I thought you might want to also. If you want. My brothers will be there, obviously. But I need one more guy."

"That's so nice," I said, but I was suppressing a laugh. Bill hated weddings. "Of course he wants to."

"Yeah, of course. Thanks for thinking of me."

I reached over and rubbed Bill's knee.

We arrived at the cabin late. After unloading the car, we headed for our respective bedrooms. I fell onto the mattress, welcoming the warmth of flannel sheets.

"Night," I said with a sniffle.

Bill closed his book and leaned over to kiss my neck. My heart jumped, but not because of the kiss.

"Bill," I said. His hand slid under the covers and over my backside.

"It's so romantic here, alone in the woods."

I thought better than to point out that Lucy and Andrew were steps away.

"I'm definitely coming down with something," I said. "You might catch it. What if you can't go tomorrow?"

He sighed and wrapped his arm around me, pulling me close. "You smell nice from your shower."

I swallowed. "Thanks, babe."

"Guess you're right, though. Don't want to get sick."

I exhaled my immense relief. I fell asleep quickly, but thought I heard him say, "I love you."

~

The next morning, I toweled off from a quick rinse, threw on a robe, and met Bill in the kitchen. He handed me a big mug. I held it close to my face and sniffed, letting the steam clear my nose. "Mmm, peppermint tea. Thank you, honey."

"How are you feeling?"

I frowned.

"That bad?" He leaned in. I offered my cheek, but he dodged it to plant a chaste kiss on my lips.

I crinkled my nose. "I'm gross."

He smoothed his hand over my wet hair. "Take this," he said, handing me Nyquil, "and go back to sleep. I know you were up blowing your nose half the night."

"Where'd you find this?" I asked, checking for an expiration date.

"Medicine cabinet in the bathroom. No clue how old it is."

Andrew waltzed in then, his spirits much too high for five o'clock in the morning.

"Have fun today," I said.

"What's wrong?" Andrew asked. "You sound sick."

"I feel it too. I'm going to try and sleep it off." I poured the green liquid down my throat and, cupping my tea, plodded back to bed.

I waited for the elixir to kick in, alone with my thoughts again. Only now, they went in a different direction.

I'd betrayed Bill. Another man's hands, another man's lips, another man's scent had been on me. Not just any man, though—one who was proving more dangerous by the minute. Why was it that David had stopped the kiss, not me?

Bill's things were around the cozy cabin, and the sheets were mussed where he'd just been. I desperately hoped I wouldn't see David again. Things felt dangerously easy with him, and I'd proven myself as weak as any of his girls.

But I had the memory, and it was unshakable. I began to drift amongst thoughts of arms and fingers, lips and eyes, skin, tuxedos, cufflinks . . .

~

I threw my hair back and dabbed a bit of makeup on my sallow skin. Unrelenting shadows circled my eyes. I gave up trying to cover them. Relaxed but still wobbly from the Nyquil, I wandered into the kitchen. I put a pot of water on the stove, prepared two cups of tea, and went into the living room.

"Hey," Lucy said, looking up from her book. "How do you feel?"

"Been better. But the drugs help. Want some tea?"

"Sure."

I handed her the extra mug. The heat was as comforting against my cold hands as the peppermint was soothing. "What'd I miss?" I asked.

"They'd caught a couple last time I spoke to Andrew. Salmon I think? Or something. I just talked to Gretchen too. She's hungover and still in bed watching a *Friends* marathon."

"What'd she do last night?"

"Went to some big museum party. For work, I think."

My ears perked up. "Oh? Where?"

"I don't know." She shrugged. "Said Kristen Chenoweth and Derrick Rose were there, and that she has juicy gossip but wants to tell us in person. Someone she met and hooked up with—oh, it was the Museum of Contemporary Art."

I forced a sound of comprehension, but inside I saw red. "That's the event David went to last night."

"That's funny," she said. "Well, not that funny, actually. They do sort of run in the same circles. Both single—wait, do you think he's the one she . . . ?"

"No." I gritted my teeth. They'd be a couple to envy. My stomach lurched picturing them side by side—her blonde ringlets and high heels, his tall, tuxedoed frame.

Lucy didn't seem to notice as the blood drained from my face. "You're right. Probably not. Have you read this?" she asked, holding up her book.

I shook my head. She talked, but I heard nothing. I was in too deep. I had no right to be angry about what was surely going on. Because Gretchen had made no secret of her interest in David, and she almost always got what she wanted.

~

"Rummy," Andrew said, placing his last set on the dining table. We all groaned and threw down our cards.

"I'm done," Bill said, leaning back in his chair. "That's three in a row. Let's play something else. Something Andrew sucks at."

"How about Texas Hold 'Em?" I suggested.

"You'd like that, wouldn't you?" Andrew asked, narrowing his eyes at me.

"Good idea, babe," Bill said, tugging on my sweatshirt. "I think I have a poker set in the car."

"You do?" Andrew asked, his eyebrows knitting.

"I think you're right, honey. Should I get it?"

"Veto," Lucy said. "Andrew was cranky for a week after the last game."

"Don't like losing to a girl?" I asked, shuffling the deck.

"I don't like losing a hundred bucks, period. Two hundred if you count Lucy."

"But I used it to buy the most beautiful leather jacket," I said wistfully. Bill chuckled and leaned over, planting a kiss on my cheek. I snuggled in the crook of his arm.

"Anyone want more salmon before I put it away?" Lucy asked. "It shouldn't sit out any longer."

"I'm full," Bill said. "We got lucky with that Coho, man. The guys next to us said they usually cap around five or six pounds."

"Yeah? Let's hope we can pull it off again tomorrow."

"If you do, throw it back," I said, pushing away from the table. "We have plenty."

"I'll throw you back," Bill kidded as I headed for the bedroom.

I grabbed my phone, shut off the alarm, and rummaged through my suitcase for birth control. When I didn't find it there or in my purse, my heart began to race. I pulled out the two neat clothing piles from my luggage and checked all the pockets. I unzipped Bill's duffel bag in a hurry and dumped his stuff on top of mine. Squatting on the floor, I rubbed my temples, trying to remember the last place I saw it. *Kitchen counter.* But I remembered checking the kitchen counter before I left the apartment, and it definitely hadn't been there.

"Bill," I called into the cabin. When he didn't respond, I yelled for him.

"Coming," he said. I crossed my arms, trying to think. If I didn't take one tonight, I'd have to recalibrate the whole month.

This time I used my angry voice when I called his name, and he came quickly.

"Yeah?" he asked, scanning the mess on the floor.

"Where's my birth control?" I heard my foot tapping against the floor but couldn't stop it.

"What?"

"My birth control. Where is it? Did you do something with it?"

His chin raised, and he looked down at me over his nose. "What would I do with it?"

"I don't know, but it's not in my bag, and it wasn't where I left it on the kitchen counter. Did you take it? Did you hide it?"

"Hide it?" he asked. "Do you think I'm some sort of monster? Shit, Olivia. When did you get so fucking paranoid?"

I swallowed, twisting my hands in front of me. "Well, where is it then?"

His eyes flashed, and I rushed over to shut the heavy wooden door to our room.

He snatched my purse from the floor and rifled through it. "Here," he said, pulling the packet out and throwing it on the floor. "There's your bullshit birth control. I put it in the zipper pocket so you wouldn't forget it."

"Oh. I—"

"Along with a shitload of condoms, because I never know with you." He pulled out a string of foil packets and dropped them at his feet. "Don't worry, we won't be needing them tonight," he added.

"All right," I said. "I'm sorry. Don't get mad."

"Really?" he said over me. "Why are you even starting birth control now? It doesn't make sense."

"Keep your voice down," I said, twisting my earlobe. "They'll hear us."

"Answer me, damn it."

"I just don't want to take any chances until—"

"Until you're ready, I know," he said with disgust. "Until everything is '*perfect.*' How could you think I would do that?" He shook his head, and his face changed. "You're acting like your mother."

My throat closed. "You're absolutely right. I'm so sorry. I thought—"

"Well, you thought wrong."

"I thought wr—look, don't patronize me. Let's just forget it. You're making a scene." I pulled the door open to leave, and he lunged forward to slam it shut.

"No. You don't get to leave the conversation. *I'm* leaving to enjoy *my* weekend, and *you* can stay here and clean up this shit."

206

I had only a second to jump out of the way before he flung the door open again. I crouched to pick up the mess, looking after him through threatening tears that subsided just as quickly as they appeared.

CHAPTER 18

THE NEXT WEEK WAS EMOTIONAL TURMOIL. Bill's anger subsided, but my guilt persisted. Gretchen and David took up a permanent place in my thoughts. Elaborate fantasies and imaginative scenarios filled my head, some fueled by jealousy, others by lustful memories. I was aroused, angry, and crushed all at once. David's rejection overwhelmed me. I knew it was irrational; I knew it wasn't fair.

At night, I tossed and turned with memories of my mother's senseless fits of jealousy. Was I turning into her like Bill had cruelly accused? I was never jealous with Bill, but when it came to David, it was slippery and out of my control. My sleep had suffered more than usual from the anxiety. I hadn't heard from David in almost a week, and I wondered if my Nyquil-drunken plea for relief had come true. Only, relief was far from what I felt.

I was glad to have the diversion of the upcoming Meet & Greet. I filled the days with minutiae, double-checking with the hotel and publicity department on every last detail. With the approaching deadline, I made sure I was working on the article every chance that I wasn't party planning.

By Thursday, I was already feeling much lighter as I made my way back from an interview with one of the bachelors.

I picked up my cell phone when it rang with my office's number.

"David Dylan is here to see you about the article," Jenny said. She lowered her voice. "I told him he could speak to Lisa, but he refuses."

"Did you tell him I'm out?"

"Yes. He says he'll wait." The phone beeped in my ear, and I pulled it away to see that Bill was calling.

"He can wait. I'll be there soon."

"Great," she said immediately.

I hung up and let Bill go to voicemail. My lightness began to fade. Maybe he just meant to apologize for . . . for what? I hadn't thought of the kiss all day, purposefully. The elevator ride seemed longer than usual as questions floated in my head. I wondered how I could ask about Gretchen without coming off as nosy or jealous. I considered not asking at all, but how could I not? The thought had hounded me for days.

When I exited the elevator, I smoothed an invisible wrinkle from my skirt before entering the lobby. David was glaring at Jenny from his chair while she wrote furiously.

"Here she is now, actually. One second." She covered the mouthpiece with her hand. "It's your husband. He has an emergency trip to New York tonight for work. Should he book you a ticket for the weekend?"

"Tell him I'm in a meeting, and I'll call him back," I said. I turned to David. "Mr. Dylan."

"He says it's an emergency, though," Jenny said.

I leaned over her desk, aware that I was giving David an eyeful. "No ticket," I clipped. I gave David an unconvincing smile. When we made eye contact, my heart thumped.

"Can we talk in your office?" he asked, standing.

"Of course," I said, leaving Jenny to look after us.

I shut the door to my office. "Sorry to make you wait," I said, picking up a paperclip from the floor. "I just finished up with another bachelor."

"Exactly how many men are you interviewing?" he asked, curling a fist into his other hand. "Never mind. I wanted to say thanks for the help with the tuxedo. I appreciate the last minute scramble." He paused. "I returned it to Lucy already."

"Great," I said flatly, sitting against my desk. "How was the event?"

"That's not why I'm here." His jaw set as I tried unsuccessfully to read his expression. "I came to find out if you need anything else from me for the article."

I blinked, mildly confused by his brushoff. "We'll need to take some photos for the spread. I think I have good gist of what you're about, but I need more hard details and—"

"Can I arrange that with someone else? I think it's best that we end our personal and professional relationship."

I cleared my throat and looked down, wanting nothing more than to hide my face at that moment. My fingers picked at something on the edge of the desk while my mind raced.

"Is this about Gretchen?" I asked and then instantly regretted it.

"What?"

"Nothing."

"Anything else?" he prompted. I shook my head, feeling suddenly indifferent about the article and at the same time, profoundly sad.

"Should we find someone else?" I asked evenly. "Beman won't exactly be pleased about this."

"I've made a commitment, and I intend to see it through. But I will work with someone else going forward."

It was the tone I'd heard him use with others, even Arnaud. But never with me. The thought made my chest contract. I put on a straight face, my practiced mask of apathy. Why I hadn't been wearing it all along, I didn't know. The self-preservation skills I'd been honing since I was thirteen had failed me for the first time.

"I understand completely." It was a struggle to get the words out, but I hid it behind my disguise. "I'll make the arrangements." I crossed my arms and waited. We were silent for a moment while he looked at me expectantly. "Was there something else?" I asked.

He laughed shortly and shook his head. "Nope. I guess that's it then."

I turned away so I wouldn't have to watch him leave. After another beat I heard the door close behind him. I went to the couch and lay down, burying my face in my hands. I should've been grateful. I should've been relieved. I thought of Bill, and I inhaled back tears. I thought of David, and it hurt in the spot my heart should be.

~

The office was dark except for amber dots of city light. Groggily, I tried to remember at what point I'd fallen asleep. I squinted at my watch: ten o'clock. I slipped on the flats I kept in my desk drawer and threw my heels in my purse.

I yawned on the elevator and wondered why Bill hadn't called the office. I closed my eyes and rested against the wall, eager to climb back into bed. It hit me that Bill was in New York.

I passed an empty security desk and pushed out of the building into a quiet night. It wasn't uncommon for me to work late, but I was never in the Loop at this time. It was a different area than during the day. Aside from a sporadic office light, it was dark and calm.

I headed to the curb to flag a cab when something caught my eye across the street. A man casually leaned against a street lamp. He peeled himself from the pole, and one thought came to mind: *Mark Alvarez*. My mind shuffled through our last meeting, identifying his short stature and inflated chest. His lips seemed to curl into a smile.

I halted at once, retreating a few steps. Panic froze my feet, and the man strolled toward me.

It's my imagination. I turned casually and started down Adams in the opposite direction. When I found myself peering down an empty road, I decided to head for the train instead. An elderly woman passed, bundled in her coat, wobbling with weighty groceries. She smiled at me.

Dread filled me as I confirmed with a backward glance that the man was following me. I broke into a sprint without warning, pushing through a surprised couple, propelled forward by fear. My heart pounded in my chest, and my feet beat the pavement as I flew across State Street, narrowly avoiding a passing car.

I mentally surveyed the area, my thoughts jumbling in a panicked mess. My face burned against the cool night, and his heavy footsteps bore down on me as if he realized we were nearing the train. The space between us seemed to close all at once.

"Olivia," he yelled.

Oh my God—it's not my imagination. I fumbled for my purse, pulling at my skirt as it inched up, and reached for my purse again, but it wasn't there—*where is my cell?*

On instinct, I turned a sharp corner toward Jackson. Panic struck as I ran headlong into an alley. I wouldn't make it to the other side.

"Olivia. Stop!"

A sudden burst of energy thrust me forward, but it was too late. His surprisingly strong hands caught my shoulders and lifted me from the ground.

I screamed with everything I had, thrashing against the hands that held me in the air. He set me down but detained me, thwarting my escape.

"Olivia," exclaimed a familiar voice. He relaxed his grip and whirled me around.

I blinked several times. I was looking at a confused David Dylan. He reached out suddenly to yank down the hem of my skirt, which had ridden up my thighs.

"What is it?" he asked. "I've been behind you since State."

I tried furiously to see over his shoulders. He turned his head, but I could see with my own eyes that nothing was there.

"Someone—I thought Mark was . . ." I paused, my breathing labored. "He was following me. I thought. But no one's there."

"Stay here," he said, retreating.

"David, wait," I said. "It could be dangerous."

He exited the alley as I struggled with whether or not to follow him. In the same moment that I heard a noise behind me, a coarse hand clamped over my mouth. The smell of alcohol burned my nostrils. I attempted to scream, but the fingers dug into my face.

"You're fast," a low voice said into my ear.

"Let go," I muffled into his hand and hurled my elbow into his ribs. He withdrew for a moment then threw me angrily onto the concrete. Standing over me,

Mark Alvarez lifted his shirt to reveal the handle of his gun.

"Don't scream," he said. A car whizzed by, and he jerked his head over his shoulder.

I needed to escape—and fast. The look in his eyes was clearer than last time, and that meant he knew what he was doing. I clambered to my feet, but he shoved me deeper into the alley. I cried out when my head connected hard with brick. I fought to remain upright, but my body slid down the wall.

When he came at me, I jumped to my feet and raised my fist, but he caught my arm and started laughing.

"Cute when you're mad," he slurred, tightening his grip. For a man only slightly taller than myself, he was wildly strong, and my knees threatened to give.

"I'm not afraid of you," I yelled and spit a sorry wad that landed just below his collarbone.

The wicked grin slid from his face, and the look that replaced it was far more terrifying. He raised his arm and hit me swiftly across the cheek. "Just shut up and do as I say," he growled, releasing my arm.

I'd never been so much as slapped, and it shocked me into silence. I held my cheek gingerly, shrinking into the wall behind me.

"You're mine now, *mami*. Bill fucked with my family and now, he'll suffer. Lou's in jail 'cause of him."

"I don't know what you're talking about," I pleaded. "Bill didn't do anything."

"No? Why Lou went away for ten years when we both in the same gang? Sell the same drugs?" He moved in closer, inches from my face. "Your husband fucked us. Yeah, we're going to have fun, you and me. And maybe if you act good, I'll let you go home to Bill after."

"Bill's not home."

"I didn't say it would be *tonight*," he said and reached out. A slow smile spread across his face when I flinched. His fingers gently brushed a strand of hair from my forehead.

"I'll go to the police."

"Baby, you think I'm some sort of rookie bitch? Those *puto* pigs can't touch me—*jamás.*"

"Lou wasn't so lucky though."

His eyes fixated on me. He quickly grabbed my shoulders and in one movement, flipped me into the brick wall. He pushed me so my injured cheek was flush against it. "We're going down the street here," he whispered in my ear, pressing his groin against my backside. "Act natural. Put up a fight, and you're going to regret it. I promise."

He locked my arms behind me in an iron grip, and I whimpered. "Please, stop," I pleaded, tears pricking my eyes. "I won't go to the police. Just let me go."

"Relax, *guapa.* You'll like it." I shuddered at his hot breath on my neck. "But one wrong move and, baby, you're done. And then I find your bitch husband and—"

He spun around at the sound of footsteps. Relief flooded over me and dissipated just as quickly when I thought of David unarmed.

I turned in time to see David lunge forward. Mark fell backward as David tackled him, and I backed against the wall, narrowly avoiding their entangled bodies. In the dark, David wrestled Mark to the ground while I frantically searched for the gun. The clang of metal hitting the ground startled me into action. I scrambled for it and just as I was within reach, a hand shot out and snatched it from the ground.

CHAPTER 19

"GET BACK, OLIVIA." David was on his feet in a flash. "Get back," he said again, aiming the gun steadily at my attacker. The self-possessed David I knew had returned, his posture straight but at ease with the gun, as though he'd done this a million times. His suit hung magically untouched, and the only thing that gave him away was his wayward hair and heavy breathing.

"Who the fuck are you?" Mark asked, struggling to his feet.

"David, please," I said with halted breath, suppressing my sobs. "Be careful."

"Get back!" he shouted. I moved away, never taking my eyes off him. In the distance was the reassuring wail of sirens.

Mark retreated toward the other end of the alley with his hands up in surrender. "Hey, man," he said as his eyes darted around. "I don't want any trouble. I promise to leave the bitch alone, just let me go before the cops get here."

David took two massive steps toward him, backing him into the wall. I gasped as he shoved the gun into Mark's neck.

"You go near her again," he said, "and you're dead. You hear me?"

"Fuck you," Mark said. "I got deals with the cops." He stared David down much more confidently than someone at gunpoint should. Even in the dark, I could see the hatred radiating from his face. "I'll be there for tonight, maybe. Then, I come back for you both."

David cocked the gun with a click and pushed it into Mark's skin.

"David," I said as calmly as I could manage. "Stop. The police are here."

His shoulders eased, and he took a step back. With his free hand, he grabbed Mark and flipped him against the brick wall. He stuck the gun in the waist of Mark's pants and leaned his forearm across his back.

Three policemen ran up, guns drawn. Behind them was a heavyset man in an ill-fitting suit.

My energy spilled out of me, and I steadied myself against the wall. My cheek smarted; I winced when I touched it, surprised to find blood on my fingertips. My head thundered with the pounding of my heart. *Blood.*

"You good, David?" I heard someone ask. I tried to expel the metallic smell from my nostrils.

"Yeah, Cooper," he said, releasing Mark to another cop. "Watch out, he's armed."

They exchanged hushed words briefly until David started in my direction, loosening his tie.

"Well, well. Mark Alvarez," the man called Cooper said gruffly. "Lou's going to love that you're coming for a visit." Four boisterous laughs filled the alley as one of them cuffed him.

"Are you hurt?" David asked, stopping mere inches from me. I stepped back automatically just as Cooper approached behind him, turning something over in his hand.

"Are you all right, miss?" he asked, concern etched across his face.

"I'm fine," I said. "How did you know to come?"

"I called him," David said.

"Is this yours?" A cop some feet away held up my purse. My hand went to my side; I hadn't even realized I'd dropped it. I thanked him as he passed it to David.

"I'm Detective Cooper," the man said. "What happened here?"

I blinked back tears, trying to decide where to start. "He chased me here from my office."

"Coop," David said softly. "Can we do this later?"

He looked up at David and then bowed his head into a nod. "Sure." He handed me a card, and I struggled to read it in the dark. *Detective Cooper, Chief of Detectives.* I peered closer. *Chicago Police Department, Organized Crime Division.* I repeated it to myself, trying to think of why it sounded familiar.

"I'll need a statement so we can book this guy right away," Cooper said. "However, it would be acceptable to do it tomorrow. If you'd like."

"Is it necessary to do it at all?" David asked.

"I need a witness account, Dylan. Otherwise I can't detain him, and I'm sure neither of you want that." He paused and turned to me, his expression smoothing. "I'll explain more tomorrow. I'm sorry—I didn't get your name."

I extended my hand. "Olivia."

"Olivia, can I give you a ride somewhere?"

"I'll take care of it," David cut me off.

"I'm asking her," Cooper growled.

"Come on, Coop. You know me." *Coop* gave David a very ungracious look.

David's words from earlier came back in a rush, stinging all over again. I had no desire to leave his side. But he'd made it clear he didn't want me around, and the last thing I wanted was to give him another opportunity to burn me.

"I appreciate the offer, David, but I think I'll go with Detective Cooper."

"Olivia, no. Wait." He grasped my arm and withdrew when I recoiled. "I'm not letting you out of my sight until I know you're home safe. Even if that means I get in Coop's car with you."

"I'm not taking you home, Dylan."

My insides quivered with indecision, thrown off by David's mixed signals. Just a few hours earlier, he never wanted to see me again. "I don't want to put you out, Detective. I can go with David."

"Are you sure? It's no problem at all."

David nodded dismissively. "You heard her."

"All right." Cooper's shoulders slumped back into position. "If you need anything else, you call me," he insisted. He slapped David lightly on the shoulder. "I'll be in touch tomorrow, Fish."

David surprised me by pulling me into his arms once we were alone. Despite my mind's protests, I allowed myself to let go a little, safe in his clutch. His muscular arms wrapped around me so that I could barely move. "Relax," he said softly. I loosened my shoulders the best I could and rested my head on his hard chest.

"Oh." I pushed him away reluctantly. "I don't want to get blood on you."

He leaned down and touched my cheek gingerly, but I flinched and pulled away.

"He hit you?" he asked.

I was quiet.

He shut his eyes, sighed heavily, and opened them again. He was so close, I smelled the brackish musk of his fresh sweat. He pinched the bridge of his nose and turned his back to me. "I should have *fucking* shot him," he said to himself. Fabric strained against his shoulders as though he might burst through it.

"If you had, it'd be you in the back of that police car."

He shook his head and turned around. "I'm taking you to the hospital," he said.

"No. No, I'm fine."

"Fine?" he repeated. "You're shaking."

I hadn't realized, but in his arms, I'd begun to tremble. "I'm really fine," I said, trying to even my tone. "Really. I'm just frightened."

He pulled me close again, running his hand slowly over my back. After a beat, he gathered the hair from my neck with his hand, sweeping it in to a loose ponytail. He pulled lightly so I glanced up. With his other hand, he lifted my chin higher to inspect the cut. My head was almost vertical, and I looked away, unsure of where to focus.

"It's just a surface wound," he said, licking his finger and wiping away some blood. "Does anything else hurt?"

I hesitated.

"Olivia."

"Not too bad," I lied, touching the back of my head. With every moment adrenaline subsided, the pain increased.

"We're going to Northwestern," he said.

"No," I pleaded with him. "Please, I've had a rough night. I can't take anymore commotion."

"Okay, shh," he said, rubbing my arms. "You could have a concussion, though."

"I don't think so," I said, and he smiled for the first time all night.

"You're a little stubborn, aren't you?" he asked. I glared at him. "All right, all right. No hospital. But tell him he *needs* to stay up and watch you tonight. It's very important, in case of a concussion. It's necessary to check on you—"

"Who?" I interrupted.

"Who? Your husband."

"Bill." I nodded. "Of course. He's in New York."

David looked at me for a moment. "You'll come with me, then. I can watch you tonight."

"No," I said. "No. I'll call Gretchen." I took out my phone and dialed. With the familiar greeting of her voicemail, I ended the call. "No answer," I said. "I'll try Lucy."

He gently took the phone from me. "It's late. They'll be asleep. Come with me." He paused. "Let me take care of you tonight."

"Don't be ridiculous. I don't expect you to do that."

"I want to do it."

"What about everything you said earlier?"

"Forget it." He smiled goofily. "We can start tomorrow." He placed his arm around my shoulders to lead me out to the street, but I stopped.

"Don't," I said, moving out from under his arm. "I can't forget it. I'm not going home with you."

"I'm sorry if I hurt your feelings," he said. "But I'm not sorry I said it. I needed to be firm. I needed it to stick."

"So? This isn't firm. This isn't making it stick. Look, it's fine. I get it. It's done. Just let me get a cab home. I don't have a concussion."

"I just said—*Jesus*, Olivia." His harsh tone was suddenly deep with bass. "I'm not letting you out of my sight, especially now that I know you're hurt. We can discuss what happened tomorrow, but please, let's just get through tonight."

I heaved a sigh. His expression went from angry to concerned to hurt, all in the span of ten seconds.

"Fine," I said, taking a step away from him. "But don't touch me again."

He showed me his palms and started walking. "This way. I hope my car's still there."

"Why?"

"That was my car you almost ran into earlier. I hopped out to chase you down."

"I don't even remember a car," I muttered.

He opened the door of the Porsche for me, and we didn't speak another word. Questions began to form as I reviewed the events of the night, but all I wanted was to lie down.

David parked in his designated spot under his building, and I followed him to double doors. He held a keycard up and they clicked audibly, opening to a marbleized elevator bank. David placed his hand on my lower back and led me to the furthest car.

"Good evening, Mr. Dylan," said a severe-looking man from behind his security desk.

"Gorman," David said with a nod.

"Everything all right, sir?"

"Yes, thank you. A small altercation near my office, but it's all taken care of."

"It's my fault, really," I said, offering my hand. "I'm Olivia."

"Pleasure to meet you, miss," he said, taking my hand with mild surprise. "And I doubt that. But one must be careful on these streets late at night. Should I have anything sent up?"

"We're all set." David's eyes were on me as we boarded the elevator, but I stood with my arms crossed, watching the numbers rise until we hit the top. The very top. The penthouse. Again, I wondered at his salary.

The doors opened to a simple, marble foyer with a single door. I noticed the sag in David's shoulders as he unlocked the door.

"Make yourself comfortable," he said, tossing his keys onto a circular table in the entryway. He motioned to the living room and disappeared through another door.

I removed my shoes and stepped from cold wooden planks onto a plush ivory carpet. Three steps down deposited me into an immaculate sunken living room with two pine green mid-century couches and a brown leather lounge chair. A monochromatic stone wall housed a cozy fireplace that was the focal point of the room. A glass coffee table, with a base fashioned from the same ebonized mahogany as the floor, held three small, colorful, abstract sculptures and a stack of design books.

The room was carefully curated, yet it didn't have the vacant feeling I'd experienced in other upscale apartments. Perhaps the most mesmerizing part was the floor-to-ceiling, white-paned windows that showcased Lake Michigan between great smooth columns.

"It's not quite what I expected," I called out. I scanned the view from the eighty-fourth floor and lifted my head to the vaulted ceilings ribbed with dark wood beams.

"Not bachelor pad enough for you?" he asked from the other room. I smiled to myself.

"Finally, a smile," he said, reappearing. He walked to the couch. "Come here."

I crossed the room but before I could sit, he touched my chin again, lifting it.

"This might sting a little," he said, showing me a towel of ice. He carefully applied it to my cheek, looking between my eyes and the towel. I inhaled sharply as he adjusted it. "Sorry. It will help, though." He paused a moment. "You must be beat."

I scrunched my face at him.

"Shit. Bad choice of words."

I laughed lightly and then winced. "I never asked if you were all right. Did he hurt you?"

He looked skeptical. "I'm fine."

"My superhero," I said, smiling as best I could.

"Hardly." He scoffed. "Although, do you know how hard it is to chase and subdue someone in dress shoes?"

I think I laughed, but I felt like I'd been sucker punched. *Chase and subdue.* The words echoed in my head. Lust reared within me at the thought of David acting out those verbs on me. Only, when he caught me, things would go somewhat differently than they had tonight.

"Here, hold this for a minute," he said, jolting me from my thoughts. He disappeared again and returned with two pills and a glass of water. I handed over the towel and gratefully took the medicine, eager for the pain to subside.

"Let's get you into bed," he said, and my head snapped up. He rolled his eyes. "I have a guest room you can stay in."

"I know that," I said with a shaky laugh. He showed me to a room furnished with just the basics.

"Bathroom," he said, pointing to a door at the other side of the room. "I'll get you something comfortable to sleep in."

"That's not necessary—I can sleep in this," I called, but he was already out the door.

I found my way to the bathroom to freshen up. After splashing my face with warm water, I examined the damage. He was right, the cut was minimal, and most of the blood had washed away. But I could already see the beginnings a bruise forming around it. I quickly tugged my fingers through my hair, carefully avoiding the tender bump on the back of my head. I smudged some dirt from my collarbone, but there was nothing I could do about the shadows under my eyes. I looked better suited for a night at the trailer park than as a guest in David's pristine home.

"I'm a mess," I said when he appeared in the doorway.

"Yes, you are."

I stuck out my bottom lip.

"Somehow you still look exquisite," he said.

It was my turn to roll my eyes.

"This is all I have," he said, handing me a folded t-shirt and boxers. He stifled a laugh. "They might be a little big, but it's better than nothing."

I raised both eyebrows at him.

His face fell. "Well, not—it's not better than . . . Never mind."

I smiled and took the clothing. "Can I have some more water?" I asked.

He shut the bathroom door and left.

Soreness descended, and I moved slowly as I changed. I furtively whiffed the shirt, which smelled of fresh laundry and David. When I came out, he was setting a glass of water on the nightstand.

"How's this for exquisite?" I joked.

"Why do you keep doing that? Rolling your eyes?"

"Because it's ridiculous. Although I don't doubt that some girls buy it."

"You do look exquisite."

I glanced down at myself and burst into laughter.

He tilted his head and smiled in a way that would get even the Virgin Mary into trouble. My laugh vanished as he looked me up and down with bloodthirsty eyes, like he might leap across the room and devour me. Standing there in a huge t-shirt and shorts rolled three times, I felt less than desirable. But the way my body responded to his perusal, I might as well have been naked.

"One day I will tell you exactly how exquisite you look right now," he said.

I clenched my jaw. His eyes lingered too long, and that empty heaviness returned between my thighs.

"Well," he said. "You're all set. I'll be back to check on you in a few hours. I'll have to wake you."

"That's why I'm here," I said, shrugging.

A roguish grin was his only response.

I climbed into the bed and got under the covers.

"Goodnight," he said, reaching for the lights.

"David," I said suddenly, sitting up.

"Hmm?"

I swallowed hard. "Did anything happen between you and Gretchen?"

"Gretchen?" he repeated, tipping his chin up.

"At the MCA event. D-did something happen?"

I jumped at his burst of robust laughter. When he saw I wasn't laughing, he stopped. His face fell. "Seriously?"

I nodded.

He stalked slowly to the bed and bent so we were face to face. My lips parted slightly.

"She's not really my type," he said, his voice low and deep. "For one, I prefer brunettes. Brunettes with big, green eyes and," he stopped to pick something from my cheek, "very long lashes." He showed me the lash on the tip of his finger.

I was now breathing through my nose to prevent any incidence of panting. In that moment, I saw myself through his eyes.

"Besides," he said, straightening up and flicking off the eyelash. "She's not tough enough for me." He winked. He strode away, shut off the lights, and pulled the door closed behind him.

My heart thumped in his wake; his fingertip lingered on my skin. I fell back into the plush bed. He didn't want Gretchen. The mixture of his smell, his touch, and his words intoxicated me. It took everything I had not to drown in the thought of him, not to touch my throbbing self through his clothing. I forced myself to concentrate on the night's events instead.

I wondered if Mark's threats were legitimate or if he'd been bluffing. Would he really be out right away? How was it that David had appeared in that moment? What would have happened if he hadn't? I curled up into a ball while the last question hung in my head.

CHAPTER 20

FUZZY, COMPLETE DARKNESS. I kept my eyes closed until I heard it again: "Olivia."

I moaned and shifted in the bed.

"Hey," David whispered.

"Hi," I whispered back. I rubbed my eyes, struggling to see in the night.

"Do you know where you are?" he asked.

"Mmm. No. Maybe."

His outline, which was becoming clearer, stiffened.

I sighed softly. "Yes, I know. I'm fine."

"All right. Just checking."

"Stay," I said before I could stop myself. I curled up into a smaller ball.

He hesitated a moment before the door closed, and I heard his bare feet cross the room. The bed dipped and after another pause, he climbed all the way on. He settled against the pillows as far away as he could get, and I wondered if it was respectfulness or if, at the stroke of midnight, our new arrangement had gone into effect. But either way, he was there, and it was dark, and somehow, none of that mattered.

"Do you normally work so late?" he asked after some time.

"No. I fell asleep at the office."

He made a noise that conveyed his disapproval.

"I can't believe I saw you," I said. "Or you saw me, I guess."

"You mean almost ran you down."

"Right. Where were you going?"

"I was also working late, except that I was actually doing work. Your office is on my way home."

"Sort of," I said, going over the possible routes in my head.

"It is," he said. "Where were you going? Don't you live in the opposite direction?"

I turned to face him, even though I could barely see him in the dark. "I don't know. At first I was running to the 'L' and then I just turned." I was quiet for a moment, reliving the moments before he'd caught me.

"What is it?"

"I was trying to get to Jackson, I think? Yes. I was." I paused, going through the route. *I took a right turn and—* "I was trying to get to you."

"Me?"

The admission surprised me. I hadn't realized it until now. I knew David's office was on Jackson. And I didn't feel embarrassed by it, although I knew I should. "It doesn't make any sense," I said to myself. "What would make me think you'd be there at that time? Or that you'd care after this afternoon?" Again, I tried working it out in my head. A beat passed. And then another before I noticed his silence. "You think I'm a stalker, don't you?"

"No." I could hear a smile in the word. "I'm thinking."

"What about?"

"Everything. Specifically about what would've happened if—"

"Don't," I cut him off. "There's no point."

"You just said you weren't sure if I would care. Do you really think that?"

"You said—"

"I know what I said. Of course I care. I would do anything—but instead, I left you alone with him. It wouldn't have gotten so far if . . ."

I covered my ears and had the overwhelming need to protect us both. "He wasn't going to hurt me," I said. "He just . . . just wanted to scare me a little."

His breathing quickened across the bed.

"I can't do this right now, David. How do you know Cooper?"

"An old friend."

"A good friend to have," I said.

"He'll take care of this for us."

"Do you think that guy, Mark, really has connections on the force?" I asked.

"He was bluffing. Cooper said they've been waiting for him to break parole."

I wanted to ask him about what he'd said earlier. About whether or not he was finished with me. But I didn't know how I could stand his answer either way, so I didn't. I sighed sleepily and shut my eyes again. Neither of us spoke for some time, and I drifted.

~

When I opened my eyes, the room was grey. David, still facing me from across the bed, was atop the comforter in a white t-shirt and light grey sweatpants. His hair was tousled, and he almost looked relaxed, except that his arms were crossed over his chest. He was so far away that he was almost falling off the bed.

I could reach out and touch him, pull him close. Snuggle into his chest. Something welled in me that was less urgent than before—less urgent, but deeper. I couldn't help myself from thinking of what he might do to me were the circumstances different. He might lean over and finish the kiss he'd started in my office, this time letting his hands wander over my thin t-shirt. He might reach between my thighs and feel my want, my need . . . .

He shifted and opened his eyes so that we were looking at each other.

"Do you know where you are?" I asked.

He laughed. "How do you feel?"

"Good," I said and meant it. "I slept better than I have in a long time."

He nodded and stretched his long limbs before leaning over me to see the clock.

"What time is it?"

"Six thirty-five."

"I should go," I said, not moving.

"Call in sick. You can stay here today if you want."

"I don't think that's such a good idea. Anyway, the party is tonight." I grimaced as I worked to sit up. I looked around the room for my clothes. He inhaled sharply, and I caught his cringe.

"What?"

"You're all black and blue," he said, sitting up next to me. He scooted closer and studied my cheek, taking my chin in his hand again. *Is it awful to admit that I'm starting to enjoy this?* "The cut looks all right, but your cheek is pretty badly bruised." He shook his head and swept the hair from my face. "Poor girl."

We looked at each other, his hand lingering by my face. The memory of our kiss swept over me again, more vivid with his vicinity. I pushed the dangerous thought from my mind but a sound escaped my lips first.

"Right," he said, lifting himself off the bed.

"Can I get ready here? It would save me a trip."

"Of course." He seemed more than happy to provide me with anything I needed. *Lucky, the girl who ends up with him.*

I pulled the covers off and climbed out of bed. His long t-shirt just met the tops of my thighs. "Shit," I said, covering myself. "I must've taken off the shorts in the middle of the night."

"Jesus, Olivia," he said, raking his eyes over me. "I'm trying to behave, but you're killing me here."

We laughed, and he turned to leave the room, shielding his eyes.

"Your clothes are around here somewhere. Get dressed, you goddamned temptress."

I giggled as he shut the door behind him.

After a quick rinse, I changed into the previous day's outfit. I was grateful to find a few makeup essentials in my purse and attempted to make myself presentable. As I never left the house without my travel hairbrush, I was able to twist my hair into an acceptable bun. I lingered over the bruise, dabbing the area with cover-up, but eventually gave up to meet him in the kitchen. He still wore a faded marathon t-shirt and the grey sweatpants that hung dangerously low. I glimpsed skin when he pulled two glasses from a cupboard.

"You have a beautiful place," I said, looking around one more time.

"Can I get you anything to eat? Or some OJ?"

I sighed. "I've got to get going."

"You should eat. I'm not a great cook, but I can whip something up."

Not wanting to be rude, I relented when I spotted a bowl of fruit behind him. "How about a banana?"

He swung around and grabbed one, offering it to me. "Anything else?"

I narrowed my eyes and smiled at him. "Bye," I said.

"Not so fast. I'll take you to your office."

"Oh, God. Can you imagine how that would look if anyone were to see us?"

"I don't give a damn. Nothing happened."

I gaped at him. "That's easy for you to say. You have nothing to lose."

"It's early. Nobody will be around."

"You're kind-of persistent, aren't you?" I mocked.

He grunted. "When I want something, yes."

"What do you want, David?"

"To see you to your office."

"It's not far. I'll go alone. But you've been wonderful. Thank you."

He shifted on his feet, visibly struggling with himself.

"You can walk me to the door," I offered as consolation.

"And down to the street." His tone was decided, although I could tell he was holding back. I wondered if he was this controlling with all his overnight visitors.

As we descended in the elevator, I tried to find the words to express my gratitude. *He obviously likes fruit. Maybe I'll send him a basket of it.* I almost laughed out loud at the ridiculousness of the idea.

This time we stopped at the ground level and were deposited into a brightly lit, bustling lobby. I passed my eyes quickly over the spacious area before I realized my surroundings. "You live in a hotel?"

"The top floors are residences."

"Don't all these people disturb you?"

He gave a short laugh. "That's not usually the first thing people ask when they find out I live in a hotel. But the answer is no. Last night we used a private entrance and elevator. So unless I come through the front, I don't normally see anyone other than my neighbors. And Gorman, of course."

"Wait a sec," I said, stopping in my tracks. "Isn't this the Gryphon Hotel? We're having our Meet & Greet here tonight."

"I know."

"Why didn't you mention it?"

He shrugged. "Why would I?"

"So if you don't show, I'm going to come up and drag you downstairs."

"I can almost assure you that that plan would backfire," he said levelly, staring ahead. "Next time I get you alone in my apartment, I won't let you off so easy."

My eyes hit the marble floor as I blushed furiously. What was with him? Did he want me or not? Was he joking? Did he usually kid around with married women this way?

"Good grief, are you red," he said, and I peeked up to see his lips spread in a devastating smile. "And go easy on that poor banana."

I looked down at the banana, which was firmly in my grip.

In front of the building, we stood face to face in the new morning, me with my hands balled around the banana, while his were shoved into the pockets of his sweatpants.

"Let me get you a cab," he said.

"No. Thank you, again. You've been beyond kind."

I noticed his hands flex through the fabric of his pants, inadvertently tugging them lower.

"I want to say I had a nice time, but that doesn't seem quite right," he said.

I couldn't stop a faint smile from touching my lips, and I nodded knowingly. "It was an emotional night. All circumstances considered, it ended up okay."

He leaned against the building pillar and nodded. "I'll call you," he said, squinting into the distance. I was about to protest until I remembered that we owed Cooper a statement. My heart skipped at the promise.

"Okay, so. Bye."

I left him standing there. I'd meant to get a cab, and I was cold, but it felt nice to stretch my aching legs. As I maneuvered through the streets, I had a morbid curiosity to pass through the scene of the attack, even though it meant going out of my way to get there.

I stood on Adams peering down the empty alley. It was grey, as the buildings shielded it from the sun, but I could see all the way down. I passed through the alley, the click of my heels bouncing off the walls in a hollow echo.

I stood, staring at the place where I'd been pressed up against the wall. The place where the gun had clattered. I pulled my phone from my purse when it vibrated, knowing it was David. I found his text along with missed calls from Gretchen and Bill.

May 18, 2012 8:09 AM
Are you there yet?

In my enchantment with the alley, I'd lost track of time.

May 18, 2012 8:10 AM
Almost

When I came through the other side, I exhaled everything brewing inside. The scene wasn't so bad in

the daylight. I hurried to the office, hoping to slip in
unseen.

—

On my way to the fourteenth floor, I smiled against all
reason. Maybe I could do this. Maybe David would
reconsider, and we could be friends, and I could be
happy with Bill. David's words the day before stung.
Bill's absence meant I could openly wallow and finally
put my feelings to rest. After our night, I felt bonded to
David in an even stronger way, and I didn't want to lose
him as a friend.

Jenny noticed my disposition and looked relieved—
I wondered if she'd been mulling over how I'd snapped
at her the day before.

"TGIF," she said as I passed. "Wow. Wait—what
happened to your face?"

I stumbled for an explanation. "I can't really discuss
it. It has to do with one of Bill's cases."

Her eyes grew, and I knew I'd have a hard time
getting out of this one. "What does that mean?"

I hushed her, not wanting to draw attention. "Don't
worry. I feel fine. I really can't discuss it. I'll be in my
office." I cursed my awful performance, deciding I should
come up with a better story.

In the office, I flopped into my computer chair and
pulled up my e-mail. Absentmindedly, I glanced at the
doorway where David had stormed out the day before.
The past twelve hours had been a whirlwind, and to stop

myself from analyzing it all, I quickly opened the top e-mail.

From: David Dylan
Sent: Fri, May 18, 2012 08:35 AM CST
To: Olivia Germaine
Subject: My banana

Did it make it to your office safely, or do I need to come check on it?

DAVID DYLAN
SENIOR ARCHITECT,
PIERSON/GREER

From: Olivia Germaine
Sent: Fri, May 18, 2012 08:44 AM CST
To: David Dylan
Subject: Your banana

I am back safe and sound, however the same cannot be said for your banana ☹ It's in a better place now though.

Thanks again.

Olivia Germaine
Associate Editor,
Chicago Metropolitan Magazine
ChicagoMMag.com

I keyed down to the next e-mail and gasped in horror.

CHAPTER 21

From: Mack Donovan
Sent: Fri, May 18, 2012 07:32 AM CST
To: Mack Donovan
BCC: Olivia Germaine
Subject: Davena Brenda Donovan

Family and friends,

As some of you know, my dearest Davena passed away
yesterday evening. I'm sorry to deliver the news this
way, but it is the best I can do at this time. Davena was a
lively girl who never let this dreadful thing get the best
of her. We will be holding a service on Monday morning
followed by a celebration of her life at our home. Details
to follow. In lieu of flowers, please make a donation to
the Davena B. Donovan Foundation, which turns one
year next month.

Sincerely,
Mack

The room spun as the words filtered into my consciousness. *Gone?* I scanned the e-mail again, reading but not comprehending. Could it be? All that life, all that light, all that love. *Gone?* My heart wrenched for Mack. His idolatry of Davena was endless. *Shattered—he must be shattered.*

I ran to the bathroom and steadied myself against the sink. My chest stuttered when I forced myself to remember our last visit and her final words. *One shot at life. Don't miss anything. Love.* She had known.

I waited for the tears. It'd never occurred to me that . . . I crushed the ceramic beneath my hands and fell into a squat. My stomach lurched with bile. My eyes burned with unshed tears. My legs threatened to collapse so I could surrender to the filthy bathroom floor. How could this happen? How could someone leave, just like that? How could she let that happen, when we needed her here? How, how, *how—*

Two raps on the bathroom door jolted me to life. I remained still, calming my jagged breathing. My knuckles were as white as the sink they gripped. I eased into a standing position when the knock came again. My lips tensed into a line as I left the bathroom, slipping by an impatient colleague.

I called Bill. I would tell him, and he would come home, and we would cry. Together we would battle the emptiness I was drowning in. Not just for Davena, but for the things I'd been holding in for too long. The weight of everything I didn't tell him was suddenly greater than the pain I avoided by keeping him at a distance. When he didn't answer, I watched the screen turn black and set the phone on my desk.

I spent the next few hours operating in a daze, doing just enough to appear functioning. The thought of calling Mack petrified me. I went over and over in my head the things I might say. How I could possibly express my regret.

"You look tired." I glanced up to see Lisa in my doorway, her face predictably drawn. "Late night?"

"You could say that."

She squinted at me, examining my face. Her expression relaxed when she made out the bruise.

"What's up, Lisa?"

"Nothing," she said. "I'm going straight to Gryphon from here, so don't worry about setup. I'll make sure everything gets done." She walked off without waiting for my response, leaving me to look after her.

Jenny stopped by next, trying to figure out what happened, but I shooed her away.

The walls of my office were almost too much to take, so I ran away. I managed to find an empty seat in the sun, far enough from the building where I could be alone. Beneath me, the bench was slightly damp but strong and supportive. The smell of dank wood and wet soil filled the air. Warmth on my colorless face gave me comfort.

How had my life directed me to this moment? My father would be disappointed to see me now, swollen eye, and fighting against the current of infidelity. It was as if my senses left me when I was with David, and they perched just out of reach to watch my demise. And, oh, how I never even tried to retrieve them. Even now, in the face of death, I thought of him. I sought somebody strong enough to carry my grief, because I couldn't do it. I shouldn't have to. It wasn't fair.

Sometimes I could hardly keep from crying out because of all the things I held inside. Bill might think I was cold, but it was far from the truth. Fear, pain, beauty, love. I felt it all, but I didn't always know how to speak it. Davena had asked me to try, but she couldn't have known how I froze in fear at the prospect. How, every day, I worried that the things I loved would be ripped from my very hands.

~

When I returned with sun-kissed cheeks, Jenny gave me a concerned look. "Can I get you anything?" she asked.

"No, Jenny. Still doing fine."

"All right. David Dylan wants you to call him. Should—"

"I'll take care of it," I said as I ducked away.

On the phone, David solemnly relayed that Cooper wanted to see us. I sighed, careful that David wouldn't hear on his end. I wasn't sure how to hold myself together during an interrogation.

"I can take you," he said when I didn't speak. I nodded into the phone.

I told Jenny I was leaving for the day, and that I would see everyone at the event later. When she began to protest, to tell me they'd be fine without me, I cut her off with a hand in the air.

I found David waiting for me downstairs, leaning against the Porsche with aplomb. He was more casual than I'd ever seen him in jeans, a t-shirt, and aviators. That is, if sweatpants didn't count. I pushed aside the alluring memory of him in his slumber party outfit.

"Well, look at us," he said as I approached. "Just a couple of kids, ditching class on a Friday afternoon."

"I wish," I said, squinting up at him. "That sounds like way more fun."

I slid into the car when he opened the door for me. The seat was low, and I tugged at my skirt as it threatened to ride up.

"Are you hungry?" he asked when we were on our way.

"I just want to get this over with," I said.

"How are you feeling?"

"All right."

"You don't sound all right." He frowned over his shoulder at me. "Did you take anything?"

"It's other stuff. I'm not really in much pain." I'd been fending off a dull headache all morning, but it was the least of my concerns.

"What's up?"

"Nothing." I waved my hand.

"Tell me," he said, unaffected by my brushoff— another tactic that often worked with Bill.

I hadn't told anyone so far. I sighed into my seat and looked out the window. I *could* tell him; that was the problem. I could tell him, knowing he was strong enough to shoulder some of the pain.

"A family friend passed away last night," I said. "I found out this morning."

His eyes remained focused on the road. "I'm sorry."

"It was cancer," I told the moving landscape.

"Were you very close?"

I bit back tears as I stared ahead. It had been so long since I'd let myself go in front of someone, even Bill. At times he goaded me, trying to get me to cry because it worried him. It wouldn't be fair to him if I did in front of David. My voice hitched when I said, "She's been around when my mother hasn't."

"You're upset. It's okay."

I looked over at him as the tingling in my nose receded. "Of course it is. Why wouldn't it be okay?"

"I mean that it's okay to cry. I won't tell anyone."

"Just because I'm not crying doesn't mean I'm not upset."

"I know," he said. "I know how brave you are. I'm sorry that we have to do this today."

"Thanks." To my amusement, he flinched slightly when I touched his arm. "You've been very brave too."

He looked at me uneasily over his arm and said, "I'm not going to cry if that's what you're getting at."

It felt nice to laugh. "No. Of course not. You saved the day, what do you have to cry about?"

~

Cooper greeted us in the waiting room. "The good news is that Alvarez number two is in custody for violating his parole. He not only had a gun on him, but a healthy amount of cocaine too. Dumbass. Since he's a felon, he's going to get it even worse." He looked from me to David. "I still need a statement for the D.A.'s office, which you guys can do individually or together—but between us, he'll probably take a plea bargain."

For the first time, I wondered if I should have Bill with me, but something about Cooper made me feel safe. And I knew enough from Bill that a statement was pretty straightforward, as long as I wasn't guilty of anything.

"I'd like to do it together," David said.

"That's up to Miss Germaine," Cooper said and they both turned their attention to me. I agreed. We followed Cooper into his office, where he poured us each a glass of water. He held up a tape recorder, letting us know the statement would be on the record.

"Witnesses Olivia Germaine and Lucas Dylan, incident involving Mark B. Alvarez on May seventeenth," he said into the recorder. *May seventeenth?* It was almost my birthday, and I'd completely forgotten. I supposed that everyone else had too, since nobody had mentioned it.

"All right, Miss Germaine," he began.

"Olivia, please," I said.

"All right, Olivia. Can you give me a general recount of what happened?"

"I left my office on Adams around ten o'clock last night. I noticed a male figure watching me from across the street. When I realized it might be Mark Alvarez, I turned and ran in the opposite direction."

"How do you know who Mark Alvarez is?"

"He has threatened me before."

Cooper raised his eyebrows at both of us. "Did you file a report?"

"My husband didn't think it was necessary."

David's chair creaked as he shifted.

"Tell me about that encounter."

"I was walking home in the evening about a month ago." I stopped to calculate. "Yes, about a month ago, and he stopped me outside my apartment building. Told me he'd been looking for Bill—my husband—and that he'd know what it was about. Bill was the prosecutor in a case against Mark's brother Lou over a year ago."

Cooper nodded. "Sounds like retaliation. Bill Germaine? I'm not familiar."

"It's Bill Wilson."

"Oh, right. I know Bill." He looked between the two of us. I realized then why organized crime had stuck out to me the night before. Bill's case had relied heavily on gang and organized crime specialists. It was likely that he'd worked closely with CPD during the trial. David's and my being together the night before wouldn't look good, no matter the truth.

"He assaulted her that night," David stated.

"Is that so?"

I gulped. "He grabbed me—I'm not sure if that's considered assault."

"Of course it is," David said.

"Okay," Cooper said, furiously writing. "Continue please."

"I ran. I was heading toward the train. I'm not really sure what I was thinking; it happened so fast. When I felt him gaining on me, I knew I'd run out of time. I turned into an alley, but when he caught me, I discovered it was actually David behind me."

"I was driving home and almost hit her with my car when she ran across the street," David said. "I ran after her and when I caught her, I could see that she was panicked." He shifted noisily and ran a hand through his loose hair, lowering his voice slightly. "I left the alley to look for whatever was chasing her."

"Had you two met before?"

"We have a mutual friend."

"Right after David left, Mark appeared from the other end of the alley. He must've guessed I would exit there." I paused when David shifted yet again in his chair. He looked more uncomfortable than I felt.

"Go on," Cooper said, not looking up from his notes. "Be specific."

"He immediately pushed me to the ground, and then into the wall when I tried to get up. That's when I hit my head. I finally managed to get to my feet and tried to hit him."

David snorted, and I shot him a look.

"I told him I wasn't afraid of him." I stopped and embarrassment hit me hard. "And I spit. On him."

"What?" David exclaimed, jumping from his seat. "What were you thinking?"

"Calm down, David," Cooper said. "You never know how you'll react in a situation like that."

"He wouldn't let go of me," I said.

"Where was he holding you?" Cooper asked.

"When I tried to hit him, he caught my arm," I said, taking an extra long sip of water so I could hide my face.

"No shit," David said.

I spit out my water and started coughing violently.

"What did you think would happen?" he asked.

I wiped my mouth. "What's that supposed to mean?"

"It means you're no match for first, a man, and second, a criminal."

"I'll kick you out if you keep this up," Cooper said. He turned back to me. "Just ignore him."

I shot a distinct scowl at David before turning back to Cooper. "That's when he hit me. He was mad that I'd spit on him."

"I can't listen to this. He's scum, Coop. Why was he even out in the first place? *Scum*." David sat back down and ran his hand over his face, pulling at his chin.

"I noticed the bruise," Cooper said, ignoring David. "Then what?"

I wavered, looking over at David. "Are you sure you want to stay?" I asked him. "You seem upset."

He only pursed his lips and inhaled loudly through his nose.

I turned my attention back to Cooper. "I think he said that Bill fucked them over and that he would suffer for it. That it was Bill's fault Lou was convicted. That they're in the same gang."

"He said gang?"

"Yes."

"This could be important. What exactly did he say?"

I racked my brain. "Like I said, that Bill fucked up. He messed with his family. Lou was in jail because of him. He wanted to know why Lou got ten years and he didn't when they belonged to the same gang and sold the same drugs. Then something about us having fun and that if I was . . ." I paused to clear my throat. "If I was good, he'd send me home to Bill afterward."

From the corner of my eye, I saw David's knuckles whiten from gripping the arms of his chair.

"I said Bill wasn't home. He said, 'I didn't say I'd send you home tonight.'"

A thunderous crack filled the room, and I almost fell out of my chair in surprise. David jumped up and cursed.

Cooper stood up. "What the . . . ?"

"Sorry." David tossed part of the chair's arm in the trash and sat down again, careful not to touch the splintered wood. "I'm sorry," he repeated, steepling his fingers and rubbing his nose. "I'll pay for the chair. Continue."

Cooper sat down again while mumbling something and looked back at his notepad. "Ridiculous. I'm sorry, Olivia. Did he make any other allusions to, ah, keeping you over night or . . . ?"

"He said to relax and that I would 'like it.' And if I fought him, I'd regret it." I exhaled, looking down at my own hands. I hadn't prepared myself to relive the night so vividly.

"What was your physical stance relative to his?"

I hesitated and briefly considered lying. "At this point he had me pinned against the wall."

"And was he restraining you?"

I looked away.

"It's okay," Cooper said. "This is a safe space. There's no wrong answer."

"He had his arm across my shoulders, and he was sort of . . . I guess, pinning me with the rest of his body. Suggestively."

"So he was sexually aggressive with you?"

David inhaled sharply and dropped his face in his hands. He released a string of muffled curse words while I tried to keep myself together. I knew then that I should have asked him to leave, because seeing him that way was almost as hard as reliving the attack.

"I'm sorry," Cooper said. "David, calm the hell down. You're upsetting her."

I wiped away an invisible tear and straightened my shoulders. "Yes. He was sexually aggressive."

"Fuck," David said softly, shaking his head. "I had no idea. Why didn't you tell me last night?"

"It's fine, David," I reassured him. "Everything turned out fine."

"Fine?" he asked, his leg bouncing up and down rapidly. "Everything is fine to you. It's not fine to me. You could have been seriously hurt or—or worse."

The room got quiet. I could tell by the look on Cooper's face that he'd picked up on David's extreme reaction. It also struck me as odd. We barely knew each other. There was no denying our attraction, but I wasn't his to protect. I wasn't his responsibility. And this wasn't his fault. So why was he so upset?

Cooper prompted me to continue.

"That's when David appeared." I put on a smile for him, but he was looking at the floor.

"Mark didn't know I was around," David said. "So I had the element of surprise on my side. I lunged at him, and after we wrestled for a minute, the gun fell from somewhere on his body. I grabbed it. I backed him up against the wall, and he said he didn't want any trouble. Then he said he had friends on the force. That he'd be out after a night, and he'd come back for both of us. That's why, like I said, I really need you to a keep an eye on this for me. I want any and all updates."

"Don't worry for now," Cooper said.

"He didn't say friends," I interjected. "He said he had deals. Deals with the cops. He didn't seem afraid at all."

"Very interesting." Cooper nodded, making more notes.

"You guys arrived then," David said. "Just in time, too. If I—"

"David," I said, "have some water." I shoved the glass at him. With a lawyer for a husband, I understood the concept of keeping quiet.

"This has been enlightening," Cooper said. "Do you have a card, Olivia?"

I fished one out of my wallet, and he rose to show us out. "That's it?" I asked.

"Yes, ma'am. If you'll follow me, I'd like to get a picture of the bruise. Got a little bit of paperwork for you to fill out, and then you're all set."

Another officer took my photo and helped me with paperwork as Cooper and David talked. On our way out, I thanked Cooper for his help.

"We'll call you if we need anything else," he said. "Like I said, I don't expect this to go to trial and if it does, it won't be for a while. But I'll keep you in the loop."

"Thanks again, Coop," David said with a handshake. "Let me know about that chair."

A grunt was his only reply.

CHAPTER 22

THE MOOD WAS HEAVY on our way out of the Chicago Police Department. That is, until I asked David if we should send a fruit basket as a thank you.

He laughed. "Cooper might get suspicious if we send a joint fruit basket."

"Oh, really?" I asked. "*That* would make him suspicious? Not running into each other late at night? Not your reaction in there?"

"He asked me, when you were getting your photo taken, if it was accurate how we ran into each other. He warned me that if you and I were hiding something, the statement could be inadmissible."

I gasped. "But it is accurate."

"I know, I told him. He's skeptical, though." He was quiet as he opened the door for me and made his way around to the driver's side.

I looked at him over the roof of the car. "Why were you so upset?"

"Not were, Olivia. Am. I *am* upset, and for a lot of reasons. For one, it pisses me off that your husband isn't—"

"Wait," I said, holding up my hand. "It's fine. I don't need to know. Let's not drag Bill into this."

"It's a little late for that. It seems this is his mess, in fact. What does he have to say about it?"

My mouth opened briefly before sealing into a tight line.

"Olivia?"

I slipped into the seat, pulling the door closed behind me.

He followed a moment later but didn't move to start the car. "Does he know?"

I shook my head. "He's been in meetings all day."

He pursed his lips and said, "You need to talk to him."

"What am I going to say?" I asked the window, tugging at my earlobe.

He started the car and reversed from the spot. "Tell him the truth."

I jumped at the sound of my phone and looked from it to David and back.

"Go ahead," he said without looking at me. "Answer it."

"Bill," I said into the phone.

"Hey. This case is turning out to be more intense than I realized. I've taken some depositions, but I might not get back until next week."

"Um," I started. "I had another incident last night."

"Incident?"

I opted for the shortened version. "I left work late, and Mark Alvarez was waiting for me on the street."

"Oh. Shit."

"He chased me down Adams and into an alley. I ran into a friend of Andrew's, amazingly, who works nearby. Together we managed to subdue him until the cops arrived."

"Holy shit. So, wait—they have Mark Alvarez in custody now? I knew that bastard would break his parole. He didn't even make it three months."

I nodded, even though he couldn't see me. "In fact, I'm just leaving the police station where I spoke to Detective Cooper."

"Cooper, yeah. I know him. You really shouldn't talk to the police without me present."

"But nothing really even happened. I just gave a statement."

"Are you all right?"

"A little shaken up, but," I paused, glancing at David, "fine."

"Good, I'm glad. I don't know why he's involving you. I'm so sorry I can't come home right now. Can you get one of the girls to sleep over tonight? I could probably be back by tomorrow afternoon. Or do you want to come here?"

"No. He's detained, and I have this party tonight that I can't miss. Gretchen and Lucy are coming so maybe I'll go home with one of them."

"I'm going to talk to Cooper and make sure this is taken care of. Promise to take it easy. Aren't you still sick from the trip?"

"No."

"Okay. Babe, I have to go if I want to get anything to eat today."

"You haven't eaten yet? It's almost four o'clock there."

"I've been seriously swamped."

I rubbed my temples with one hand and took a deep breath.

"Liv?"

"There's something else," I said, lowering my voice. "Bill, Davena passed away last night."

Silence on the line conveyed his surprise. I stared hard out the window as I waited.

"Honey. Jesus. I'm so sorry."

"It's terrible. Poor Mack."

"Yes, terrible. Did you know it was that bad?"

"I knew, but, no. I didn't really know."

He moaned. "I'm so—oh, God. You must be, just . . . . Should I come home tonight?"

I set my jaw as I continued to watch the passing cars. I'd been strong for years, keeping the hurt inside and managing from one day to the next. Couldn't I make it one more night before dissolving? Because that was what I wanted to do. To let someone else take over for a while.

"I'll be fine until tomorrow," I said.

"When's the service?"

"Monday."

"I'll see if I can get a few hours off."

"I don't mind going alone if you can't."

"Babe, of course I want to be there. We can talk about that later, though." He sighed heavily into the phone. "Stay in tonight. Ask one of the girls to come over."

"I can't." I shook my head. "Go get lunch. Or dinner, whatever."

"I'm sorry for your shitty week. But maybe this time it'll stick with Mark. And then it's done."

"Let's hope so," I said with a sidelong look at David. "Call me later, okay?"

I hung up and sat in silence, waiting for David to speak, but he didn't. I thought about Bill's words—*shitty week*. It was a shitty week, exhausting both physically and emotionally. But shitty wasn't the right word. It felt . . . something unidentifiable.

We pulled up to my complex, and David turned off the car. "He's not coming back?"

"Tomorrow." I sighed. "He's got so much on his plate. He was happy to hear about Mark being in custody. Sounds like he won't be free anytime soon."

I watched David's jaw muscles tense just as his grip on the steering wheel tightened. "What about after the event? Will you be okay tonight?"

"Yep. Will you?"

He smirked at me.

"No, really," I teased. "Will you be? I'm worried. Do you have someone who can stay with you?"

He looked away and . . . blushed.

"Wait, do you?" I asked when he didn't respond.

"I'm having dinner with someone," he said, looking through the windshield. "And I may bring her to the party."

I forced a smile and swallowed. "That's good," I said slowly. My surroundings focused sharply as I tried to respond. "Are you sure you've thought this through, though? I mean, she probably won't like the theme of the party . . . seeing as how it's to celebrate your bachelorhood. Although, it's rather convenient that you live right upstairs."

He gave me a reproachful look.

"Also," I continued, "don't forget to tidy up my guest room." I palmed my forehead with exaggeration. "Shit. What am I thinking? You won't be needing it."

His chest heaved with a deep sigh. His expression reminded me of the face Gretchen's brother would make when we pestered him as kids.

"I'm not fucking around, Olivia. What about tonight? Can you stay with Gretchen or someone?"

"I'll be fine," I said, crossing my arms over my seatbelt.

"Does he really accept that 'fine' bullshit?"

"What?"

"You're always saying everything is fine even though it's not. It's fine that you were attacked last night? It's fine that somebody you obviously care a great deal about passed away? Does *anyone* care enough to question whether or not you're actually fine?"

"Excuse me?" I asked. "What are you saying? That Bill doesn't care about me?"

"That's not what I'm saying. Just . . . I don't think he, or your friends for that matter, know you as well as they think."

"And what, you do? I've known you all of a month."

"I didn't need seconds to know you better than them," he snapped. "And it's two months. I saw everything I needed to in that moment at the theater."

It was the first time either of us had ever mentioned it, and the car thickened with tension.

"You are impossible to read if you're not paying attention, but I am. And I may not know the details yet but *I know you.*"

I reeled back as my mouth hung open. "Does that seriously work for you?"

"That's fine." He sat back, unruffled. "If you want a satisfactory marriage with someone who is incapable of loving you the way you deserve, then that's up to you. What can I do about it?" He shrugged his shoulders as my jaw hardened. Nobody had ever spoken to me that way and certainly not about Bill, who, everyone knew, adored me.

"Satisfactory," I cried. "Bill adores me!" I faltered, completely flustered. "I don't know what—what you're trying to pull, but he's an amazing husband who treats me—"

"How?" He leaned in and looked me full in the face. "How does he treat you?" he demanded, his eyes boring into mine. His voice lowered into a rumble. "You have no idea what I'd do with you."

My legs began to sweat against the gummy leather, and I shifted in discomfort. I was transported back to the theater, when the red velvet seats had pricked my thighs, and his lingering presence had clung to me. He was too close and too comfortable.

"I—I . . . ," I stammered, looking for the words. The way he looked at me was too much to take, and I fumbled to escape from the seatbelt.

"Here, let me," he said coolly and slipped his hand down between my thigh and those sticky leather seats. His fingers lingered against my bare skin, and my pulse pounded. He bent closer so that I could almost touch my lips to his neck. His faint, earthy scent left me dizzy and pining for more.

He grazed along my outer thigh as he searched for the release, and it was all I could do not to shudder. My breath caught in my throat. *Do not squirm, do not squirm. That's exactly what he wants.*

He pushed the button and the seatbelt jumped into my shaking hands. David leaned back into his seat and stuck his chin in his hand, looking back through the driver's side window. I huffed as I pushed the door open and hastened out.

I took a deep breath and leaned back into the car. "Maybe you were right yesterday," I said softly. "Maybe any type of relationship is impossible."

He looked over at me. "And maybe I'll skip tonight."

I nodded. "I think that's best." *That's it. It's done. Shut the door and walk away.*

And I did.

CHAPTER 23

I WOKE UP STILL SHEATHED in my bath towel and with my head on a damp pillow. For once I was glad for Lisa's help, since it had given me the opportunity to nap. The clock on the nightstand told me that I needed to get up immediately if I was going to make it to the Meet & Greet on time. I closed my eyes. *Five more minutes.*

It was an apt ending to my turbulent relationship with David. His accusations were fresh in my mind. *How dare he? He's willing to destroy a marriage, and for what?* It pained me to wonder if he'd done this with other women. And where were they now? I couldn't shake the image of David asking another woman out to dinner, flirting with her, flashing her that seductive grin.

My stomach flipped when I thought about the upcoming event. I needed it to go well, since it was my idea. I wished then that Bill could have made it. *But he would have hated it anyway.*

My phone revealed several missed texts from Gretchen and Lucy confirming our plans for the evening. At least I would have them for support.

~

"What happened?" Ava squealed when she opened the apartment door. Her eyes shone with excitement as she questioned me about the bruise, and I attempted to give her the shortest version possible. "Then what?" she asked. And then asked it again.

"I'm going to let Gretchen know I'm here," I said finally, desperate to escape. I followed the sound of Gretchen's blow dryer and found her bent over, a mass of blonde hair.

"Gretch," I yelled as I stood in the doorway.

She flipped her head back and looked at me, startled. She held up her hand. "Five minutes."

I dropped on her bed and glanced around the familiar room. It was surprisingly unremarkable for Gretchen, with white walls, a bed, a dresser with a vanity, and a hamper in the corner. I picked up *US Weekly* from the bedside table and scanned the first few pages.

"Shoes," Gretchen exclaimed suddenly, motioning to my feet.

"Brian Atwood. A little gift from me to me for all the stress," I said. "Do not tell Bill."

She dropped her towel. Without her heels and makeup, she seemed smaller than I ever remembered, but trim too, like she'd been working out more. I watched her wrap herself in her robe and tried to see her as a lover might. My nagging suspicion hadn't gone away. Did he find her attractive?

She started toward her vanity and paused. "What is that?" she asked, staring at my face.

I frowned. Apparently I'd done a poor job of covering it up. I resolved to invest in better concealer. "Mark Alvarez again. The guy from Bill's case."

"The guy who confronted you last month? Are you okay? What happened?"

"Can I explain when Lucy gets here? It's a long story."

"No."

"I'm okay, don't worry. All intact."

Her mouth sat open for so long, that I began to count the seconds. She made a noise finally. "Okay, but no excuses when she arrives."

She sat down and shook a bottle of foundation. "How was your week otherwise?"

"Great," I said. Without warning, I began reciting Mack's e-mail in my mind. I shook my head forcefully to make it stop.

She laughed. "Okay?"

"How was yours?"

"Mine actually *was* great, liar," she said. "Our biggest client complimented me in front of my boss—you know what a witch she can be. Then a headhunter contacted me today. I'm seriously considering leaving, I mean . . ."

I had the sudden urge to hear from her that nothing had happened with David. Despite his assurance, it still gnawed at me. I squirmed inwardly as she talked, itching to ask about Friday night. The more I thought about it, the more it made sense that he must be the surprise guest. A player like him and a single girl like Gretchen, who always got her way when it came to men. They belonged to the same social circle—it only made sense.

"How was fishing?" she asked, making a gagging face.

"Fishing?" I asked. It felt like a lifetime ago, until I remembered it was the same night as the gala. "You don't want to hear about that. Lucy said you had an interesting night?"

"I'll wait 'til she gets here," she said, tenderly brushing blush onto her cheeks.

"No," I demanded, causing her to look at me. "I want to know now. I'm excited."

"You're acting weird," she said. "Why are you all pitchy?"

"I'm fine." There was that word again. I'd never realized how often I said it. "Tell me about Friday night."

"So you can wait, but I can't?"

"I bet you love telling your story. Mine is just depressing."

"All right, but don't tell Lucy I told you first or she'll be mad. Guess who I hooked up with? You never will."

My teeth clamped when I experienced the overwhelming feeling that David had lied to me. Another act in the David Dylan show. My head began to purr with a dull vibration. Did he actually think I wouldn't find out? Did he care? Once she said it aloud though, it would help cut the cord once and for all.

Anxiety ate at my insides and in my head, I screamed at her to spit it out.

"One of the hottest guys in Chicago," she continued. "Any guesses?"

I wrung my hands.

"Even hotter than Frat Guy," she said, referring to an infamous one-night stand from college. Her fingers pulled at her lids as she skillfully smoothed on liquid eyeliner. "Or remember that guy David from Lucy's engagement party?" My heart hit the floor and tears pricked my eyes. *How could he—*"Even hotter than him," she said.

I blew out an exhale. A tear made of pure tension fell before I could stop it. I was overcome with relief, followed by body-racking embarrassment.

"Olivia—God, what is the matter?" she asked, peering at me in the mirror.

"Nothing," I said, furiously wiping at my eye. What was I thinking? I felt ridiculous. And after last night, I was ashamed. How did I think I couldn't trust him? He'd put his life on the line for me.

She turned in her chair, eyeliner in hand, and glared at me. "Tell me," she said.

"I'm just PMS'ing," I lied. "Who's the guy?"

"Graham Broderick," she said flatly. I'd ruined her moment. I looked up, racking my brain. She snatched the magazine from my hand and opened it to an earmarked page. She held it up an inch from my face.

"Oh," I exclaimed. "From that movie—what's it called . . . ? He's like a real celebrity! And you're right, very gorgeous."

Definitely not hotter than David.

She smiled smugly and turned back to the mirror. "He was at the event, and my date knew him from high school. He was totally flirting with me so eventually we ditched the party, got drunk, and ended up back at his lakefront apartment."

"What about your date?" I asked, trying to keep my interest level high in an effort to distract her.

"Oh, I don't know. He was just a friend. I left him at the party."

I tsked and shook my head at her.

"Anyway, Graham's my date tonight. That should get you guys some good publicity." She expertly whisked on mascara, glancing back and forth between her reflection and me. She screwed the cap back in and came to sit by me on the bed. "Tell me. What is it?"

I struggled with myself. If I voiced my feelings for David, they would be real. And after the way we'd left things, I didn't know if I'd ever see him again—so did it even matter? What if I were to tell her for nothing?

But the weight of my rollercoaster feelings since day one had me questioning everything, and it was beginning to scare me. Since the moment I'd laid eyes on David, he'd been an inescapable presence in my thoughts.

"I don't know how to say this," I said to myself. "I think I'm . . . I don't know. I'm attracted to someone else."

"Oh, sweetie. That's okay. That's perfectly normal." She smiled gently and patted me on the knee.

"No." I sighed. "I'm falling for this person. I have feelings for him." It was the first time I'd let myself think it. And definitely the first time I'd said it aloud. I didn't expect it to feel so true. I looked down at my fingers, which I'd wrung red.

"What?" she breathed. "But, Bill . . . you guys are happy, aren't you?"

"Yes," I said emphatically. "I think so. Yes. It's not really about him at all . . . ."

Her composed face didn't reveal the judgment I'd expected to see. I reminded myself that this was Gretchen I was talking to, not just anyone. Lucy, wholesome and trusting as she was, would have the opposite reaction.

"But," I started again, feeling the tears returning. "I don't know what to do. I love Bill, and I've never even felt the urge to be with anyone else. *Ever.*"

Gretchen nodded thoughtfully. "And you think you feel that strongly for this guy? Why?"

"I feel . . ." I paused, my eyes darting around as I thought. "Connected to him in some way. I think he feels it too. It gets stronger whenever I'm near him, and I can't stop it. I can't stop it," I repeated to myself. "And we kissed and it was . . ." I exhaled, letting the sentence hang.

Those Windex eyes grew bigger than I'd ever seen them. "Wow, Liv. You kissed? I've never even heard you talk about another guy since you met Bill."

"It just sort of happened, and I feel so . . ." Words filtered through my head until I chose one. "So guilty."

"Oh, Liv." She wrapped my forearm in her hand. "I can't tell you what to do, but . . ." She stopped as if searching for the words. "Bill has always been . . . safe. You fell in love slowly and without any hiccups. I saw what your parents' divorce did to you. You stopped taking risks. You stopped knowing how to open up. Bill was—*is* safe. He has always loved you, and he'd never hurt you."

Her words were eerily similar to Lucy's. As if there was some reason why Bill shouldn't love me as much as he did.

"That doesn't mean you owe him anything though," she continued. "I know how you can get. Stop being so hard on yourself. Take some time to think about what you really want. Not what you think others want, but what you really want deep down."

A little of the struggle lifted from my shoulders as Gretchen took it on, but it was hard to ignore the question burning in her eyes.

After another moment of silence, I spoke. "I can't tell you who. Then there's no turning back."

She looked disappointed. "My point is, I remember that passionate side of you; I know it's there, and it was hard to watch it die during the divorce."

"My parents fought a lot at the end, but I never expected it to get so bad," I said. "I didn't know they would split. I thought they loved each other."

"It was for the best, honey. They were miserable and they were making you miserable. Seeing you almost cry right now, well, I'm shocked. It's been a long time."

It hurt my heart to hear her say it out loud. "I know, I'm sorry. I hate crying in public."

"Public? Liv, it's me. This isn't public."

"Yes. That sounds stupid, doesn't it?"

"I remember when we were kids, you assumed you were going to have it all," she said, looking up. "The best job, the best house, and the cutest husband. You said he was going to be the best guy in the world, and the tallest too, and that you would love each other more than anyone. Do you feel that way about Bill?"

"Bill is tall," I said, smiling.

"Liv?"

I blinked furiously at her. "Gretch, that's childish stuff. Everyone thinks that way when they're ten years old."

"Not me." She shook her head. "I just wanted to be happy. I thought that being happy meant finding someone to marry and a good job. I didn't know other kids who said they would *be* the best at everything, *have* the best of everything."

I laughed lightly and nodded. "I had high expectations because my dad did. I didn't want anyone to ever think that I wasn't good enough."

"Nobody thinks that. Everyone loves you."

"Do they?" Gretchen looked hurt so I touched her arm. "I know you do. I love you too, so much. I never would've survived without you and John. You're the reason I made it through."

She gave me a beautiful smile, and I was sure I saw tears in her eyes. "So what about Bill? Is he all of those things?"

"I don't think anyone can be all of those things. I think I may have been a bit idealistic." I rolled my eyes. "But he is as close as it gets."

She bit her lip, and her eyes avoided mine. "What are you going to do?" she asked.

"Move on. What choice do I have?" I paused. "But for now, I'm going to have a carefree night with my girlfriends. You'd better get dressed, or I'm leaving your ass behind. I can't be late for my own party."

Her eyes lingered on me a moment before she stood. I watched her sort through her closet in an unusually silent manner, pulling out article after article. "Thanks for listening," I whispered.

Lucy's voice floated in from the other room. On my way to the kitchen, I was almost knocked over by Bethany when she rushed up to hug me. "I heard you were attacked in an alley downtown by a murderer rapist."

"What?" Lucy screamed. She rushed over and skidded to a stop in front of me. "Your face!"

"That's an exaggeration," I said, glaring at Ava.

276

"Wait," Gretchen called from her room. "I haven't heard the story yet." She raced in, clutching at her robe as it threatened to fly open.

"This is the last time I'm going to tell this," I prefaced.

They listened intently as I recounted my story. It sounded so grim as I told it, and I felt awful for bringing the mood down. When I got to the part about David, I sniffed and rushed the words out.

"What? That's crazy," Lucy said.

"Well, you know he works by us. We're profiling him for the 'Most Eligible' issue," I explained to Ava and Bethany. "So, he was on his way home from the office—"

"At ten o'clock at night?" Lucy asked. "That's an extreme coincidence."

"I know." I shrugged. "I was very lucky. Anyway—"

"Wait, hold up," Gretchen said. "Since when is David part of that issue? This is the guy from Lucy's party, right? Is he going to be there tonight? I didn't know—" She gasped loudly, and we all looked at her. "Oh, my—"

"What?" Bethany asked.

Her eyes grew wide and she covered her mouth, staring at me. "Oh my God," she said, the words muffled by her hand.

I grabbed her arm and pulled her into the bedroom. "Give us a minute," I said to them, pushing Gretchen with more force. Shock covered her face, and I shut the door behind us.

"David Dylan?" she hissed. "*He's* the one you've fallen for?"

My brows knit as I stammered for a response.

"Oh, Olivia. No, no, no. Forget what I said earlier. He's a total womanizer."

"How do you know?" I asked.

"I can just tell. I know tons of guys just like him. Someone like that can be . . . dangerous. He knows how to make you feel special. Believe me. He's handsome, charming, and sexy. There's no way he's not single for a reason."

"Sounds familiar," I said with intent to hurt.

"Well," she said, seemingly unfazed, "I learned from experience. From guys like him."

"Look," I started. "We can talk about this later. I don't want anyone else to find out."

"Is that story true?" she asked. "Or were you with him that night?"

"It actually is true, weird as it sounds. I was at work late, and we did run into each other." I decided not to reveal just yet that I'd spent the night in his apartment.

"And when you asked me to cover for you?"

"I met him for a drink to explain that nothing could happen between us."

"It takes a drink to explain that?"

"Olivia?" Lucy called from the other room.

"Come on, before they get suspicious," I said, pulling her arm.

"We're not done with this conversation," she said.

We were met with a sea of confused faces when we returned. "Sorry," Gretchen said. "I—I thought I forgot to. . . turn off my curling iron."

I rolled my eyes inwardly and continued my story to distract them. I left out as many details as possible, telling the story as though David were less impassioned.

When I finished, they were stunned. Lucy was almost in tears, but I assured her that I was feeling better and that the police were taking care of it.

"Next time that happens, you call me right away. David is a hero," she said with starry eyes.

"No," I said, trying again to downplay his involvement. "Anyone else would've done the same thing."

She shook her head. "He is something else. I always thought he was so polite. He's just a good guy." I looked at Gretchen imploringly.

"I'm almost done getting ready. Lucy, make me a drink?"

Thank you, I mouthed.

"Are you sure you're feeling up for tonight?" Lucy asked me quietly, and I nodded. Though the weight of the morning's news weighed heavily on me, I knew better than to reveal it. Lucy would send me home if she found out Davena had passed.

"I need to have some fun," I said. "Plus, I really need to be there. This whole thing was my idea."

"Thanks for inviting us," Ava said. "All my friends are super jealous. Is there going to be dancing?"

"Yep." I nodded. "And I think dancing might be just the ticket."

Lucy bit her lip. "I haven't been dancing since that spring break we went to Mexico."

"Oh, this will be nothing like Mexico," Ava chimed in. "I've been to the club upstairs at the Gryphon. Very classy."

Bethany nodded. "It is."

"Good, because I'm scarred for life after Tijuana."

I laughed and squeezed a lemon into the drinks. While delivering one to Gretchen, I paused to admire my sleeveless leather mini-dress. It hugged in all the right places and nude pumps elongated my legs. I needed more cover-up on the bruise, I decided. My lips were glossy and colorless, and the bulk of my hair was pinned at the top of my head, with a few pieces escaping to frame my face.

I thought that for someone whose insides were so tangled, I could pass for a normal, happy human being. And maybe I'd have to for a while. Gretchen stepped out then in silver skinny jeans, a white over-sized tank, and red, sky-high stilettos.

"Let's do this," she said after a long sip of her drink.

CHAPTER 24

THERE WAS NOTHING IN THE WORLD like the feeling of bass pumping against your brain, reverberating throughout your entire body. The fast and steady beat pulsed through me, entangling with the fiery alcohol, manipulating my limbs, and looping my hips. The darkness of the dance floor was sporadically pierced with flashes of red, green, blue. A white spotlight flickered over glowing, sweat-dampened skin.

Gretchen's petite figure moved against Graham Broderick while her eyes closed blissfully. A group of girls, who didn't look old enough to drink alcohol, *and oh, I should check, but I just don't want to leave*, they stayed close to us, trying to cut in for a dance with the movie star.

I'd had a lot to drink, but it was hard to care. With the week I'd experienced, it was the best medicine. I'd already been all around the event, checking in with the necessary people and mingling with the guests. The party was in full swing. David's non-presence was almost palpable to me, but the alcohol numbed the disappointment. It numbed the pain. It numbed everything.

Davena. I blocked the name from my mind and focused on the music, letting it wipe everything in my head. Just then, someone bumped me, causing my glass to drop and shatter at my feet.

I groaned. "I'll be back," I shouted to no one in particular. I squeezed my way off the dance floor.

Minutes later, drink in hand, I made my way around the party. I stopped now and then to converse with the guests of honor and then checked on Serena, who was firmly positioned at the front.

On my way back, Beman motioned me over. "I must say, I'm pleased with what you've done here. Not too over the top but a fine guest list. And how did you manage to get Graham Broderick? There are actually paparazzi out front."

"Oh, he's a mutual friend," I said, waving my hand nonchalantly.

He nodded and grinned tightly. "Very nice. Keep up the good work."

"Thanks," I called as he sauntered away.

I headed out to the back balcony. I was in conversation with a Bachelorette when someone tapped my shoulder.

"Brian Ayers," I exclaimed, wrapping him in a warm hug and planting a kiss on his cheek. "I'm so glad you could make it."

"Hello, Olivia. Thank you for the invite. Sorry I wasn't here earlier." He eyed my face, squinting at my cheek.

"No problem. You did miss my speech, though."

"And for that I will be eternally sorry. Can I refresh your drinks?"

"Sure," the Bachelorette said. She waited until he walked away. "He's cute, Liv. He must be in the issue too. He's too cute not to be. Is he gay? He is, isn't he?" She cringed.

"No." I smiled. "He's straight and available."

"Oh, good." She laughed, twirling a piece of auburn hair around her finger. "Because one time, I was flirting with this guy all night long, and I thought we were really hitting it off until someone finally told me—" Her eyes changed as she looked over my shoulder. I inhaled deeply, feeling his presence strongly at my back.

"Hi," she said dumbly.

"Ladies."

I looked up at David from the corner of my eye. His expression was smoother than his bristly jawline, and his dark hair was tousled. I rolled my lips together to keep from gaping.

"Are you a Bachelor, too?" the girl asked. I peeked around him stealthily to search for his date.

He cleared his throat. "Can you give us a moment?"

"I'm waiting for a drink," she said.

"I'll make sure you get your drink. Do you mind?"

I crossed my arms and tapped my finger against my forearm once she'd sulked away. "I'm surprised to see you here."

"Are you?" he asked, taking a sip of something dark.

I looked away. "Yes. You said you wouldn't come."

"I said maybe."

"I just didn't think I'd see you again, at least not this soon. Where's your date?"

"Why not? Because we had an argument?"

I glanced back at him. "An argument?" I squeezed my fingers into my arm. "That wasn't an argument. That was a finale. With fireworks."

"Not for me, it wasn't."

"Well, it was for me," I hissed under my breath, glancing around the balcony.

His back straightened then. "Brian Ayers," he said, holding out his hand and clapping him on the back.

"Nice to see you, fellow Bachelor. Here you are, Olivia," Brian said, passing me a glass while balancing two others.

David's gaze darted between us, and his face darkened.

Brian blew a piece of hair from his forehead and looked around. "Where'd she go?"

"She's over there by the ice sculpture," I said, pointing. We all looked, and she waved. Brian held up the drink to her, and she came scurrying over.

"So, aside from this speech, what did I miss?" he asked us both.

"Can't say," David said. "I just arrived."

"Not too much, just a lot of dancing and miniature hamburgers."

"I could definitely go for some food right now," David said, rubbing his stomach.

"Didn't you come from dinner?" I asked.

He shrugged. "I'm a growing boy."

"Well, what've you got there, young man?" Brian asked, taking David's drink from him. "Iced tea?" David snorted as Brian whiffed the drink and made a face. "Whiskey. That's potent shit." He shook his head and passed it back. Brian put a damp hand on my shoulder. "I'm a gin and tonic man myself."

His fingertips brushed against my neck. The look returned to David's face with a blaring intensity, and it was beginning to make me uncomfortable.

"And how about that portrait, Miss Bacall? When are you going to let me take it? You'd look just right hanging in my gallery room."

I blushed, looking into my drink. "I don't think so."

"Don't get shy on me, Olivia. You have magnificent eyes, they really are unusual. The camera would love them. Aren't they magnificent, David?"

"They are." In those two words, his tone of voice said everything. His drink swirled in measured circles. He wore a charcoal, V-neck sweater over a slate-grey button down. It showed the knot of a matching tie, which he now loosened as his eyes burned into me. He made no effort to hide the fact that he was infuriated by Brian's behavior. And it had my body utterly thrumming as a result. The way he looked at me, like he couldn't control what might happen next, almost brought me to my knees.

"We had the most fateful meeting," Brian went on. "It was like something out of a romance movie. This one was walking her dog and got tangled in the leash. It took off after some poor fluffball, and Olivia here fell flat on her ass. Luckily I was passing by and gave her a hand up."

"How romantic," David said, deadpan.

"It wasn't my dog," I started to explain but was cut off.

"I'm loving this party." The auburn-haired girl accepted her drink and prattled on about something or other. I wasn't listening. David was looking at me in that way, penetrating and lusty with a twist of somber, and I was suddenly remembering the seatbelt. His hand grazing my skin, so close to the hem of my skirt. I shuddered. He raised an eyebrow at me.

"What do you say, David?" Brian asked.

"Hmm?"

"About taking this nice young lady to see the view of the water. I don't think she's ever been this high up before."

She giggled. "Yes—"

"Run along, you two," Brian said.

Brian winked, and I caught the tail end of David's glare. David stuck out his elbow and the woman took it, smiling with giddy abandon.

"I don't know what's up his ass," Brian said once they were on their way, "but he needs a good lay, and he isn't going to get it hanging out with us."

"How long have you known him?" I asked, scowling spitefully after Ritz, my new nickname for the redheaded ditz.

"Years. A good man. One of the only guys in Chicago I trust. There are a lot of bullshitters, Liv. Don't be fooled. May I call you Liv? It feels so natural."

"Of course."

"Enough about Dylan, though. Should I be worried about the monstrosity on your face? I admit you did a nice job of covering it up. Perhaps I need to throw down the gauntlet?"

I laughed. "It's all taken care of. I prefer not to discuss it, however."

"Very well, that's your call. So I know you have the scoop on the ladies here. Fill me in. That one wasn't my type, not very bright. Seems much better suited to Dylan." I bit my cheek at the comment. "Who do you suggest? I need a girl like you, smart and beautiful, but edgy too. Come on, I know you're a little wild," he said when I started to protest. "Look at you, in your leather dress."

I couldn't help but laugh before breaking down the guest list. "And, you know," I said when I'd finished, "my best girlfriend is here. She's a real catch, but she came with someone." I looked around the room and pointed her out to him. David, standing on the opposite balcony with his back to us, caught my eye.

"And you say she's clever?"

"She is, though she might try to fool you," I said distractedly. I sent Gretchen a text, telling her to come over alone. I could see David's profile now through the glass, and he was laughing with the woman. To my surprise, they seemed to be enjoying themselves.

"Hey," Gretchen said, waltzing up.

"Gretch, this is my friend Brian. He's one of our Bachelors."

"I'm aware," she said with a killer smile. "I've already had Liv fill me in on the best attendees."

Brian laughed boisterously. "I just had her do the same for me."

"He did," I confirmed. "I'm a good friend, don't forget it."

"And why aren't you in the feature, Gretchen?"

"I was a couple years back."

"Funny, I think I would have remembered."

While they got acquainted, I checked for David again, but neither him nor the woman were anywhere in sight. I rose onto the balls of my feet to get a better view.

"I'll be back," I told them. "Listen, I need him single until June. Don't get any ideas, G."

I reentered the ballroom, looking for Lucy but hoping I might spot David and reassure myself that he wasn't hitting on Ritz. I stopped in my tracks when I was met with the unpleasant image of him handing her a drink with one hand as his other hand rested on her back.

Is that his type? Redhead, curvy and reeking of desperation?

I bemoaned the fact that I had actually selected her as one of Chicago's most date-worthy singles. How could I argue with my own taste?

I pounded the remainder of my drink and plunked it on the nearest table. I turned to leave when I saw two arguing guys in the corner almost knock over a table. "Hey," I yelled, running over to them. "Stop—what are you doing?"

"No worries, babe," replied a young, stocky blond. "We're just fucking around."

"Who're you here with?"

"We used to work in the restaurant downstairs, so we snuck in."

"Dude, shut up," the other one said. They burst into laughter. "What's your name? You're hot." One of us was swaying.

"You guys aren't supposed to be here. I have to throw you out," I said. "Find somewhere else, preferably far from here."

"Hang on," the blond said, moving to block my way. "Let's get a drink. I'll buy."

"The drinks are free. And no."

"Come on," he pleaded. "What's your name?" My eyes darted around him, searching for security. He sniffed.

"Liv," I said.

"What is it?" the friend asked.

"Liz," replied the blond.

"Liz, where's your drink?" he asked, not bothering to hide his slurring. "Didn't this asshole offer to buy you one?"

"I'm good," I yelled. "But, seriously, you guys have to go."

"Lighten up. You need a drink." The friend laid a heavy arm over my shoulders. I moved to lift it off, suddenly reliving Mark's hands on me.

"Stop," I said.

"What?" he asked into my ear, causing me to wince. "You're not leaving are you? I'm getting you a drink."

"And I'm getting security if you guys don't leave. This is a private party."

"No, dude, don't get security," he said, tightening his grip.

"Please, get off."

"Huh?"

"She said get *off*."

I looked up just in time to see David yank the guy's arm from me and twist it before throwing him into the wall. He positioned himself in front of me and towered over the stocky blond, whose face flashed with a new alertness. "What the fuck don't you understand about *get off?*" he yelled, pushing him into the friend.

"David?" I cried in shock.

The friend yelled something, holding up his palms, but I couldn't hear over the music. They hurried away and ran right into security.

David had regained his bearing and was now towering over me. "You need to start paying more attention to—"

"What the hell are you doing?" I sizzled. "I can take care of myself."

"Clearly you can't," he said. "Those guys—"

"Were completely harmless."

290

"You don't know that."

"You know what?" I pivoted on my heel. "Forget it—I'm leaving."

"Hang on," he started.

I spun around to cut him off. "Stay here. Enjoy the party." I couldn't help casting an obvious glance at Ritz, who was biting her nails by the bar where he'd left her. "You shouldn't have any problems meeting someone," I muttered. I craned my neck to look for Lucy.

"Someone like Brian Ayers? There's a match made in heaven."

I paused. "What business is it of yours? I like him."

He shrugged. "I didn't think he was your type."

"I don't have a type, David. *I'm married.*"

He took a step closer and the thrumming returned—only now, it gave way to a full body vibration as he stared down at me. "So you keep saying. I'm beginning to wonder if you flirt with all of them the way you flirt with me."

I balled my hands into fists on each side of me. "Again, not that it's any of your business, but I was trying to set him up. He's over there talking to Gretchen right now." Even though I was making no secret of my irritation, I'd lost his focus. He was looking at one of my hands, which I now realized was nervously playing with the hem of my dress. "And I don't."

"Don't?" he repeated, riveted as my fingertips grazed against my bare thigh.

I lowered my voice and rasped, "Flirt with them. Flirt with anyone, actually, the way I flirt with you." He blinked from my hand to my eyes. I had his attention now. "Goodnight, David."

"Goodnight?"

"I'm going to say good-bye to everyone."

"Olivia," he commanded, but I was already leaving. "Stop running away."

I turned around to find him one step behind me. "Leave me alone," I whispered as calmly as possible.

"No." He lightly grasped the wrist of the hand he'd been tracking.

"Don't touch me," I said, withdrawing. His touch was too intense, and I didn't know what it would take to send me over the edge. I searched the room for an escape, deciding to forgo the formalities. I ended up at the elevator bank, impatiently punching the button.

"What—where are you going?" David asked my back.

"Home. Just go back to the party, David." When he didn't budge, I bolted for the service stairwell. I burst through the door and jumped when it slammed against the wall. I rushed down a flight of stairs and had to stop myself from turning back for my coat.

"Olivia," he called from above.

I held my purse to my breast. "Leave me alone," I called over my shoulder. My heart leaped when I felt his unmistakable hand on my arm. He was damn near impossible to outrun.

"Stop. I'm not letting you run away. Are you mad at me? And where is your coat?"

I whirled around to face him on the landing, shivering from the stark surroundings and from the emotions that were beginning to escape. "Am I—am I mad?" I asked, seething. "What do you think?"

"Is it about this afternoon?"

"No. Y-yes—it's about everything. Why are you here? I thought this was done."

"I tried. Believe me I did."

"Tried what?"

"To stay away," he said steadily. "I tried to stay away, but I can't." He glanced down at his feet, and when he looked up again, his eyes were blazing. "Spend the night with me."

The breath flushed from my lungs, leaving me cross-eyed with lust. I could almost hear my body vibrating now, so coiled with desire that I knew I would snap if he touched me. "Why, so you can humiliate me again? Toss me aside like day-old garbage?"

"What the hell are you talking about?" he asked.

I watched him closely. "I don't understand. Is this some sort of game for you? You pushed me away in Lucy's office and then told me you never wanted to see me again. That you were finished with me. And now suddenly you want me?" A fluorescent light flickered somewhere above us, as though channeling my anger.

"Jesus, is that what you thought? I left you that night because there was too much on the line, not because I didn't want you. I was afraid of pushing you into something you might regret. But, Olivia, you make it so fucking impossible," he said, pleading up to the ceiling. His breathing was ragged, and he looked back at me with stormy eyes. "I can't be around you anymore because you drive me crazy every second of the day." He ran both hands through his hair. "Fuck, if I don't distance myself from you, I'm going to lose my sanity."

I took a step backwards.

"And when I ended things, you just took it. You didn't even care. Just let me walk out. Tell me you care, Olivia, and that I'm not completely delusional."

"You know I can't," I whispered. How could he think I didn't? It was oozing from my pores all the time, how much I wanted to touch him, how much I thirsted for his attention.

"Then show me," he said.

"What do you want from me?" I asked. "You expect me to jeopardize everything—*everything*—for . . . for what?" My voice bounced off the empty walls. "Sex? My marriage, my work, my friends . . . my marriage." I swayed slightly as I yelled, at the mercy of the alcohol that ran through me. "I can't do it, David!"

"How many times do I have to say it? Did you hear a word I just said? *It's not like that, and you know it.*"

"Oh, okay," I said wryly, sweat forming on my nape despite the cold. "Where's your date? Did she stand you up? Is that why you're here now, in this stairwell? To see if I'll fuck you?" I stepped up to him, coming right under his chin, my temper flaring and my thighs burning. "Well, what's stopping you? Why not take me now? I bet you don't even have the decency to bring me upstairs." I put as much venom as I could into the words, and they felt bitter leaving my mouth.

"So help me God, Olivia," he whispered, stepping back infinitesimally and locking his hands under his armpits. "Don't test me. That date was over before it began, thanks to you. And I know what you're doing. I know you're afraid."

"Afraid? Afraid of losing everything, yes."

"You're afraid of this. I am too. I want—"

"Stop," I shouted, covering my ears. "This has to stop. Why won't you stop?"

"Olivia, listen to me." His face became calm as he took a deep breath. "I am afraid. I've never touched a married woman. You might not believe me, but this has been hard for me too because it goes against all of my beliefs. My parents, who are my world, have been happily married for thirty-seven years. I would kill anyone who tried to come between them. But it's nothing compared to keeping it inside. I can't hide it like you. And if I honestly thought he was the right person for you, I would walk away right now."

My heartbeat pounded in my stomach, reverberating throughout my body as he paused.

"I have real and deep feelings for you, and . . . I want to be with you."

CHAPTER 25

DAVID'S WORDS HIT ME PHYSICALLY, like a blow. *"I want to be with you."*

"How can you say that?" I asked, incredulous but no longer yelling. "You barely know me. You have Maria, yet you see other women. You're Chicago's bachelor of the goddamn year. Everything you've said tonight—they're just words. They don't mean anything. Give up already."

"No."

"Give up," I pleaded.

"No," he said through gritted teeth.

"You know what," I spat, "at the end of the day, you're a player, and you only want what you can't have."

"You think I can't have you?" He stepped into me.

"Wait," I said, panicked.

"Is that what you think?" he asked, leaning a little closer. "*I* don't think so. I want you. And I think you want me too."

He didn't wait like I'd asked. He was upon me in a moment, consuming me with a hard kiss that tasted of thick whiskey and sex. The warmth of his hands on my arms spread through me. He whipped off his jacket, never taking his lips from mine, and wrapped me in it so I was drowning in him, in a mossy blend of pine and aged leather.

"Show me you care, Olivia," he breathed. "I need it. I need you." He kissed the spot beneath my ear that made my knees buckle. Feather-light kisses along my jawbone lit chills over my body, and he stopped at my lips. He stilled there, as I became painstakingly aware of the empty feeling between my legs I wanted him to fill.

I looked into his eyes, and for a moment, everything else fell away. He took away the pain, all the things that hurt, that I could never say out loud. Brown eyes pleaded with me to let him take over, to let him ease the hurt.

He squeezed my arms mightily, reminding me with a flex of strength that if he wanted, he could take me whether I agreed or not. "Show me, Olivia. I need you. *Only you.*"

"I . . . " Desperation for him filled me to the brim. The instant I surrendered to it, he engulfed me in a primal kiss that was all mouth, saliva, lips, teeth.

Our hands, for the first time, explored each other furiously. His traveled behind my neck, over my shoulders, and along my arms. They grazed the crease of my ass as he bunched my leather dress. He pulled me against a hard erection, but I was already there, tugging his shirt from his pants, reaching underneath, touching his firm stomach—oh, how I had longed to know what his skin would feel like beneath my fingertips. He withdrew suddenly, ripping me from my adulation.

"This isn't right," he said.

"What?" I asked with breathless shock.

"Come upstairs with me," he said. He wrapped me up again and put his lips against the curve of my neck. My face burned deliciously from his stubble and only more of it would soothe the sting.

"Come upstairs," he whispered. My eyes rolled up to the ceiling as if the answer might be written there.

Before I could respond, he was pulling me down the second half of the stairs by my hand. I tried desperately to match his long strides, almost breaking into a run behind him.

David hit the 'Up' button when we'd reached the floor below. He slid one hand under the jacket that hung from me, sternly placing it on my shoulder as though I might try to run.

I opened my mouth to protest—say something, anything—but I was heady from the hand fastened to me and from the intoxicating, overwhelming scent of him. And then he looked down, comforting me with his eyes and his nearness. "You're so beautiful," he said, as though to remind me of it.

The elevator doors parted and David guided me inside with another couple. He swiped his card to the penthouse and we stood at two separate corners during the ascent. My mind raced faster than I could keep up. *Now's the time. Say something, Olivia. Stop this.* The elevator charged with tension. The people in front of us exchanged a knowing look.

I opened my mouth again . . .

He was a wall of exquisite beauty, his hands tentatively rubbing his brow and then pushing through his obsidian hair. He frowned, and then exhaled, and then frowned again, all the while watching the numbers rise, glancing at the couple in front of us, and then letting his eyes drift to me. His expression was pained—not just lustful or wanton, but pained, and yet . . . adoring, as though I were finally his, something he'd acquired after a lifetime of longing. These were the things I thought I saw, they were what occupied my thoughts during the fateful elevator ride. With him, it didn't take much; it was easy, it was right, it was as it should be.

He wasted not a moment, but pulled me to him once we were alone again. Voracious lips locked on mine as his hand found the hem of my dress. Stiff leather crackled audibly in the silence of the elevator, diminished only by the treasonous moan that escaped my lips when his rough hand moved against the soft skin of my inner thigh. Suddenly he was moving me backward out of the elevator, and somewhere in the distance, bells chimed or keys jingled.

Inside the apartment, he shut the door and leaned his forehead against it for a weighty moment. He didn't bother with the lights, just turned to me in the dark. I was sobered by his stare, and the gravity of the situation began to set in. After this, there would be no turning back.

I stepped back, just enough for him to notice. "I can't do this," I said, but my voice wavered. "I don't know how to do this." I could barely form the sentence, due to an all-consuming desire. "David." In that one word, I pleaded with him to have the strength I couldn't.

He wet his lips and paced toward me, forcing me back into the wall like a scared kitten. His hands brushed over my arms, and the jacket fell in a heap on the floor. He outstretched his arms against the wall, trapping my body with his. I'd been pinned to the wall not long before, and I'd been terrified. This time was different. This time, there was nowhere else I wanted to be. Still, I ignored my body's impulse to submit.

Carefully, he reached down and encircled my wrists with each of his hands. He pulled me forward and quickly folded them behind my back, stilling my body with his.

"I have to leave," I said.

"So leave."

My hands strained in his strong grip as I thrashed against his hard body. I realized that this time, instead of walking away, he intended to fight against me, to fight for me.

My chin quivered, and I shook my head, lightly at first and then harder. His head was pulled back so his mouth hovered above mine. I focused on the door across the room. "Olivia," he whispered thickly into my ear, the hairs of his cheek tickling mine. Nothing rivaled hearing my name on his lips. I yearned for the burn of his face on mine. I wanted this, I couldn't deny, but I also knew that it was irreversible.

I kept my head turned toward the door, knowing that one look into his eyes would be my undoing.

Shifting my wrists firmly into one hand, he reached up with the other and slowly dug his fingers into my hair. My breathing shallowed as he slid each bobby pin from its designated place. He dropped them, each one chiming as it hit the floor. My hair fell plentifully around me, and he tucked a handful behind my ear. He gripped my chin, turning me to him. With the gentleness of a saint, he kissed my wound.

I gasped as he pushed his pelvis against me. He leaned in, our mouths all hot air and desire, but was careful not to let our lips touch. I squirmed, but he waited, patiently asking me to make my final decision.

I twisted my hands and he released them, standing back slightly so that we were no longer touching. I lifted my palm and flattened it tenderly against his heart, feeling the buttons through his sweater.

I closed my eyes for a short moment. "I'm sorry," I whispered. Agony crossed his face before I balled the fabric in my fist and pulled him to me, slowly raising my mouth to his. For the one precise second that we contacted, we sighed into each other, and then his hands were under my thighs, lifting me effortlessly so my legs wrapped around him.

He kissed me hard as we moved, and I furiously undid his tie before being thrown on the bed. Our mouths reconnected as I landed into fluffy down, and my shoe hit the floor with a loud thud. We ground into each other until he sat back to pull off his shirt. I took in, for the first time, the perfectly formed muscles that pushed and pulled with every movement. He was lean and muscular, hard but graceful.

Those muscled arms imprisoned me against the mattress allowing me to run shaking hands along a coarse, marble chest. I leaned up into his earthiness, inhaling a heady pine scent a second before he reattached his mouth to mine. Greedily, my hands ran over his warm, naked skin, relishing the firm muscles that detained me.

He pulled the dress up my hips and disconnected from me. With a quick glance down, he groaned at the white lace panties glowing against my skin. His fingertips hooked under the elastic, and I sucked in a breath. They dragged along the waistband, sending me into soft convulsions. His hand reached beneath the lace to find me slick with longing.

He kissed me again. I bit his lip softly when he slid a finger along me. Clumsily, I pulled at his belt buckle until it gave. Metal struck the floor when I threw it, ringing through the room.

"You think since the moment I laid eyes on you," he said hoarsely between kisses, taunting me with his finger, "that I haven't wondered," he paused, rubbing me harder, "what it would feel like to be inside you?"

His words cut to my core. Scorching eyes fixed on me as he stood and speedily unbuttoned his pants, stepping out of his clothing in one graceful movement. His erection was big, impossibly big, and the thought of taking all of him inside me sent a ripple of heat up my aching body to my face.

He impatiently pulled at his socks and left me panting before returning barefoot with a condom.

Disappointment flooded me. "I'm on birth control."

"Trust me, there's nothing I want more . . ." He leaned over the bed and planted a kiss on my pout. "But we have to be extra careful."

I nodded, waiting with my hair fanned out beneath me, lustily watching him affix the condom.

He took my arms and tugged me to him. Reaching back to unzip the length of my dress, he drew a sharp breath. "No bra," he said, lifting it over my head. I sat before him with drawn knees, hugging my arms to me. He unfolded them, drinking in my naked body. "You're incredible."

His fingers crooked into the elastic of my panties again. I lifted up as he dragged them over my bent knees and down to my ankles, where they fell to the floor.

He climbed over me, guiding my back onto the mattress. His tongue ravaged my mouth, and I pushed back, letting my teeth nip at his bottom lip. He covered my quivering body as he slid his arms underneath, pinning me to him. His hips moved against me, and his kiss matched their hastening pace. I became even wetter under his control—he was so maddeningly rigid against the inside of my thigh, rubbing his length up me, sliding along my opening before hitting my clit. I thrust upward when I could no longer take it, opening my legs wider, steepling them for him.

"David," I exhaled. "Please, David. I can't . . . I can't take it."

He eagerly spread my legs further apart with his, baring me to him. He reached between us and deftly inserted the tip of himself into me.

"Olivia," he growled, looking to the ceiling in pleasure. "You're so wet. So ready."

"Please." My voice was high-pitched, impatient to fill the endless ache.

He moved onto his elbows. A small sound escaped me as he eased all the way inside. I breathed in sharply as he exhaled. I clenched the sheets in unforgiving fists. My walls molded around him, and he felt like heaven inside me. It was what I'd been missing all this time.

I didn't know how my face looked in that moment of pure bliss, but he whispered, "Are you okay?" We remained that way, momentarily immobilized by the sensation, until I managed a quick nod.

His breath quickened as he sought my mouth, kissing me as though it were the last thing he would ever do; it was needy, tender, and fast all at once.

He pulled out almost entirely and drove inside of me with a guttural groan. I gripped his arms and had only a second to wrap my legs around him before he thrust again, wrapping me up into his rhythm. His pace accelerated quickly, giving me exactly what I wanted and more than I knew I needed. Within seconds he was mercilessly driving into me over and over, *yes yes yes*, he moaned as though he were reading my thoughts. He reached for my hair and yanked it, bowing my head to allow him access to my mouth as we fucked.

Our bodies moved greedily after months of built-up tension. I cried out brokenly, warmth building within me. My orgasm mounted swiftly and without mercy, pulling me into a world I'd never been.

He kissed that perfectly sensitive spot behind my ear, and I licked and sucked the wet saltiness of his neck. He whisked my forearms above my head in an iron grip, pushing them into the mattress. Our fingers intertwined, squeezing together as the thrusts came more and more frantically.

"Oh, God. You are so beautiful," he rasped. "Open up for me, baby."

Thoughts of opening and closing, inadequacy and flaws began to rush over me. Here I was, underneath the most beautiful man in the world, and I was certain he was the answer to questions I'd stopped asking long ago. Could I do this for David? Warmth receded as I gave into the anxiety, knowing that I was too flawed, even for him.

I heard my name and opened my eyes, not realizing I'd been squeezing them shut. "Come back," he said, never breaking our rhythm. "Come on, Olivia. Look at me." I met his eyes as he moved into me, slightly slower but with more force. The change in momentum had me gasping for air and the heat rekindled, drawing me into him. "Olivia," he moaned with such intense need that I moaned back at him. My legs pulled him closer, urging him deeper.

"That's it," he said, picking up his pace again and never losing eye contact. "Oh, God. That's it."

"David," I cried suddenly. My bloodless fingertips tingled in his grasp; my thighs shook with the force of an impending explosion. He kissed me with the same force, giving me the push I needed to surrender.

"Let go, baby," he uttered against my lips. Holding onto the edge, I instinctually constricted myself around him. "Fuck, Olivia," he shouted, and I lost control.

My entire body seared with fire and the world went white around me. I gave myself over to the first blissful wave of pleasure that ripped through me as he called my name over and over, coming fast and hard with me.

~

I didn't know how long we'd lain there. When I fell back to earth, I found our breathing had synced. As our fingers were still linked, he was still inside of me, securing his collapsed weight to me.

Just as I began to doze, he drew back and smoothed his hands over my hairline, brushing the strands from my face. He kissed the place the hair had been, then my cheek and my neck, lingering with each contact. "I have never," he whispered into my neck, "*never* come that fast. You drive me wild."

Gently, he reached down to pull out of me. He threw the condom on the ground and sat back on his knees. The world slowed when I sat up to face him. A heavy pit formed in my stomach as we watched one another, and the scope of what had happened hit me.

I looked down at my naked body, examining my adulterous hands. My face contorted as tears threatened.

I shook my head and covered my face, trying desperately to hide from him what was coming. "No," I whispered into myself.

"Olivia," David's voice begged. I lifted myself from the bed, wanting only to run away, but fell to the ground as my shaky legs buckled beneath me.

"No," I wailed. "What have I done?" My entire body shuddered with sobs as I curled myself over my knees. Tears spilled from my hands and disappeared on the floor. The coarse wood dug into my skin; it gave when David stepped down to grasp my folded hips with his immense hands. He lifted me up and turned me to him, hugging me tightly as I shook.

"I'm here," he whispered feverishly. "Let me in, let me help."

"You can't." Despair squeezed my chest, making its way up to my throat. "I don't know what you think you see in me, but I'm not that."

He placed his hands on both sides of my head and guided it back gently, clearing the hair from my tear-streaked face. "I see a girl who wants to let go."

His words struck something buried deep inside, and I shook my head harder, stepping back without breaking eye contact. "I'm not that. I don't want that," I said, pressing my palm forcefully against my chest. "I'm black inside, David. You don't understand. There's nothing there to give, I'm too fucked up. And you, oh, God. You're so *beautiful*." The confession knocked the breath from me as the words pulsated through my body. I trembled under his loosened grip. He was drawing out my closely guarded secrets, charming them from me like poisonous snakes.

David looked equally horrified. I didn't know what to see in the way he looked at me. I only knew that I had finally managed to drive him away, but not soon enough.

The damage was already done.

CHAPTER 26

I EXPECTED DAVID TO RELEASE ME, to make some excuse about having to work early while gathering my things and ushering me back into the night. Instead he grabbed me to him and kissed me with a heated fury. He lifted me off the ground to his level and held the nape of my neck with his free arm. He grew hard as stone between my legs, prompting me to wrap all of my limbs around him. His fingers dug into my back, and I cried into his mouth as the pain gave way to pleasure. He charged me against the cold plaster, knocking against the nightstand and overturning a lamp.

"I need you," he said through gritted teeth, adjusting my weight with his hips. I released him and flattened my palms and upper back against the wall. He stepped back with my legs still clinging to him and reached under my buttocks with one arm. Holding me steady, he used his free hand to sink himself into me without checking to see if I was ready. I was wetter than water, but I gasped with surprise from the unanticipated feel of his unsheathed cock inside me.

Immediately he was pumping his hips against me, propelling me up and down the wall as he thrust into me with urgency. He leaned over my hips to catch my lips in a furious kiss. "You feel so good," he panted. "Fuck. You're amazing."

He drew me to him and wrapped his arms underneath mine, taking a shoulder in each hand. We straightened against the wall as he pushed me deeper onto him until my ass connected with his scrotum. I vainly grasped at his slick back, trying to hold on as he continued to buck.

My insides tightened deliciously with each naked plunge, bringing me quickly to the edge. I threw my head against the wall, wincing in pain as it hit directly on my bump.

"Shit," he said, backing us away from the wall.

"It's fine, don't stop." I wrapped my arms around him and buried my face into his neck as he rounded the bed. He bent over suddenly, cradling my back so I wouldn't fall, and I gasped with new awareness of his depth. With a light laugh, he drew back to kiss me quickly on the lips. He stuck a packet in his mouth and tore it swiftly, producing a condom.

Still dangling from his body, I gave him an exaggerated pout. He looked me evenly in the eyes and pulsed into me once with a groan. My lips split as I drew a sharp breath.

He leaned over and pecked me again. "I can't wait to come inside of you," he said, kissing the underside of my jaw, "one day, when you're mine."

I nearly lost my grip at his words. I was so aroused, I feared I might faint from the sheer extent of my need.

He withdrew from me and set me on my feet to roll on the condom.

His gaze swept over me in the moonlight, and he licked his lips as I wrung my hands. "Clasp your hands behind your back. Like that." He shook his head, sending a rapid blush up my exposed body. "God, you're even better than I imagined. And I imagined a lot."

I had imagined too. I took in his towering frame and broad, solid torso. Dark curls started at his chest and thinned into a delicious trail. His stomach was flat with a hint of a six-pack, and the muscles in his arms were perfectly formed, just as I'd fantasized. His massive erection seemed implacable, and my mouth moistened just looking at it. I tucked my hair behind my ear as I let him examine me back.

He turned me around, and I yelped as he smacked me on the ass. "On the bed."

I climbed up and sat facing him, running one foot down my other leg. When he didn't make a move, I bit my lip and whimpered, nearly crazed with aching.

He exhaled a short, forceful breath and took a large stride toward me. "Christ," was all he said as he took an ankle in each hand. In one movement, he had spread my legs and yanked me to him so I fell back on the comforter. I shut my eyes and groaned when I felt his lips on the inside of my ankle, making their way up my knee to my inner thigh. His mouth jumped to my stomach, brushing my scar, and my ab muscles clenched fiercely. *No, no, no. Stay with him.*

He moaned and released my legs. He pressed his chest to my stomach and took my breasts in his hands, running his thumbs under my nipples. I pushed my hips into his torso, desperate to feel him again. His mouth encircled one nipple and then the other; I bowed into the bliss of his tongue, softly crying out as I grasped handfuls of his soft hair. He let me pull him up for a hard kiss. He shoved a finger into me and massaged, feeling me from inside.

I writhed beneath him as he added another finger, bringing me back to the edge. I arched into his body, fighting off the urge to come from his fingers. I needed to feel him again, to watch him grunting as he hammered me.

"Come for me," he rasped against my neck.

"No." I grabbed his solid ass in both my hands, urging his hips toward me. "I need you inside me."

"So fucking stubborn." He stood upright again, pulling my hips to the edge in one motion. His fingers spread my swollen lips for the head of his cock. He shackled my ankles in a steadfast grip and slowly swirled his hips twice. "Beg for me."

"Please," I said. "Fuck me, David."

He plunged into me and released my legs. His shoulders leaned on my feet as he deepened his range. He gripped my hips, nailing me into the mattress so fast that I had to grab the sheets.

"Look at me, Olivia."

My ears roared as I squeezed my eyes shut, trying to prolong the impending orgasm.

"I'm going to come any second," he said. I felt his hand grab my jaw as he demanded, "Look at me."

I broke myself from the darkness and opened my eyes for him. Wildfire tore through my body, throwing me into a violent orgasm that had me coming twice as hard and long as before. He continued to pound me through the climax, never losing eye contact. He seized my waist as my spent body threatened to slide up the bed with each thrust. With gritted teeth and a punishing final thrust, he came feverishly, holding on to me until every drop had left his body. It was the most erotic thing I'd ever seen.

~

Sinewy arms propped David over me as his chest heaved. I ran a hand through my sweat-soaked hair and over my undulating breasts, trying to catch my own breath. I jumped when he brushed my clit to pull out of me and throw the condom next to the other one. I hooked my legs onto the edge of the bed, where I was still dangerously close to slithering off.

"You're going to fall," he observed, looking me up and down.

"I can't move," I replied between heavy breaths. He reached over and pulled me into a sitting position. A hand swept under my knees, and suddenly I was in his arms. He carried me to the bathroom and let me down at the toilet.

"What?" I asked.

"You should always pee after sex. Go."

I sat down, more out of exhaustion than compliance. "A little privacy?"

"Just go."

I crinkled my nose at him. "David."

"Fine." He turned his back.

"Really?"

"I just fucked the shit out of you. Who cares?"

I hadn't had to pee before, but now that I was in position, I couldn't hold it any longer. It was oddly intimate even though I'd peed in front of Bill countless times. And I had the advantage of admiring David's toned ass as he waited, obviously magnificent, even in the dark.

"Aren't I heavy?" I asked when he was carrying me back. He laughed heartily. My arms tightened around his neck when he tossed me in the air a little and caught me.

"No, honeybee. You are not. You think I could've fucked you that long standing up if you were?"

"The wall did most of the work," I pointed out, as he held me over the bed.

"Is that what you think?" he asked, nipping my unharmed cheek with his teeth. "Should we try it again and see?"

My eyes widened, and I bit back a giggle. "Can you?"

"I could have you 'til the sun comes up, but you need to rest. We both do." He dropped me then, and I let the giggle out as I hit the springs. "First, I have to pee though."

"What, I don't get to watch?"

"You can if you want," he said.

But my lids were heavy, and my legs were leaden and *did he call me honeybee again?* and the sheets must have been a thread count somewhere in the thousands because they were *oh, so . . . .*

I was disoriented when I felt the mattress give underneath me. Suddenly David was climbing in next to me. I reached across the valley between us to touch him and said, "I'm cold."

"Come here." He pulled me to him, and I complied, fitting myself against a body I wasn't used to. I rested my bent arm on his torso and lay my face on his shoulder.

"How do you feel?" he asked into my hair.

I sighed. "Sore."

"Good. I want you remembering this all weekend."

"Can I tell you something?" I asked.

He rolled onto me and looked me straight in the eyes while his chin rested on my chest. His body seemed miles long with him below me, his legs likely hanging off the edge. "I've been waiting for that question for weeks. Please, tell me something that I don't have to beat out of you."

I swatted his shoulder and snickered. I cleared my throat, feeling suddenly on the spot. "It—that was . . ." I curled my arm up to touch my earlobe, but he caught it without even a glance and kissed the inside of my wrist. I held my palm out instead. "That was my first orgasm with anyone. Well, first and second," I added, looking up at the ceiling.

"What?" His tone conveyed his shock. "You can't be serious." He moved off me and sat back on his calves.

"It's true. Does that freak you out?" I asked. My hand fell back on the bed, and I shivered, suddenly cold.

"Sorry," he mumbled, snuggling back between my legs and tucking my arms underneath him. A huge smile crossed his face, that broke only long enough for him to kiss me quickly on the lips. "No," he said emphatically. "I just can't believe it. How?"

I faltered, wondering if it was possible to explain. "I've orgasmed on my own obviously, just never with a partner. I always thought Bill and I would get there, but he stopped trying after a while. Not that I blame him. The harder he worked, the less turned on I became. I let him watch me, but I could never get into it." I was quiet. "So I might be on another planet right now." He kissed the base of my neck more times than I could count. "I guess it helps that it's been building for two months."

He stopped. "Oh, yeah? Then how do you explain the second one?"

I gave him a shy smile and his face turned serious.

"You have no idea what that means to me," he said, placing another kiss in the hollow of my neck.

"It means you're an experienced lover," I kidded, even though I knew it wasn't the reason. I had blossomed for him. Beneath him, clasped to him, we were in our own world, and I felt safe.

"No." He sighed, exhaling against my neck. "It's different." His voice was so soft, that I had to strain to hear. *Is it different for you too, David?* I wanted to ask, but I just enjoyed the feeling of his lips, his breath, him, on my body. He lifted his head to give me a mischievous look. He moaned, grinding his hips against me softly, alerting me that he was hard again. "That might be the sexiest thing I've ever heard. Even better then banging a virgin."

"David," I squealed.

He laughed, and it was such a playfully uncharacteristic comment that I couldn't help but join him.

"I mean it. You're gorgeous. If you were my girl, I'd have you coming every chance I got."

My laugh melted, and my mouth watered at his words.

He slid down my body and nuzzled my breasts, sighing into them and scraping his facial hair against my skin. "Did I tell you you're incredible?"

"I'm thoroughly worked over, is what I am."

"You know, when I looked into your eyes at the theater, I was stunned. Nothing like that has ever happened to me. And when I saw you in that gold dress, at the restaurant, I knew you were the most beautiful thing I had ever seen. You were glowing. But right now, in my bed, naked and undone . . ." He leaned forward to kiss me softly on the lips. "You are perfect. I never want you any other way."

I ran my hand over his cheek and through his hair. It hurt me that I couldn't respond the way I wanted, so I just touched, memorizing him with my fingers.

His gigantic hands splayed over my ribcage. "So smooth," he commented, moving his fingers over my skin. *Everything is smooth in the dark.*

My body jolted when his index finger ran over my scar. "Except for this. What is it?" he asked.

I gulped and squeezed my eyes shut, thankful for the night to hide whatever nuances might give me away. *Why is he asking me this? Who cares what it is?* I balled the sheets in my fist and willed that he would leave it alone.

Instead, he leaned closer and examined it. "What's it from?"

"Wasn't that enough for one night?" I asked, half-joking. His silence was response enough. I sighed and pushed his hand away. "It's ugly, and I don't like talking about it. Let's not."

"What happened?"

"I don't want to lie to you. So please don't make me."

He laughed softly and buried his nose in my chest, placing a feather light kiss between my breasts. "Don't lie. I'm not easily scared." Suddenly his body against mine began to feel heavy, and his breath on my skin was grating, as though it hit a nerve with every exhale. I must have moved, because he said, "Stop. Don't pull away. Tell me what happened."

I was quiet for a moment, debating. "My mother accidentally stabbed me when I was a teenager." It felt ridiculous to say out loud. I hadn't had to since that night at the hospital. *All that blood.* "My parents fought a lot the year leading up to their divorce, but it had never become violent until she pulled a knife one night. I don't think she meant to do anything with it, but I jumped in the middle and, well, you can guess the rest."

With the words out of my mouth, I no longer felt cornered, and his body began to feel less like a trap and more like a shield. I glided a hand over his smooth upper back. I'd said it aloud, and the world hadn't come crashing down.

"What's the rest?"

Again with the questions. "You ask a lot of questions," I said. I moved my hand to his hair, letting the silky strands sprout from between my fingers. "Why, are you going to rescue me from my past, David?"

I pulled lightly on his arms, and he snaked back up to my face, settling on top of me. He pecked me on the lips softly, lingered there a moment, and then kissed me again. Slowly, he caressed my tongue with his while running his hand along my jawline.

"You're hard," I whispered into his mouth. He nodded without separating from me. He weighed heavy on me and I took it, wanting nothing more than to stay securely underneath him as long as he would let me.

When the kiss grew more urgent, he tore away from me. "You're distracting me. What's the rest?"

"Hmm?" I asked sleepily. I opened my eyes, wondering if I could convince him to keep kissing me. "The rest? Hospital. Blood. Screaming." I closed my eyes again. "Really, that's all the detail I care to remember. I hate hospitals. Blood scares me blind."

"Does it hurt?"

I puckered my lips and cocked an eyebrow at him. "No, of course not."

"You flinch when I touch it."

"A reflex, I guess. I can't control it." The room quieted, the only sound a pair of mirrored breaths.

"To protect you from your own mother," he said finally. "I don't know anyone who could do that."

"It was a long time ago. It never happened again. My dad left her the next day, and I went with him."

"Your dad sounds like a smart man."

"He is," I agreed. "But she never got over it. She thinks we abandoned her."

"What is it?" he asked gently, noticing my change in cadence.

"It's weird to talk about. I haven't in so long. I guess since it happened."

"How? What about . . . ?" He hesitated. "What about Bill?"

I looked down at him. "*Now* you can say his name?" I let out a laugh, which promptly turned into a yawn. "No, you're right. I forgot. Of course I told Bill."

How could I tell him that that wasn't true without scaring him? That Bill had never asked? That I'd just told him one of the most personal things about myself—something I hadn't even shared with my husband?

CHAPTER 27

WHEN I AWOKE, I felt the puffiness of my eyes, the unfamiliarity of the silky sheets under my skin, the raw stickiness between my legs. Hard, strong arms clutched me from behind, locking me to a strange body. Guilt flowered within as I remembered, but my muscles clenched at the memory. Before I could fully recall, David stirred behind me. His hand lifted my hair, and he touched his lips to the curve of my neck, causing my eyes to flutter shut and a moan to escape.

"Perfect," he whispered into my skin.

My body tensed instantly, and my eyes flew open. In the cruel sunlight, the darkness had lifted and all that lay there was the truth.

"Oh," was all I could say as I lifted my body onto weak arms, carefully avoiding his stare. My eyes stung with lack of sleep, but my weariness was only physical. I looked at my watch, wondering how anything on my body could have survived the night before. Six o'clock. The shame weighed on me so heavily, that it'd woken me up, not allowing me to forget for more than a few hours.

"I have to leave." It came out coarser than I'd intended, but all I could think was that my husband would be flying back later. That, and the fact that I didn't know how I'd be able to leave David in that moment.

I let myself look at him then. The white sheets were pulled up to his muscled stomach, and his head rested back against his arm as he watched me. Matted hair fell over my shoulder, and I imagined that mascara had smeared around my eyes. He looked perfectly unaffected meanwhile.

"Stay," he said, no pleading, just flat. I knew that if I allowed myself, my worries, my fears, my inhibitions would melt away under his gaze. I would melt away.

But I no longer felt adventurous or sexy. I just felt wrong. A dull pain began to throb behind my eyes as I looked for something to cover myself up. I heard David get up and when I turned, he had put his underwear on. His muscular body, now that I could see it in the daylight, was robust and ridged, and it took every shred of my willpower not to drag him back into the bed. He gathered up his side of the sheet and offered it to me.

Wrapping myself in it, I stood. We stared at each other from across the bed. I might've expected that the electricity between us would diminish, but it didn't; if anything, it intensified as my body recalled the night before. I longed to submit myself to him again, to feel the weight of him on top of me. I knew without words that he felt the same—by the way he looked at me, and by his twitching but restrained erection.

"Bathroom," I said, shifting on my feet. He nodded. I quickly glanced around a bedroom that was all sunlight and whiteness, except for a wall of grey-shaded stone behind the bed. In the bathroom, I shut the door behind me. It was just as beautiful and immaculate as the bedroom, with a rock and glass shower that overlooked the water.

I sat on the toilet and ran my hands over my face. I'd actually gone through with it. I'd betrayed, deceived, lied. And with someone like David, who was no stranger to casual sex. I wondered if he normally let women spend the night. I pushed the heels of my hands into my eyes until I saw white. It didn't matter; he'd gotten what he wanted. And hadn't I? It was a moment I'd furtively fantasized about, yet my daydreams were nothing compared to the reality. The reality of his skin on mine, his length stretching and filling me. The reality of him working my body as if he owned it.

I shook my head hard. No. I'd done so much more than acted out a fantasy. I had a husband, and a family, and a life to answer to. What had I done? Something profoundly wrong. Something bigger than myself. Something that could never been undone.

I stole a quick glance at my reflection as I washed my hands. I was right about my smeared makeup, red eyes, and tangled hair. The bruise on my face was ripe, but it didn't shock me anymore. Did I look different? How did adulterers look? Would a scarlet "A" appear, branded into my skin somewhere?

I wet my thumb and wiped the smudges from under my eyes. I raked a hand through my hair, starting at the roots. I *needed* a brush. My hair was the only thing within my control at the moment. My fingers stuck on several tangles, and I bit my lip to keep my crying out; underneath, a slight wave had developed from my sweat.

When I opened the door, David was waiting on the edge of the bed in those disarming sweatpants. I leaned against the doorway.

"I liked the bedhead," he said, jutting his chin at me.

I shook my head. "Left to its own devices, my hair would put me in an early grave. It does not know how to cooperate."

"Well, I like you that way. Disheveled."

"David. Last night was . . ." I let the sentence hang, wrapping the sheet tighter under my arms.

"It was," he said, his head bobbing slowly. "I meant what I said."

"About my hair?" I joked.

"No."

"Then what exactly?"

"Everything. That I want you in my life. That I have feelings for you. That you're incredible." A lascivious smile formed on his lips, the perfect partner to his tousled, inky hair. "I want more."

My mind raced. Our connection only intensified once we'd given into it. For the first time, a question I'd been battling broke through: *does he actually care for me?*

"And I meant what I said. I'm not good for you. I'm, I don't know . . . broken, and—and married. Trust me when I tell you, there is no other way."

He closed his eyes for a moment and then whipped them open. "You're broken?" he asked with a look of disgust. "And you have nothing to give? How the fuck can you say that to me after last night?"

"I understand. Being with you last night was . . ." My voice hitched as I tried to find the words. "A release, and I don't just mean sexually. But that doesn't change the fact that I belong to someone else."

He stood from the bed.

"Don't." I held up my hands, stepping back instinctively. His eyes narrowed into a closed face, and because of it, my heart tightened. He took a measured pace. "This isn't how this goes," I explained. "It can't happen again."

"Olivia." It was a command; he must have known what it did to me. He reached for me confidently, gone was his moment of hesitation. He gathered me in his arms and kissed my wounded cheek, my neck, my shoulder. I cherished the feel of his lips on my skin, knowing it would be the last time. With that, I began to weep silently in his arms. This time I cried for what I was losing, not from guilt or regret. He held me closer and let me cry into his chest, his large hands caressing my back as the sheet fell to my hips. My nipples tightened against him, and I felt his equal desire hard against my stomach.

"Shh," he whispered in my ear. He bent and kissed me fully on the lips, pressing my wet face against his and sharing the tears. The slow and sensual tempo of his kiss turned urgent and deep. His hand slid down my back and under the sheet, massaging my ass and inspiring the fervor again. My legs quivered instinctively.

I'd been with boys before; I'd been with boys I'd thought were men. But this was different. David kissed like a man. He tasted, he smelled, and he fucked like a man. It would take all the strength I had and then some.

I understood now that I was the one who would have to be strong for everyone—for David, for Bill, for myself. It had been unfair to ask him to be. It was all on my shoulders.

"No," I said resolutely and pulled away, drawing the sheet over my shoulders, hiding in it. I felt so small, looking up at him from under wet lashes.

"Olivia." His tone was softer, and I could see the struggle within him. "I've waited . . . it's not—I don't want to lose you." He ran a hand through his hair.

I stared at him. "We have to forget about this," I said. "We barely even know each other."

"You keep saying that, but I know it's not how you feel." He waited, his brown eyes searching mine. It was true, but it was an argument I couldn't afford to lose, so I didn't say anything.

After a few moments of silence, he looked at me calmly and asked, "Is this really what you want?"

I looked back, urging myself to speak, urging myself to put an end to it once and for all. Just one word. His expression changed as he waited, and I recoiled into my sheet. "Is this really what you want?" he intoned with increasing volume.

I nodded, and he grasped my blanketed arms forcefully. "Tell me, then. Tell me you want this."

I opened my mouth but the words failed me.

He shook me once, pressing his fingers into me. "Look me in the eye and tell me you can forget," he said. "If you can tell me that, I promise—we're through."

My knees and my resolve began to buckle. I reached deep inside for a modicum of strength. Any woman would be lucky to have this man standing in front of her, asking her to stay. Any woman would be horrified to know that I might be willing to give up my life for someone I'd met only months before.

I squared my shoulders, still firm under his grip, and looked him in the eye. "I-I . . ."

"I can't hear you," he said, backing me into the doorjamb.

"You're hurting me," I said.

"Say it, Olivia," he said. "Say it."

"Yes," I yelled. This is what I want! It's over."

He released me, and I hastily grabbed my belongings from the floor, running out of the bedroom. He didn't come after me this time, and I was grateful. I didn't think I could ever look into those eyes again without remembering the look I'd just seen. I ran into the foyer, hit the 'Down' button, and, dropping the sheet, dressed speedily as the elevator ascended.

Once inside, I bit my lip to hold back the tears. I tried, in desperation, to push David's expression from my mind. The doors parted to the regal, eerily quiet lobby that echoed with the click of my heels as I raced through.

I sensed eyes on me, but I fixed my gaze on the revolving door ahead as though it would get me there faster. When I pushed through to the other side, I was forced to shield my eyes from an unrelenting sun. Stumbling down the block, I stopped to lean my back against a cool, scratchy brick wall to catch my breath. It was then that I sank down to the ground, put my head in my hands, and sobbed.

AVAILABLE IN PAPERBACK
FROM AMAZON.COM

Come Alive

THE CITYSCAPE SERIES: BOOK TWO

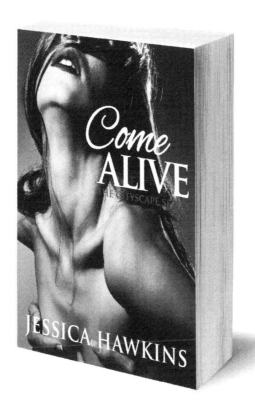

CHAPTER 1

I BLINKED MY EYES OPEN and quickly squeezed them shut again. Knowing I'd been caught, I fluttered my eyelids as though I hadn't been about to feign sleep. My husband stood over me, watching, but I focused on the nightstand to avoid his stare.

"It's nine," he said gently. "Better get a move on."

I rolled over and faced the wall with a small sigh, unable to handle his soft expression. "I'm not going."

"Liv," he started.

"I have to work today."

"Work?"

"Things are crazy at the office."

"It's the weekend, and I told you about this birthday party last month. Can't it wait 'til Monday?"

"No. I'm under deadline."

"I'm sure you could spare a Saturday afternoon," he said wryly.

"Call Serena if you don't believe me."

"Of course I believe you," he said, taken aback. "But you're working too much. You need to take some time off, babe. It's been over three months of this."

I gulped. *Has it only been three months?*

When he continued, his tone was tentative, hedging. "I know it's been hard, but this isn't what Davena would have wanted. She would want you to move on."

I almost laughed out loud, but I didn't. I never did. The mattress dipped when he sat. Hesitant fingertips touched my shoulder, and my skin pebbled. I couldn't remember when he'd last touched me. When he'd stopped even trying. His caress was strange; unexpected but not unwanted. It triggered a wave of guilt that left my heart pounding. Because of what I knew. Because of what I'd done. Because, after three months, I still burned with desire. But it wasn't for him.

I braced myself as David's image appeared. I wished I wouldn't think of him every morning and dream of him at night. I wished his memory would fade, the way he had from my life. *Three months.* Three months since I had stormed from his apartment, since *that night.* My insides flurried as I remembered, the details still fresh in my mind despite the time that had passed. Despite the fact that every time they surfaced, I dashed them away immediately.

"Well, I have to go to the party." Bill's voice cut into my thoughts. "You know how my sister can hold a grudge."

"Of course you do, sweetie." The endearment was forced, unnatural, but Bill wouldn't notice. "I wrapped Jimmy's video game last night; it's on the kitchen counter."

"Thanks. I'll bring you back a piece of birthday cake." When I didn't respond, he stood and left the room. Soon after, I heard the front door slam. I exhaled a long breath.

Hours were slow; stretched and elongated like a rubber band that never snapped. On the better days, I woke up numb. *Today is not one of those days*, I thought as I dragged myself from the bed.

Dressed in an outfit much too crisp and binding for the weekend, I meticulously applied my makeup. Every strand of my golden brown hair was combed into obedience. Inside, I had cracks, but I wouldn't let them break the surface.

I was on the train within the hour. Through the windows, I found comfort in the way everything blurred together. A child's squeal had me blinking from my trance. Across from me, a young man wrangled two toddlers as his wife cradled a baby on her lap. It was chaotic and messy, but she watched her husband with obvious love. The woman smiled goofily as he dodged apple juice spray. I looked away, fiddling with the clasp of my purse.

The morning after my night with David, I'd cried my eyes raw against the brick wall by his apartment. I hadn't known up from down, left from right, love from despair. But I'd locked it up so tightly I could still feel the chains digging into me with every movement. When Bill returned from his trip that day, I mustered the biggest, most convincing welcome I could manage. But I couldn't look him in the eye. And I couldn't pretend to want his hands on me. And though Bill was never one to pick up on my subtle cues, I had made it impossible for him not to.

Somehow, the week passed. After a late night at work, I walked into an apartment filled with twenty of our closest friends and family. I gritted my teeth and let them wish me a happy twenty-eighth birthday, barely making it through the night. Not even Lucy or Gretchen, my closest friends in the world, could scratch the surface. I could only put my energy into acting normal. I had scoffed to myself when I'd overheard Gretchen and Bill in the kitchen toward the end of the party.

"How's she doing?"

"I can't tell, Gretchen, and it freaks me out. She won't talk about Davena at all. She keeps to herself and pretends nothing is wrong."

"Well, Davena was like a second mother to her," Gretchen said. *"There are times in her life when she was closer to her than to her actual mom."*

"I think that's why she's taking Davena's death especially hard. She and her mom haven't been getting along."

"She doesn't look well."

"I haven't seen her eat in days. I'd feel better if she at least cried, but she does nothing except smile and laugh in the weirdest way."

"She was like this when her parents divorced. I tried to tell you. She's hurting. She doesn't deal well with loss."

"I don't know what to do."

"Have you tried talking to her?" Gretchen asked.

There was a pause. "She leaves the room when I do."

"It's still fresh. Just give her time, Bill."

After the last guest had left, we fought. I'd made some empty promise to come home early from work and unknowingly missed half the party. I asked him how he could have possibly thought a party was a good idea.

I started leaving for work early and coming home late every day. With my recent promotion, it wasn't hard to find projects at the magazine. Days turned into weeks, weeks into months. And not a day went by that I wasn't reminded of him. Of *that night*. And of the irreversible thing I'd done.

As the train barreled along, I tried not to remember. After all, the separation from David had been longer than the time I'd known him. Surely that was enough time to move on?

But it was impossible to forget. I fought myself as I always did when the memory threatened, but in that moment, alone on the crowded train, I wasn't strong enough to stop it. I remembered the pain in his hard brown eyes when he'd demanded that I speak up. That I tell him I wanted nothing more to do with him. I rewound through our final conversation, when he'd said he wanted me in his life. He wanted us to be together. I remembered how he felt pressed against me and how I'd wished he would take me again.

His hands on my hips had held me steady as he'd mercilessly driven me to orgasm . . . twice. It was unforgettable. Haunting. Relentless. Under his affection, under his touch, I'd come alive. And since then, I was slowly drowning; hounded by the memory I tried to repel and weighed down by the guilt.

-

I was alone in the *Chicago Metropolitan Magazine* office. Maybe it wasn't necessary for me to work on a Saturday, but the thought of sitting through a child's birthday party with Bill's family was daunting. I weaved through the empty cubicles until reaching the door to my office. *Olivia Germaine*, it read. *Senior Editor.*

I flopped into my big chair and rubbed my eyes tensely. On the days I wasn't numb, everything seemed sharper, more excruciating; shame, grief, desire. It was a constant battle to swallow the emotions that rose up my throat one after the other.

My fingers flew over the keyboard, but my mind was occupied with other things. I owed Bill more than I gave him. He'd been patient, and I knew he was becoming concerned. Whenever things turned intimate between us, I pulled away without an explanation. He attributed my distance to Davena's death, but there was more to it than that.

When my cell buzzed, I glanced at the screen and ignored the call. Within moments, my office phone began to ring. I sighed with defeat, knowing Gretchen wouldn't give up.

"What's wrong?" I asked when I picked up the receiver.

"Good afternoon to you too, Liv."

"Seriously, Gretchen. Is everything okay?"

"Yes," she said with feigned irritation. "I'm downstairs."

"What? Why?"

"Bill texted me that you were coming in today, so I thought I'd surprise you for lunch."

"You should have called first. I'm in the middle of something."

"So take a break, and pick it up later."

"Later I have other things to do."

"How? You work nonstop, and it's *Saturday* for God's sake. What could be so important? I haven't talked to you in weeks."

"My schedule has been full with this promotion. Beman has me under impossible deadlines. They need me."

7

"I know they do, but I need you too. We need you. Come on—lunch is on me."

"Fine," I said, exhaling forcefully.

There was a brief pause on the line as I saved the document on my computer. "Fine?" she repeated after a moment. "What the fuck is wrong with you? I made a special trip over here to take you to lunch."

"I didn't ask you to do that."

"No shit. I miss you," she said, her voice softening.

"Look, I said I'd come. Just give me a minute." I hung up before she could respond and locked up the office.

Downstairs, I felt mildly better after a deep breath of fresh air. She was waiting in a sleeveless tank top and denim cut-offs. Despite her casual outfit, her bright blonde hair was curled into perfect ringlets as usual. I tucked some hair behind my ear as I approached her.

"Aren't you hot?" she asked.

I pulled my sweater closer. "I only have an hour."

She rolled those big blue eyes of hers and pulled on my arm. "Then you'd better get talking."

"Talking?"

"Yes. It's time to have a conversation, and that's why I'm buying you lunch."

"What's the topic of this conversation? And don't say Davena, because that's all anyone ever wants to talk about."

"Because you won't," she whined. "You won't talk to Bill about it, you won't talk to us and you refuse to see a shrink. Forget about poor Mack." She waved her hand.

"He's beside himself, and you can't even pick up the phone."

My heart stopped along with my feet. "Who told you that?"

"Bill."

"Wow," I said. She continued walking, so I ran to catch up to her. "No wonder you sound exactly like him. Do you guys get together and talk about me? Have little powwows about how to get me to spill my guts? Well here's a tip: get a new hobby, because there's nothing to spill. I loved Davena, but I've made my peace with her passing. Life goes on, Gretchen."

She muttered something under her breath.

"What?" I challenged.

She sighed. "Liv, you can talk to me," she said in an atypically delicate voice.

I glanced down at the pavement as we walked, willing myself to stay calm. "Everything is fine. You don't need to worry."

"I do, though. You never talk about her, and you haven't seen Mack since the funeral. It's not healthy and . . . it shows." I pursed my lips and rewrapped the sweater as I crossed my arms. "Lucy needs you," she continued. "With the wedding next weekend, she has to know she can count on us."

"Of course she can," I said defensively. "I've been there every step of the way—did I not host the wedding shower, and have I not done everything she's asked?"

"Yes, you have, it's just obvious that your heart isn't in it. And it hurts her feelings."

9

"She said that?"

"She doesn't have to."

I swallowed. "Okay, I get it."

"Good. So let's start with how you felt when you heard the news. Maybe you can explain why you hid it from us that night. It's no wonder you got wasted and went home early. Nobody can keep something like that inside, not even you."

"No—what I meant was that I get it. I'll change. I'm not up for this random therapy session."

"You can't change without talking about it."

"Again, there is nothing to talk about," I intoned. "People grieve in different ways, so please just drop it. As far as the wedding, I get what you're saying. I will try harder. For Lucy."

Gretchen heaved a deep sigh and looked away as she bit her thumbnail. "You're a stubborn bitch," she muttered.

An unwilling smile found my face. "Where are you taking me anyway, Milwaukee?"

"Nope, we're going to a place with the largest, juiciest burgers around. You need some nourishment," she said, tugging at the hem of my sweater. I almost gagged at the thought of a hamburger, but I figured this was what choosing one's battles meant. My heart dropped, however, when we rounded the corner. I was standing in front of the restaurant where David had taken me to lunch months before.

"Hello?" she urged, holding the door open.

I fumbled for an excuse. It was Saturday, though, and David wouldn't be working nearby, so I followed her inside. I recognized the red-lipped hostess, despite the fact that she wasn't nearly as cheery as she had been when I was with David. I wondered if she was trying to place me, since she gave me a curious, narrow-eyed look. I scanned the restaurant furtively as she led us to an open, conspicuous table.

I ordered a burger, or rather, Gretchen ordered one for me, but I found it hard to stomach. After making a show of the first two bites, I nibbled on the side salad while Gretchen caught me up on the last two months of work at her public relations office.

"You've got to come with me next time," she was saying. "California in the summertime is the shit. I even took a couple surf lessons."

"Doesn't sound like work," I muttered.

"It's all about schmoozing, Liv, and—"

I froze. *Was that . . . ? No.* It came again from behind me, and I stiffened instinctively.

"David, my man!" the voice boomed.

My heart whipped into a violent pounding, filling my ears as blood rushed to my head. Gretchen looked at me with her head cocked. Her mouth moved, but I heard nothing.

With slow precision, I turned my head over my left shoulder and looked back. Two men I'd never seen before were pumping hands emphatically. Through my decelerating heartbeat, I heard one call the other 'David.' I shook my head quickly and returned my attention to

Gretchen. She was still talking about California, though now she was looking at my plate. To preempt another argument, I forced myself to take another bite. I chewed the patty methodically until it was mush in my mouth and swallowed because I thought she might notice if I spit it out.

"Well, that's an extra hour on the treadmill," she groaned to her empty plate and covered her tummy with her hand.

CHAPTER 2

DAVENA'S FUNERAL HAD BEEN like every funeral before it. I'd sat in the pew, staring forward as Bill clasped my hand in his. At some point I had looked over to find him in tears, but my hands were lifeless in my lap, and I didn't have the words, so I returned my eyes forward. My only moment of reality was when her husband, Mack, had hugged me. He'd squeezed the breath from my lungs, holding me too tightly. And when he'd let go, I felt nothing again.

She was predictably lovely in her open casket, with heavy makeup and untamed, sheared blonde hair. Cancer had not tainted her in life or in death. I wondered how she didn't even look vulnerable from that position; I wouldn't have been surprised if her eyes had popped open, and she'd invited me out for a cocktail at Sunda.

But she didn't. And eventually they eased the coffin closed and took her away. Back at their place, Mack did his best to turn the reception into a celebration of her life, but the pain in his eyes was searing. It was unavoidable, even when I looked away. We left early.

Although my belief in the afterlife was dubious, I sometimes prayed to Davena for relief. In my head, I confessed everything—that I was a sinner, an adulterer and a liar. That I only felt remorse for deceiving Bill, not for the crime itself. Sometimes I believed maybe she heard me. Sometimes I imagined she would make everything right.

"Did you look at the article yet?" Lisa, also known as my toxic co-worker, glared at me from the doorway of my office, arms crossed, lips drawn.

Her words rattled in my head a moment as I shifted back into reality. "Which one?"

She exhaled her annoyance. "The guide to Logan Square."

"It's on your desk already."

"Oh." She pivoted and stalked away, revealing Serena behind her.

"She's always super grouchy on Friday morning," Serena said with a warm smile. "And Monday. And Tuesday. Wednesday, too . . . . You get the idea."

"Where did your hair go?" I asked.

"I'm taking a cue from Hollywood and embracing the pixie cut. What do you think?"

"Cute," I remarked, turning back to my computer.

"So, boss lady, are you excited for this weekend?"

I blinked my attention back to her. Serena had taken to calling me 'boss' since her recent promotion from intern to assistant editor.

"The wedding?" she prompted uncertainly.

"Yes. Lucy has been planning her wedding for as long as I've known her, so it should be impressive."

"I love weddings, I mean they are just, so romantic, and everyone is just like, so happy to be there. And it's supposed to be a gorgeous weekend, I mean—"

"Serena, I'm really swamped here."

"Oh. Sorry. Actually, I have an idea I want to run by you."

"Shoot," I said while tapping out a quick e-mail.

"It's about the *Chicago's Most Eligible Bachelors and Bachelorettes* issue—"

"What?" I froze mid-keystroke.

"Well, um—I think we should do a follow-up piece on the website. I'm sure the people we featured like, went on dates and stuff. Maybe some even found relationships because of the article. We could even do, like, a teeny-tiny article in the mag next month."

I shook my head rapidly. "No, that won't work. Let's try and come up with some new concepts, not beat the crap out of old ones."

"Oh, okay, cool. I like that too."

She lingered a second longer and then scurried away. I hadn't meant to shut her down, but I couldn't risk a run-in with David Dylan: Bachelor Number Three. I didn't want him anywhere near me.

I had gotten lucky at the launch party for the *Most Eligible* issue two months earlier. Every bachelor and bachelorette had shown up to the event, the best in the magazine's history. Except for David Dylan. I'd overheard Lisa say that he accepted a job in New York and absolutely could not attend, even though she'd begged him. Knowing he was out of town was no more painful than knowing he wasn't right next to me. He was gone forever, and the physical distance wouldn't change that.

I couldn't ignore his presence at the party, though. Despite his non-attendance, his smiling photo, which far outshone the other attendees' pictures, was everywhere. Lisa had gleefully taken over David's segment for me, and the way she'd styled the photo shoot, it could have been an ad for any top menswear designer. He was all teeth and hard muscles in the three-piece suit Lucy had sold him. Clutching his jacket casually at his side, he was the definition of roguish businessman.

I'd given my boss the issue for final approval without ever proofing David's spread. The wounds were too fresh. Even now, I still hadn't had the heart, or the guts, to read about David Dylan: wealthy, charming and handsome Chicago bachelor. Every girl's dream catch.

I got up and locked my office door, allowing myself a minute to lie down on the couch. I was thankful for my weighty sweater to block the blasting A/C unit above.

I'd told David I was black inside, but I was wrong. I hadn't known it, but I was empty. And for one stolen moment, he had filled me with himself, physically and emotionally. *Now* I was black. Now I was poisoned. I was so reprehensible, that instead of the constant regret I should have felt, it only came in fleeting waves.

I recalled his hands in my hair, his breath on my skin, his mouth between my breasts . . . . *Just fucking stop*, I pleaded with myself. *I have to forget, please, I can't do this anymore.*

The reason I didn't feel was because I didn't want to, not because I couldn't. The scorching memory of our one night would destroy me if I let it. The guilt was already a steady drip through my system, seeping into the cracks of my interior.

The ringing of the office phone shredded through my thoughts. I pinched the bridge of my nose and sat upright. Work was the one thing in my life that never let me down, never judged or condemned me. I returned to my desk and hit the speakerphone button.

"What time is the bachelorette party tonight?" Bill's voice filled the office.

"Seven o'clock," I said, wiggling my mouse to wake up the computer. "When is Andrew's?"

"Same. Think you can get off a little early? I have a surprise for you."

"A surprise?" I repeated cautiously.

"Yeah, can you?"

"I don't know. I'm sort of backed up here." I rubbed my eyes and refocused on the screen.

"Please? I'm really excited."

"All right," I relented. "I can work through lunch."

"I'll pick you up downstairs at four, k? Love you."

~

I waited downstairs for Bill on a street-facing concrete bench, wondering what the surprise could possibly be. When the car arrived at the curb, I could hear Bon Jovi on full volume: that was a good sign.

"Hey," he said when I climbed in. "Ready for your surprise?"

"Yes." Because I had promised myself to try harder, I took his hand.

He squeezed it. "It's a bit of a drive, so sit back and relax."

As we discussed our impending parties, it became evident that we were leaving the city altogether. I recognized the point when we were entering Oak Park, but I still had no idea what his intentions were. It was when we turned onto a familiar street that I recognized my surroundings.

"Don't get any grand ideas," he warned.

Our search for the perfect home had been put on pause after Davena's death. Now we were on the block of the last house we'd seen over three months before. I recalled the afternoon with our realtor Jeanine—the awkwardness at her suggestion of a nursery and the ensuing argument where he'd tried to convince me that we were ready for children. That house had sold though, he'd told me bitterly back in June. Unless it had fallen through, and . . . *Oh, no. Don't let the surprise be a house. Would he go that far?*

He pulled up to the same spot we had parked with Jeanine months before.

"Bill—"

"No, no," he stopped me. "Just wait." We both climbed out of the car, and he turned around. "I've been working on this with Jeanine for a while." He wasn't looking at the house we'd visited last time, though. I followed his gaze to the eyesore of a house across the street from it.

It was still as ugly and unkempt as before. Ferns drooped heavily, blocking the front door. Grey stone crumbled in some spots. Paint under the windows peeled. But it had that same draw. The same endearing character that had appealed to me the first time I'd seen it.

"The owners are big shots in Hollywood," Bill explained, "who don't even care about the property. They told her they'd be willing to sell it for a good price because of the poor shape. Since they rarely get to Chicago, they granted her access to show it to us."

I looked from Bill to the house. He had remembered my comments that day. To my surprise, I smiled. "Wow. Honey, this is so thoughtful."

"It would be a lot of effort, and we'd probably have to stay in the apartment another year or so, but . . . I just can't stand to see you this way anymore. I want you to be happy, and if this is what it takes, then we'll do it." His voice was laced with sadness. I'd been punishing both of us for my crime, but it was the first time I realized just how much he was hurting.

I loved what he'd done for me, so I took his hand. "Let's go see the inside."

The interior was almost empty with the exception of some covered pieces of furniture and an antique grandfather clock as tall as Bill. The main room's greatest feature was a toss-up between the expansive, central fireplace and a ribbon of windows that made up the back wall separating the backyard.

The sprawling wood floor creaked with each step, and it was cold inside, but I could tell it must have been very warm once. Dust caked the surfaces and dead insects were scattered on the floor. I stepped into a decent-sized backyard that was overrun with weeds and in dire need of some attention. But it was large enough for outdoor entertaining, and I envisioned strung Chinese paper lanterns, a concrete and rock bar, rose bushes, a trickling fountain . . . .

When I reentered the house, Bill was standing with his hands in his pockets. I watched as he inspected the stairway railing and kicked at a loose floorboard. The corners of his mouth tugged, suggesting a frown. I scanned the room around him. Honey-colored flooring would complement the warm light that flooded from antique lamps. Heavy, earthy furniture made of oak and aged leather would fill the open floor plan.

And, yet . . . something felt off, though I wasn't sure what. The house had potential, and I was already wondering what it looked like in the early morning when the light was just starting to filter in. Still, I struggled to complete the picture.

"What do you think?" he asked.

I froze, and seconds passed; I could hear the soft ticking of the grandfather clock. Maybe it was my imagination. Maybe once we'd overhauled it and made it into the beautiful place I knew it could be, things would be different. They had to be. Bill had been right all along. It wasn't going to be perfect right away or maybe ever. It would take time for it to feel like home. I took a step backward and pointed to the second floor. "Upstairs?"

I followed as he carefully climbed the noisy steps. The master bedroom, located at one end of the hall, was spacious—bigger than any others we had seen, which I knew would appeal to Bill. It had a large, unobstructed view of the backyard and a corner window on the opposite wall that faced the street.

He reported that there were two more rooms down the hall. I nodded, taking his words in but still studying him. "Can we afford it, really?"

"No," he said honestly. "The house, yes. But I have no idea about the remodel. It's outside our budget, I'm sure. It would mean cutting back on some things for a while."

"Is this what you want?"

He squinted his eyes while his tongue ran over his front teeth. "I don't know how I feel about taking on a project like this when we're both so busy. But I really want to get out of the city, and I want you to love your new home."

It was undoubtedly the nicest thing he'd ever done for me. I shifted, and a floorboard groaned beneath me.

The bedroom was growing dark, and I blinked at his disappearing silhouette. "Okay," I said. "Yes. Let's do it." I crossed the room and hugged him close for an overdue moment of intimacy. We walked to the stairs arm in arm before separating to descend.

~

"Open mine next."

Lucy squealed with delight as she accepted the overstuffed party bag from Bethany, who had a playful gleam in her eye.

"Oh, my," she groaned as she pulled out a pink, feathered tiara with the word 'Bachelorette' branded across the front. We were ten girls at a noisy restaurant downtown, egging Lucy on as she unwrapped gifts between sips of her pink Cosmo.

"You're wearing that now, and you're wearing this too," Dani said, placing a necklace with mini phallic-shaped candies around Lucy's neck.

"Dani! It's definitely inappropriate for my little sister to be draping me in penises."

"It is perfectly appropriate," Dani retorted, clearing a mass of brown, glossy ringlets from her shoulder.

I picked up a green gummy penis and popped it in my mouth before scrunching up my nose. "Sour apple," I lamented. "Yuck."

"Oh, no you don't, Olivia Germaine. You will swallow that penis," Gretchen scolded, waving a finger at me.

I laughed and gulped the candy down exaggeratedly before chasing it with my Cosmo.

I sat between Lucy and Gretchen as Dani, maid of honor and official party planner, stood to raise her glass. "There will be no toast tonight because between the rehearsal dinner and the wedding, I'm running out of material. Lucy is too good, and there aren't enough naughty stories to go around. There's only one decent one from high school, involving her bedroom window and a football jock named Jack, but I'm saving that for the big night."

"Dani, no! You wouldn't!" Lucy cried, her face a veritable bright red.

"I'm teasing, sis. That one isn't nearly good enough for a wedding toast. Anyway, please raise your glasses for my non-toast, and let's get this party underway."

"I can't believe you're getting married in two days," Gretchen said to Lucy, leaning into my lap.

"Me neither. I never thought I'd say this, but I'll be glad when it's over. It's been so much work."

"Yes, it has, but you've done an amazing job," I reassured her. "Sunday is going to be beautiful."

"It had better be," she said. "What are you doing about a date, Gretch? You RSVP'd plus one, so you must bring a plus one."

"Actually, I'm just going to bring John. Is that cool?"

"Of course! I love your brother."

"Why don't you have a date?" I asked skeptically.

"No reason," she responded with a shrug.

"Hey, whatever happened with Brian?" I was embarrassed that I'd never asked about the date they'd gone on months ago.

"Who?"

"Brian Ayers. I introduced you at the magazine's Meet & Greet."

"Oh, that guy? No. Yuck."

"Yuck? He's hot. He's like freaking Hemsworth hot, if you're into blonds, which you are."

"Agreed, but he's a pretentious prick."

"Oh," I said with surprise. "I don't think so at all."

She shrugged. "Then you fuck him."

Her roommates, Ava and Bethany, giggled from across the table, but I gave Gretchen a reproachful look.

"Who are you bringing, Dani?" Ava asked.

"This guy I've just started seeing," she replied with a half-smile.

"He's coming from Milwaukee?" Bethany asked.

"He lives here," Lucy interjected. "You guys know him from my engagement party. David Dylan." For the first time, our end of the table was silent, and I was sure they could all hear my heart drop. "It's still new, which is why I didn't mention it."

Ava looked confused, but Bethany reminded her that he was 'that tall, gorgeous hunk from that one restaurant's soft opening' before declaring that she was supremely jealous.

I fielded a sidelong glance from Gretchen. She and I hadn't discussed David beyond the night I'd confessed my feelings to her. I hadn't let our conversations go that way again. She didn't know about what I'd done, but I hated that she knew anything at all.

"You . . . You lucky bitch," Gretchen joked awkwardly. "I've had my eye on him for a while. How did that happen?"

Dani's eyes brightened. "Well, I was in town last month for some wedding planning, and Lucy set us up. He took all of us on his sailboat, no big deal," she said with a giddy grin.

"Can you imagine having David Dylan as a brother-in-law?" Lucy asked. "I'd never stop staring!"

"Hands off," Dani kidded.

"I'm trying to convince Dani to move to Chicago, and this is part of my plan," Lucy said proudly.

Dani rolled her eyes. "She acts like Milwaukee is another country."

"You're here all the time anyway," Lucy pointed out.

I was spinning my wedding ring at the same pace that my mind was whirring. I glared at the girl across from me. She was Danielle officially, but insisted on being called Dani. She had Lucy's dark brown hair and green eyes like mine. I had always been worried about Gretchen catching David's attention with her blonde curls and Windex-colored eyes, but now David's words from a few months back rang through my head: '*I prefer brunettes with big, green eyes . . .*'

"I'll be honest, I thought David was something of a womanizer, but they've been out twice, and he hasn't made any moves," Lucy revealed.

"He's such a gentleman," Dani boasted.

Gentleman. My insides tightened at the term, and I gripped my thighs. He was no gentleman. He was rough and harsh and callous but tender and sweet and considerate. The adjectives flowed through me, and I bit my lip. He deserved someone like Dani, who was cute and spunky and most importantly—available.

"He's flying back just to take her," Lucy said, and everyone twittered.

"Where is he?" I asked hoarsely before I could stop myself.

"New York," Dani answered as though the information was nothing. "He's an architect, and he's working on a project there. Originally he said he couldn't make it because of work, which I thought was weird because it *is* Labor Day weekend, but he changed his mind all of a—"

"Excuse me," I said, standing.

"Do you want company?" Gretchen asked, moving to get up.

I sighed inwardly, wanting nothing more than to run away and cry, but my self-preservation instincts kicked in. "No. I'm fine." I gave them a big smile. "I'm going to call Bill and tell him I miss him."

The table cooed harmoniously. Lucy nearly melted in her chair.

"What can I say, all this wedding talk has me feeling romantic."

I made a show of retrieving my phone and went to stand outside in the warm night. Warm, yes, but I was cold. I was always cold to the bone lately. I didn't call

Bill as I had said but took a moment to collect myself. *Dani. And David. Me. And Bill.* It made perfect sense. I wondered if he had even considered how it might hurt me to hear that. Surely, after all this time, he didn't consider my feelings anymore. Why should he?

And would it matter if he did? In the end, things were as they were supposed to be. Who was he to me? A mistake. A mark that could never be erased for the entirety of my marriage. Long after I will have forgotten him, he will remain a part of my past.

Long after I've forgotten him . . . . When will that be? How much longer until I forget?

It felt like a lifetime had passed already since that night. But though I worked hard not to think of him, the way he'd made me feel persisted. When I was near him. When I watched him watch me. Kisses, whispers, sensations in the dark.

I looked up at the night sky for a long time. In moments like these, I longed to be back in the suburbs of Dallas, where I could lie in the backyard and blanket myself with millions of stars. Tonight there were few. *So this is how it goes.*

When a prick of light shot across the sky, leaving a faint silver streak in its path, I didn't bother making a wish. I just turned and went back inside.

ABOUT THE AUTHOR

Jessica Hawkins grew up between the purple mountains and under the endless sun of Palm Springs, California. She studied international business at Arizona State University and has also lived in Costa Rica and New York City. Some of her favorite things include traveling, her dog Kimo, Scrabble, driving aimlessly and creating Top Five lists. She is the helpless victim of an overactive imagination that finds inspiration in music and tranquility in writing. Currently she resides wherever her head lands, which lately is the unexpected (but warm) keyboard of her trusty MacBook.

CONNECT WITH THE AUTHOR

http://www.jessicahawkins.net
http://www.twitter.com/jess_hawk
http://www.facebook.com/jessicahawkinsauthor